BLAZING TRAILS

With his dying breaths, Nat Ellis charges his
nephtters
cachone,
handna's
unfibar,
Wyowith
Clerurns
outNat's
interand
styliand
Littlown
thrugers.
Fornder
Basig in
nearrun
then, Big
Mor. . . .

BLAZING TRAILS

FRANCIS W. HILTON

SAGEBRUSH
Large Print Westerns

First published in Great Britain by Isis
First published in the United States by Kinsey

First Isis Edition
published 2015
by arrangement with
Golden West Literary Agency

A catalogue record for this book is available
from the British Library.

ISBN 978-1-78541-015-4 (pb)

11899087 2

PUBLISHED BY
F. A. THORPE (PUBLISHING)
ANSTEY, LEICESTERSHIRE

SET BY WORDS & GRAPHICS LTD.
ANSTEY, LEICESTERSHIRE
PRINTED AND BOUND IN GREAT BRITAIN BY
T. J. INTERNATIONAL LTD., PADSTOW, CORNWALL

This book is printed on acid-free paper

Table of Contents

CHAPTER
ONE

Mysterious Letters

Through the stifling heat of late August, "Montana" Ellis roweled his jaded mount toward Elbar. Save when the pony slowed down of its own accord to blow, not once in hours had the furious pace slackened. Sweat rimmed the brute's eyes and ears, lather flew from its jaws. Dirty foam webbed its flanks, trickled from beneath the sodden saddle blanket. Swarms of flies and mosquitoes clung to its sweat-streaked neck.

Dust scuffed up by hoofs leaden, mechanical with weariness, rose in choking clouds to go drifting away before a slow, hot wind, then settled down in a low-hanging streamer along the back trail. Patches of alkali glared blindingly in the sun, a wilting, blazing orb crawling through a sky of glittering tin. The air was pungent with the odor of blistered sage and greasewood.

Yet for all the merciless heat, the tormenting flies, the sweat that beaded his own brow and streaked his grimy face, Montana pushed on tirelessly, relentlessly, his gaze fixed on the broken country ahead. Far behind him now lay the Bear Lodge mountains. The Big Horns were but etchings on the smoke-blue horizon ahead.

About him was a region wild, desolate — dreary, sun-baked flats, steep, grottoed bluffs, towering gumbo buttes — ugly piles, drab and corrugated as molten metal that had burst its mold and cooled as it ran. Hogbacks, bristling with shelf rock and cacti, gave off shimmering rays of heat like a griddle. Majestic pine and spruce long since had given way to straggling, stunted cedar and an occasional gnarled cottonwood that bent thirstily toward the dry bed of one of the countless writhing ravines. Lilies with waxen petals fought for life beneath clumps of greasewood that grew gigantic where other vegetation withered and died. It was a region bereft of beauty, awesome in its vastness.

There was something savage in the way Montana rode, his body slapping the saddle, arms flapping with the rhythmic motion of the horse.

Tall, but of well-knit frame, he was broad of shoulder, slender of hip. Dust powdered his gray flannel shirt, thrown open at the throat to reveal a muscular, sun-blackened neck. Dust covered his brush-scarred chaps. His bronzed face was lean and firm, for all its present grimness, marked with pleasantness, the confidence of carefree youth. Yet there was about it a premature hardness; a hardness increased by smoldering blue-gray eyes which, one sensed, could grow cold and expressionless; eyes, the friendliness in which seemed to veil a cruel gleam that could, on occasion, blaze with livid flame. His lips were thin, braced. A thatch of sunburned sandy hair lay damply on a sweat-beaded forehead beneath a wide-brimmed hat. His almost too square jaws bulged with the pressure of

2

set teeth. Except for his eyes, in which now lurked something of a half-anxious light, his whole attitude was one of reckless determination. And save for an apparently abstracted observation, which yet took keen and critical note of everything within range of vision on the limitless expanse, those eyes always were set on the dreary flats ahead.

Where Tongue river crooked a sullen arm about a small Wyoming cow town, he reined in to shift sidewise in his saddle and sweep the hazy horizon. When a careful survey failed to reveal any moving thing save small bunches of prowling range cattle, he swung down, allowed his thirsty horse a few sips of water and squatted on his dime-thin rowels beside the stream.

"I reckon that town will be Elbar, horse," he told his blowing pony, after the manner of men of the silent trails who make companions of their mounts. His glance snapped from the animal — which stood with its weight on three legs, head drooping wearily, flanks heaving — to the village across the river, its shabby, weather-beaten buildings swaying like a mirage through shimmering waves of heat. "Now just what in the devil do we do?"

Again the question that for days had been uppermost in his mind. Hour after hour on the long hot trail he had tried to answer it. To no avail. He was still as far from that answer as ever. For the hundredth time he fished from the pocket of his shirt a worn envelope, extracted a letter.

"Go to Elbar, Wyoming," he read aloud the almost illegible scrawl. "At the crossing of the Tongue river, just outside the town, wait till you meet Clem White. Then —"

There the letter ended abruptly. And therein lay the cause of the uncertainty in Montana's eyes, which again had resumed their survey of the greasewood.

"Wouldn't that stump you, horse?" he pondered aloud. "Go to the Tongue river crossing at Elbar, Wyoming. Wait outside the town till you meet Clem White. Who in all get-out is Clem White? And what the devil do I want to meet him for? Damn it all, horse — Why couldn't Uncle Nat have lived until he told me instead of shagging me way off down here on this wild-goose chase? Sometimes I think he was a little locoed in the head when he died."

The hoofbeats of a horse, which suddenly had popped up out of a dry wash to his right, brought him to his feet with a swift movement, the swift, agile movement of a lunging puma. He whirled. His hand shot down to close about the butt of the forty-five revolver holstered at his hip, thonged down securely to his leg. But that hand jerked upward quickly to search for papers and tobacco in the pocket of his shirt at sight of the newcomer who drew rein beside him.

"Gosh-all-hemlocks, you're nervous, mister," came a frightened voice. "I didn't aim to scare you thataway. Thought for a minute you was going to drill me."

In a swift glance Montana sized up the newcomer, a slightly built boy barely in his teens, with deeply tanned face and mild gray eyes. He was clad in a tattered shirt and patched overalls hitched around his slender waist with a piece of rope. A shock of hair protruded from a

4

torn hat. His boots were sadly worn, run over at the heels. Yet aside from his clothes — ragged enough to arouse the pity of any man — there was about him a pride that commanded admiration.

"I am nervous, buddy," Montana confessed sheepishly. "I'm waiting for somebody. Kind of figured when you rode up, quick-like, you might be him. Not seeing you coming, I just —"

"I'd hate to have you waiting for me if you was any faster going for that gun of yours, mister," the lad returned soberly. "Are you aiming to shoot who you're waiting for?"

"I don't know," Montana admitted. "Because I haven't any idea in the world who I am waiting for."

"I'm waiting for somebody myself," the lad remarked with sudden chumminess, swinging down out of a battered saddle-held together with bits of rope and baling wire — to stretch out lazily on the ground and regard Montana inquisitively.

His nerves calm again after his start at the boy's appearance, Montana squatted back on his rowels to tap a measure of tobacco into a paper, pull shut the sack with his teeth and twist a cigaret.

"So you're waiting for somebody too, sonny?" he observed, striking a match on his boot sole, cupping the light in his hand, extinguishing it with a puff of smoke, and grinding the match in the dirt with the caution of men born to the fear of fire on the prairie.

The youngster nodded.

"Funny we'd both be waiting for somebody at the same river crossing, ain't it, mister?" he ventured.

"It sure is, Button," Montana agreed. "But then, I reckon you know who you're waiting for — that's a danged sight more than I do."

"That's the funny part of it," the boy said, staring at the puncher with childish frankness. "I don't know any more who I'm waiting for than you do. But I'm plumb glad it ain't you; because if I'd of been the jasper you was waiting for mebbeso you would have reason to plug me."

"Shucks!" Montana grinned. "I'm not so tough, buddy. Just skittish, like a green colt. Been in the saddle so long I'm plumb tuckered out." His sharp blue-gray eyes whipped along the reclining figure. "You look like you've done some tall riding yourself. Who you waiting for?"

"For a jasper by the name of Ellis — Montana Ellis."

"Montana Ellis? That's me! So you're waiting for me? And me, I'm waiting for a feller by the name of — But then it couldn't be a kid like you."

"I'm Clem White," the boy volunteered quickly.

"Clem White!" Montana exclaimed incredulously. "Hell! Here I've been all keyed up for days figuring to stack up against some tough walloper who would be snorting to knock over my cob pile. And here you —"

"So that's why you are so skittish?" The boy attempted a chuckle that ended in a nervous note. "Figured you was due for some gunplay? But me being just a kid you ain't scared any more, huh? So you're Montana Ellis? I'm sure glad to know you, Montana." He sprang up to offer his hand in a frank, boyish gesture. Montana shook it gravely.

6

Then from the pocket of his ragged overalls the youngster extracted a crumpled envelope.

"I got a letter from some feller by the name of Ellis up in Montana," he said. "The only letter I ever got in my whole life. And was I some proud? This jasper wrote for me to be sure and meet Montana Ellis at the Tongue river crossing outside of Elbar, Wyoming, on the twenty-fifth day of August and I'd learn something that would more than pay me for my trouble. So here I am. And now that I've met you, what is it, mister?"

"And now you've met me I'm danged if I know what it is, buddy," Montana admitted truthfully, sucking hard on the cigaret, his gaze evading the disappointment that flared into the youngster's eyes.

"You — don't — know?" the boy cried, dangerously near tears.

"I just can't say for certain as to that, either," Montana hedged. "It won't take long for me to show my hand. It's thisaway. My uncle, Nat Ellis, died up in Montana a while back — A stroke — Come on sudden like. Before he cashed in, Uncle Nat tried hard to tell me something, something it seemed like he just had to get off his chest before he faced the Big Tallyman over on yon side of the divide.

"But he couldn't get it out. He just mumbled and muttered and begged with his eyes. But one thing he did manage to make me understand. That was that he had three letters cached under the mattress of his bed. One of them was addressed to Clem White, Lonetree, Wyoming."

7

"And it told me to come clean up here and I'd learn something that would more than pay me for my trouble," the boy blurted out. "I come — and I ain't finding out anything."

"Never mind, sonny," Montana consoled him. "There is something back of all this, you can just bet the ace. It's up to us to find out what it is. But as I was saying, Uncle Nat managed to tell me about those three letters. I got them out from under his mattress. One of them was for you, one for me, and the third one was addressed to a jasper by the name of Al Cousins, Elbar, Wyoming. Do you happen to know this Al Cousins, Button?"

"Never heard of him. Don't know a living soul around these parts. I'm a plumb stranger hereabouts."

"Well, we've got to locate Al Cousins," Montana said. "For Uncle Nat made me understand that I was to mail your letter, read mine, and deliver the one to Al Cousins personal."

"And all your letter told you was to come down here and meet me just like mine told me to come up here and meet you, huh?" the boy demanded, struggling gamely with tears. "And now neither one of us knows what for. Somebody is crazy — or playing a dirty joke on us."

"Mebbeso," Montana conceded, "but I've got a different hunch. If you could have seen Uncle Nat lying there with a pleading light in his eyes, trying to make me understand before he died, you'd believe, like I do, that there is something behind it. What it is I haven't any more idea than you. But it's up to us to find out."

"And just how are we going to find out?" the boy cried. "Your uncle is dead. Besides, I never knew, or even heard of, any Ellises."

"Yet it is a dead mortal cinch that Uncle Nat knew your name," Montana reasoned. "And he also had your address. If he didn't know you, how do you account for that?"

"I can't," Clem admitted. "But what gets me is what he wanted me to come up here for to meet a jasper who don't know what for any more than I do!"

"Where you from originally, Button?" Montana asked.

"Nowheres." There was a touch of sadness in the boy's voice. "I reckon I just kind of growed out in the greasewood. I don't even know how old I am; never had any way of telling. First thing I recollect I was doing chores on a cow ranch on Powder river. The foreman used to kick me until I was black and blue. I sneaked away from that job and got another one working for a jasper over near Lonetree. He isn't any easy walloper to work for; he busts me just plenty, but at least I've et and had a place to sleep. But coming up here thisaway —" He stopped, biting his lip.

"What, buddy?" Montana encouraged.

"Oh, nothing," The boy resumed, his chin quivering, "only I've come clean up here expecting to hear something and — and the old man fired me. He told me if I went I didn't need to come back. Damn your uncle. I wish he'd have minded his own business and left me alone. I would have had a job and wouldn't be on the drift, not knowing where my next meal was coming from."

Montana got slowly to his feet to flick away his cigaret and grind it under his heel.

"Never mind, buddy," he said. "We'll be pards from now on. We'll stick together and either find out Uncle Nat was talking sense or that he was crazy in the head."

"You're on!" the boy cried, seizing the puncher's hand. "I never had any jasper who wanted me for a pard before. I'll stick to you forever; because I know you ain't the kind who'll kick hell out of me. But —" New tears welled up in his eyes. "I'm broke — and I ain't et for two days."

"You haven't got me beat much at that," Montana grinned. "I figured when Uncle Nat died that I'd have the ranch. But I reckon I was the only thing on the whole place that the bank didn't have a mortgage on. I've got ham-and-egg money, though. And the two of us ought to find enough work to keep us eating. Come on, buddy. Throw a leg over that crowbait of yours and we'll put on the feed bag right now."

The boy hung back.

"I ain't never been around much," he said timidly. "I ain't got any guts at all when it comes to bulling my way through."

"Just you leave that to me, buddy," Montana reassured him, dropping an arm across his shoulders. "I've never missed any meals yet — although some of them have been delayed for quite a spell. I'm really to blame for getting you up here."

10

"That isn't any sign you've got to feed me," the boy flashed. "If I'd had any sense I'd —"

"It isn't a question of sense," Montana cut him short. "It is a question of victuals. And that's what we're going to get the most of quick. Pards split the kitty all the time. We've got work together. Say?" he asked. "What am I going to call you? You aren't from any place in particular and —" He stopped, thoughtfully. "Montana is a pretty good state, kid. You've never been there yet, but I suppose that is where two old side-kicks like us will wind up. Supposing we just call ourselves the Two Montanas?"

"That would be great!" Clem exclaimed with childish enthusiasm. "You be Big Montana and I'll be Little Montana. Gosh-all-hemlocks, mister, I never thought when I rode up here and saw you going for your gun that you were the kind of a feller who would play make-believe with a little walloper like me. When you were clawing for that gun you had a nasty eye. It just plumb froze me so I couldn't holler. You looked tough and —"

"I am tough," Montana growled with mock severity. "And you'd better not give me any of your lip, Button. I'm boss of this here Two Montana gang." He seized hold of the youngster and tossed him onto his horse. Then he threw back his head and laughed, a jolly, contagious laugh that brought a chuckle of delight from the lad. "And I'm ordering my gang to plank themselves down to ham and eggs at the first restaurant we can locate in this here town of Elbar." He swung into his own saddle. "After that we'll find this Al

Cousins and see what is in the letter I brought him. If it doesn't tell us any more than our letters we'll shag it north, buddy, north to Montana, together."

CHAPTER
TWO

A Warning

Dusty garbed, their faces streaked with sweat and grime, Montana Ellis and the boy, Clem White, rode across the rickety plank bridge that spanned the sullen Tongue river and pushed their weary ponies into Elbar.

The village was a counterpart of other hamlets that dotted the prairies, their only hope for existence the trade of the big cattle outfits in the surrounding territory — a shipping point at the roundup's end — a rendezvous for freighters, cowhands bent on a spree — a hideout for fugitives who scoffed at the law from the fastness of the wild region beyond.

A single street, deep-rutted by wind and rain, flanked on either side by dilapidated boardwalks, was uninviting, dreary. A cluster of buildings, with high false fronts, huddled together as though for protection against the merciless suns of summer and lashing fury of winter blizzards. A ramshackle church, the sign proclaiming its denomination long since effaced by blasting sand — stores, saloons, the inevitable livery stable, harness shop. Beauty there was none. Paint and civic pride were things unknown. Everywhere was evidence of weather, the buildings but blackened hulls, shingles warped, torn paper flapping on their roofs, driftwood and débris banked against their sides by the Tongue in its annual rampages.

Save for a dozen saddle horses drowsily fighting flies at the hitchrails, rumps to the stinging sand that whirled along the street before a whining breeze, the village seemed devoid of life.

"It isn't just what you'd call crowded with folks," Montana mused dryly to the wide-eyed, staring boy beside him. "But mebbeso the gents hereabouts do most of their work at night and take a siesta in the daytime. It must be the place though, because that two-story building yonder," he shifted his weight, stood in one stirrup, "the biggest in town, is the Elbar Hotel. I don't allow that Uncle Nat was loco this far."

They rode slowly down the street, Montana reading the signs as they went.

"Saloons just plenty and regular," he observed, "but no restaurants or human beings. I'll lay money to —"

The violent shying of his horse checked his words. The form of a man came lurching through the swinging doors of a saloon to sprawl face downward in the street. When Montana had succeeded in quieting his snorting mount, they rode back. The stranger still lay motionless in the dirt. Dismounting, Montana dragged his reluctant horse forward and stooped over the fellow.

"One sheepherder helping another!" came a raucous bawl followed by a roar of laughter.

At that moment the prone man — a wizened, poorly dressed fellow — recovered his senses. Montana helped him to his feet, picked up his battered hat, slapped the dust from it, and placed it on his grizzled head. Muttering his thanks, the man slunk away into the crowd which suddenly had collected from nowhere.

"I say it takes one sheepherder to find another!" came the booming voice again. "It's the smell that does it, I reckon. Where did you do your last herding job, drifter?"

Montana's gaze traveled upward slowly from a pair of flashing, inlaid spurs, along bangle-studded chaps and blazing purple silk shirt finally coming to rest on the swarthy, weather-pitted face of a man who had swaggered from the saloon to stand directly above him on the boardwalk — a man of ponderous bulk with massive shoulders and great thighs that glistened with ornamental conchas. A loosely knotted neckerchief of red, a great-brimmed beaver hat with silver band, and fancy wristlets of stamped leather completed his attire.

But the flashiness of the garb drew only the passing interest of Montana. It was the fellow's eyes that held him; little glittering black eyes, set deep beneath beetling brows and low, narrow forehead, peering out from over high cheekbones — cruel eyes, scheming.

As Montana's gaze met that of the stranger the fellow started violently. His gloved hands dropped to hook, thumbs down, near the butts of two pearl-handled forty-fives holstered in a studded cartridge belt at his waist. The strange light that flared into the glinting eyes puzzled Montana. It was as though the fellow had recognized him. Yet for the life of him he could not place him.

15

The stranger's gaze darted on to the boy, who had swung down to stand timidly beside Montana. The unfathomable gleam in those eyes deepened. Montana dared a glance at Clem. But if the lad ever had seen the big puncher before, was even conscious of the recognition in his eyes, he gave no indication of it.

Montana broke the silence that was deepening ominously; silence unbroken now save for the occasional shifting of a roweled foot on the plank walk or the whine of the breeze chasing eddies of dust up the street.

"You guessed it, pardner," Montana said goodnaturedly, yet with a strange glint in his own blue-gray eyes. "I come from a sheep country, all right. But being a cowman I never have been accused of having any keen affection for the woollies. Even a sheepherder though, is better sometimes than no humans at all. I figured until I saw this one come bouncing out from that bar that everybody around here was dead." His steady gaze never left the man while his faculties were groping about to account for the veiled light of recognition that shone in his eyes.

"There are no dead ones in Elbar," the fellow snarled, taking an uncertain step to plant himself spread-legged, weaving on his feet. He licked weather-cracked lips, a gesture that somehow suggested a lion gloating over easy prey. It was obvious that liquor had put the big cowboy in an ugly mood. "But snooping strangers have a way of turning up missing."

Montana's eyes jerked along the huge frame before him. Gone now was their quiet pleasantness. A shafted light, sinister, warning, lit their depths. But his thin lips were smiling; a set and frozen smile. And if the big puncher calculated to intimidate him with his threatening manner he was sadly disappointed. When Montana spoke his voice had taken on a soft brittle tone. His words came cold, clipped.

"Figured you already had me pegged the way you sized me up," he said.

Again the cowboy started. Again the unfathomable gleam flared into his eyes.

"I'm asking your name," he demanded, thick-tongued. "And I'm telling you plain — we don't cotton to strangers around Elbar."

"Is that so?" Montana asked quietly. "And me with the unfortunate habit of going wherever I please." In a quick movement he stepped up on the walk, onto an even footing with the big fellow. His eyes swept the length of the street, now lined with people. White faces peered from windows and doorways.

"It doesn't pay to get mouthy," the big puncher snarled. "I'm demanding to know your name. And the name of this brat," indicating the boy, who had edged closer to Montana to stand trembling with fear.

"I'm not asking your pedigree," Montana flung back softly. "And I don't aim to have any roaring bull like you prying into mine. Come on, buddy." He drew the boy up beside him and pushed him ahead into the saloon. "We came into this town to eat, if you recollect."

"Hold on!" the big puncher rasped. "What brat is that?"

Once the lad was safely behind the swinging doors, Montana spun about.

"You'd like to know, wouldn't you, walloper?" he taunted in a voice that even those nearest now strained to catch. "If it's causing you any particular worry, find out!"

The snarl of a beast left the puncher's thick lips. He bounded toward the swinging doors to pull up short, weaving drunkenly on his feet, gloved hands still hooked in his cartridge belt. The onlookers crowded back, opening a lane between the two.

"For the last time, jasper," he bellowed, "I'm demanding to know your name and the name of that brat!"

Livid flame leaped into Montana's eyes. His smile broadened, froze.

"And for the last time," he mocked, "I'm telling you — it's none of your business!"

The retort threw the big cowboy into a rage. Montana gaged him with a coldly glittering eye. The onlookers stood rooted in their tracks.

The puncher made a threatening gesture toward his forty-fives. Montana leaped squarely in front of the doors, jerked straight. His hand shot down — a movement so swift it baffled sight. The crowd, which had stood on the deadline of tragedy before, sensed rather than saw that movement, plunged to safety.

The corners of Montana's braced lips quirked. His Colt came from nowhere into his ungloved hand. The muzzle jerked up. The big fellow's forty-fives seemed to freeze on the rims of their holsters. A nervous foot scraped explosively.

"You're asking for it, walloper," Montana purred. "And you're detaining two hungry pilgrims from dining. We haven't et since the Lord knows when. We're going to eat now. You get it, pardner. It's your move. Fast!"

A sound rumbled in the big puncher's throat. His leathery face became saffron. Slowly his guns settled back into their holsters. His gloved hands jerked away, moved into the air.

"You can't come into Elbar and yank a gun on me," he snarled.

"So I see," Montana flung back softly. "Now lay off your bellyaching. Sober up and come back. If you still feel like hunting trouble, I'll be around somewhere. Shag it, jasper!"

"I'll get you for this." The big cowboy backed down the walk.

"Any time," Montana threw after him. "And if I've finished my business and left your peaceful little village you can always find me on the Yellowstone."

Sputtering with rage, the big fellow whirled and stamped away, spur rowels raking the plank walk angrily. Montana slid his Colt back into its holster to stand facing the onlookers, who, one by one, slunk away, leaving him alone with the boy, who came trembling from behind the swinging doors.

"Now that's what I call a royal welcome to this enterprising little city, buddy," Montana said grimly.

"Gosh, that was great," Clem blurted out with childish admiration. "You sure did call the turn and make that feller eat crow. When I grow up I want to be just like you. Wasn't you scared of him?"

"It doesn't make any difference how big you are, Button," Montana said soberly. "It's guts that gets you through. That walloper could eat me up feathers and all in a rough and tumble."

"But with a gun," the boy breathed. "Look how you covered him."

"Being fast with a gun isn't anything to admire in any man, kid. Don't ever tote one. Then you won't ever have any reason to use it, mebbeso do something you'll be sorry for."

"But if you hadn't of had yours?" the lad persisted.

"That jasper wouldn't have done a thing more than he did. You can tell grade stuff from pure bred every time. That walloper is plumb low grade. The only thing I'm regretting is that he has kept us from eating this long." Turning abruptly, he secured their horses, tied them to the hitchrail and started off down the street. A few paces and he stopped. "Here we are, buddy," he said. "Mother Hope's Café. Here's where we throw a slug under our belts."

He opened the door of a neat appearing little restaurant to the clang of a bell overhead and stepped within, the lad crowding his heels. The place was deserted. Moving to the lunch counter, Montana straddled a stool, picked up a menu card and fell to studying it. The boy followed suit. Presently they were aware that someone had come in quietly from the kitchen in the rear.

"What'll it be, buddy?" Montana asked, still engrossed in the bill-of-fare.

"Ham and —" the youngster began eagerly.

"That's the ticket," Montana exclaimed, eyes still downcast. "All the ham and eggs in Elbar, cookie," he ordered. "And a son-of-a-gun pudding with a ton of raisins served in relays for two hungry Montana wolves who haven't et since they were pups. We're so danged hungry our —"

He glanced up to meet the amused eyes of a girl upon him.

"I — I —" he blurted out, flushing. "I reckon we'll take two orders of ham and eggs, miss," he repeated lamely. "And —"

"Son-of-a-gun pudding served in relays for two hungry Montana wolves," she smiled. "I got your order, mister."

She moved away to the kitchen. Montana's embarrassed gaze followed her.

CHAPTER
THREE

Low-Down on Trouble

For a time after the girl had gone into the kitchen, Montana stared after her in moody silence. He could catch glimpses of her moving about, hear her talking to an elderly woman he could see bending over a stove, and whose voice rose above the sudden sizzle of frying ham.

Occasionally the girl turned to surprise his eyes upon her. His gaze shifted quickly in embarrassment.

But in the sly glances he had at her she reminded him somehow of a rose in her freshly-starched pink house dress and spotless apron of white. Her even features were framed in a mass of auburn hair that lay in tiny ringlets on her forehead. Her eyes were large and brown and frank, fringed with long dark lashes that accentuated their wistful beauty. Her face glowed with healthy color. The prettiest, most interesting face he ever had seen, Montana decided. Her hands, too, he noted, were finely formed, delicate yet strong and capable as they moved about preparing the food. Her movements were graceful, supple with the freshness, the strength of youth.

He found himself wondering what her name was. The sign over the door — *Mother Hope's Café* — could the large woman in calico bending over the stove be Mother Hope? And the girl? There was something of a resemblance. Hard work and care that had seamed the older face had failed to erase all trace of its former beauty.

He tore his gaze away from her presently to regard the boy who sat beside him staring into the street, deserted again after the brief stir of excitement precipitated by their arrival.

"Sonny," he said thoughtfully, "that big jasper I locked horns with thinks he knows me. I saw it in his eyes. And he thinks he knows you, too. But I'll swear I never met up with him before. Are you dead sure you've never been around here?"

"Honest," the boy replied. "Seemed to me that he thought he knew me, too. But I never saw him. He's just mistaking us for somebody else."

"Mebbeso. Either that or he's so drunk he figures we're long-lost cousins or something. He —"

"Much obliged for helping me, stranger," came a voice at his shoulder.

Montana broke off his conversation to whirl on his stool. Behind him stood the wizened man he had picked up in the street, and who obviously had entered the café through the kitchen.

"Shucks." Montana smiled in a friendly fashion. "I didn't help you any. Sit down and have a bite to eat with us. We've ordered all the ham and eggs in town. It's your last chance till the hens lay again."

"No, thanks. But I'll pull up and talk for a spell if you don't mind." The old man seated himself beside Montana where he could keep an anxious eye on the door. "I'm Joe Lewis from over Cutbank way. And I'm giving you a tip — be mighty careful while you're in Elbar."

" 'Pears like it might stand a feller in hand," Montana returned. "The gents I've met up with so far don't seem to be just what you'd call friendly."

"The walloper you tied into isn't friendly to anybody," the old fellow growled, peering at Montana closely. "You've made a deadly enemy of him. He'll get even or bust something trying."

"So I figure," dryly. "Who is he — the mayor or sheriff? The way he's all rigged up in those fancy store clothes he looks like a circus buckaroo."

"It's Smokey Tremaine!" Lewis said in a lowered tone as though utterance of the name itself was forbidden.

"Smokey Tremaine!" Montana repeated. "Now what am I supposed to do, bust out in a cold sweat or leave town?"

"Smokey is foreman of the Diamond A — the biggest cow outfit in Thunder Basin."

"Reckon I'd better steer clear of the Diamond A then," mockingly. "But if I do it won't be because of —"

He stopped as the girl came from the kitchen with a trayload of steaming food. He attempted not to stare, but for all he could do his eyes had a way of straying to her as she placed the plates before them.

"Coffee?" she was asking.

"Don't care if I do, miss," Montana gulped. "That is — What will you have, buddy?"

"He's already drinking his milk." The girl laughed, a friendly, musical laugh; and her voice was low, sweetly low and husky.

He fell to eating ravenously to cover his embarrassment, cursing himself under his breath for being such an idiot before this strange girl, a waitress in a cow-town café. Yet never before had he seen her like. Never before had he seen a woman that routed his last vestige of control, although, he admitted to himself, he never had been entirely at ease around women.

"By the way, Lewis," he said presently. "I'm looking for a jasper by the name of Al Cousins. Know the gent?"

"Al Cousins!" the old fellow exclaimed. "Why, Cousins is the big squeeze of the Diamond A spread. Smokey Tremaine is his foreman."

"Huh?" Montana grunted. "And to see Cousins I've got to go right into this Thunder Basin country under Smokey's nose? Now isn't that a tough break?" he demanded of the boy in mock seriousness. "Glad you came along, Button?"

"I'm not afraid as long as I'm with you," Clem was able to mutter for all his crammed mouth.

"Shucks, you'll be getting me stuck on myself if you keep on." Montana grinned. Then to Lewis: "What makes all these folks so hostile to strangers?"

"Elbar and Thunder Basin have never been healthy places for outsiders," the old man answered in an undertone. "They're even worse right now."

"Why?" There was careless indifference in Montana's voice.

The herder looked around cautiously, although they were alone in the café.

"For a good many reasons," he said. "Mebbeso that is one of them." He jerked a gnarled thumb behind him. Montana glanced across the neat room with its plank floor scrubbed almost white. On the wall was a placard. He strained to read it.

$5,000 DEAD OR ALIVE!
For "Three-Finger" DeHaven, alias "Slick" Nogstrum, alias "Butch" Franklin. Wanted for murder and rustling. Identifying marks first and second fingers of right hand missing. Fugitive is a killer. Officers are warned to take no chances. Notify

JIM CROWE, SHERIFF,
JAMES COUNTY, WYOMING.

When he had finished reading, Montana shrugged and shot a glance at the gaping boy before his gaze shifted to a second placard — a glaring placard in red, with the picture of a pitching horse — the announcement of a rodeo. Before he turned back to his food he caught the name, *Diamond A Rodeo*.

The herder watched him closely for a moment as though trying to read his thoughts. But Montana's face suddenly had become expressionless, veiling every thought or emotion.

"I'm not saying Three-Finger DeHaven is back in Thunder Basin, understand," the old fellow offered. "I'm just tipping you off that the Basin isn't any place for strangers."

"How's that?" The words were the only evidence that Montana was even listening. He finished his steaming coffee in a gulp and pushed his cup across to the girl, who was hovering near by, attempting, with poor success, to find something to interest her outside on the dust-swept, blistered street.

With a smile that again brought the blood into Montana's face, she refilled the coffee cup and placed it beside him.

"Thanks," he muttered.

Another dazzling smile was his reward.

"Because you might be another detective, that's why," the old herder whispered when the girl had moved off a short distance, to busy herself polishing the lunch counter. "I'm telling you, strangers are about as welcome as blackleg in here. It's a bad mess, feller."

"Rustlers?" Montana asked indifferently, his fascinated gaze, over which he seemed to have no control, following every movement of the girl.

"They've been working in the Basin for years," the herder replied. "You see, the Diamond A owns danged near the whole of Thunder Basin, Al Cousins and King Kent — Al's a fine old gent, common as dirt. Kent's a stubborn bullbat and uppish. They do what they can against the rustlers. But they don't seem to get

27

anywheres. Nor the law doesn't, either. The detectives they've hired to go in there just naturally disappear. So do the cow thieves. They must have wings. Nobody ever gets so much as a glimpse of them."

"What's the matter with their foreman, Smokey Tremaine?" Montana asked. "He's tough enough to tangle with rustlers, ain't he?"

"They don't come any tougher," the herder growled. "And you're the only jasper who ever had the guts to call his hand that I know of. He's cock of the Basin; and Kent swears by him. Cousins don't say much. But it don't take only half an eye to see he hasn't got any use for Smokey. Reckon he only puts up with him because Smokey is the best cowman in these parts; knows cows to a fare-you-well. But then again, poor old Al hasn't been accountable for years."

"Loco?"

"Sane as you or me. But he had a kid — a little shaver of a boy. Raised him by hand after his ma died. Some ten years back the kid, just then learning to walk, turns up missing. They hunt high and low for him. Finally, they fish his hat out of Piney river, near the Diamond A, making it pretty certain that he fell in and was drowned."

"Knocked the pegs out from under the old gent, Cousins, huh?" Montana surmised.

"Plumb. Thought for a while he was going loco. After that he just seemed to lose interest in everything. His foreman — let's see, what was that jasper's name? Danged if I recall now. But anyhow, he pulled out about the time the kid disappeared; Kent, who was a common puncher, just kind of oozed into charge. He's the big bull on the range now; head of the Stock Association and everything else. He goes to managing the Diamond A and snakes Smokey Tremaine, his side-kick, up from a thirty-dollar job as top rope and makes him foreman. Al just seemed to turn everything over to them."

"Still owns an interest, doesn't he?"

"Nobody knows, because Al isn't the talking kind. Kent's the one who shines at that. Al just sort of slides along moping and grieving for that lost kid. But, even then, I've always said they'd better look out for him. There's fire in the old boy, you see." He indicated the placard on the wall advertising the rodeo. "As far back as anybody can remember, the Diamond A holds that rodeo. Folks from all over these parts come to see it. It used to be open to all comers. But Smokey Tremaine has cleaned up so long now nobody will compete with him. He's as good a bronc peeler as ever threw a leg over an outlaw — good as he is a cowman. Al don't make any bones about hating to see Smokey take top money every year. So the rodeo has just settled down to a war betwixt the two of them. But for all Al has been able to do, Smokey is the champion twister on Tongue river. Smokey cleaned up completely in the rodeo, held just a couple of days ago. That's why he's in here celebrating, raising hell. He's cock of the roost for another year."

"I'd fire him if I was Cousins," Montana growled.

"So would I," Lewis agreed. "But then, we ain't on the inside and don't know the whole deal. Al and

Smokey don't go at it hammers and tongs. They're more like a couple of prize fighters waiting for an opening so they can tangle for a knockout. But this man Kent — he's where Smokey gets his drag, because Kent thinks the sun comes up and goes down in him. And Smokey is slick enough to keep Kent egged on to holding the annual rodeos just to show old Al up. But Al is game even if he is heart-broke. He thought the world and all of that kid of his."

"How do you get down to Thunder Basin?" Montana asked shortly.

"Thirty mile due east. But if you should happen to be a detective hunting Three-Finger DeHaven and those rustlers, take a fool's advice and stay out." Lewis got up from his stool.

"Much obliged," Montana said, offering his hand, which the old fellow took eagerly. "I can tell you in danged few words I'm no detective. But I have got business in these parts. And I may be crazy enough to hang around — if I can land something in the way of work."

"Work? Say — But then I don't reckon — You wouldn't mind a little trouble with that work, would you?"

"I'm not dodging any," Montana said.

"I'm not deliberately steering a man into a mess," Lewis responded. "But if it's work you're really wanting, why not lope down to the stockyards? There's a fellow down there I used to know when I was in cows. He's unloading some stuff. That's the other reason they're not particularly struck on strangers in Elbar right now. But that fellow is white — all white and square. A man to be proud of on any range. If you really want a job, I'll put in a bid for you — tell him you're riding down to see him, if you want."

"Do that," Montana said quickly. "I'd sure be much obliged."

"I wouldn't do it without I'd seen you back Smokey Tremaine down," Lewis countered pointedly. "This newcomer is going to need help, because of snakes of Tremaine's caliber. Either that or they'll run him out."

"Tell him I'm his man," Montana said. "The reception I got here don't make me particularly loving on any of the citizens. But I'm crazy enough to want to stick. You tell that jasper I'm dead anxious to work and r'arin' to go. And you — So long. We'll probably meet up again sometime."

"I hope so. I'm proud to shake hands with the man who made Smokey Tremaine eat crow — and to know his name."

"My name?" Montana chuckled. "Shucks! I'm Big Montana. And this here is Little Montana. We're just the Two Montanas, giving your Wyoming range the once-over."

He smiled after the old fellow as he turned quickly and ducked out through the kitchen into the alley.

"Are you through, sonny?" Montana heard the girl ask the boy as he turned back to the counter. Clem gulped down a huge mouthful of pudding and spun around. "Sure you're full up? Can't eat any more?"

"I can chew but I can't swallow," the boy mumbled. "I don't reckon I ever et so much. Did you, Montana?"

"I've done right smart, buddy." Montana grinned. "And now we'd best —"

"Come in again, Little Montana," the girl invited cordially, leaning across the counter to pat the youngster on the shoulder.

"How did you know my name?" the lad demanded, startled.

"I just heard this gentleman telling Mr. Lewis that you were Little Montana and that he was —"

"And what's your name?" the boy interrupted to ask. "You knowing mine, I ought to know yours."

"Sure you had," she laughed. "I'm Sally Hope. Mother runs this restaurant."

"You're awfully pretty, Sally," the boy blurted out, much to the embarrassment of both the girl and Montana. "About the prettiest woman I ever saw. And I'm sure proud to know you. I want you to meet my pard — the best pard a little jasper ever had — Montana Ellis."

The girl nodded and then — Montana choked on his last mouthful of pudding. For no reason at all that he could see she extended her hand. Her shapely white fingers were lying in his great bronzed paw. He clasped them gingerly. She drew her hand away.

"I'm sure pleased, Miss Hope," he found himself saying above the sudden staccato pounding of his heart. "Hello, we've got visitors in town," he observed as a large group of horsemen came thundering down the street.

32

"It's the Diamond A boys," the girl said, moving quickly to the window and peering after the riders. "It looks like there is trouble brewing."

"Trouble?" Montana queried.

"That new outfit moving onto the range that Mr. Lewis mentioned," the girl said. "The stockmen are up in arms about it. I hope there won't be any —"

"Come on, sonny," Montana said suddenly. "We've got to trot along and tend to our horses. Good-by, Miss Hope."

"Good-by."

The two quit the restaurant. As he turned to pull shut the door, Montana looked back. The girl stood gazing after them. And she smiled sweetly to his nod.

CHAPTER
FOUR

The New Ramrod

Outside the restaurant Montana and the boy secured their horses, mounted, and rode on up the street to the livery barn. During the time they had been in the café the deserted village had become crowded with cowboys, while horsemen still came thundering in from the greasewood.

"Things sure have picked up since we rode in," Montana observed as they reached the livery stable and dismounted. "Must be a meeting of the cowmen on that new spread the girl and Lewis were telling us about."

Turning their ponies over to a hostler the two went back outside and started down the street of Elbar, which had jerked itself from its lethargy, and plainly was in a tempest of excitement.

Broad-shouldered, lean-hipped cowboys paced about. Punchers squatted on their haunches, backs to the gusty wind that chased sheets of dust across the brush-clotted flats. In the alleyways cowboys leaned idly against their ponies, which stood three-legged, heads down, rumps to the stinging blasts. About the livery stable were other punchers riding in or surveying

34

the score of gaunt buildings in silence. The air was impregnated with a tenseness that threatened momentarily to explode and send the crowd clawing for the guns holstered at every hip.

"I'm taking you over to the hotel, buddy," Montana said shortly. "I don't like the look of things around here."

"But what are you going to do?" the boy asked anxiously.

"Mill around and find out what's up. There's trouble in the air sure as shooting. I never saw a storm come up any quicker. Everybody's got blood in his eyes."

"You don't suppose your scrap with that Smokey Tremaine started it, do you?" the youngster asked as they strode along toward the hotel.

"A little set-to like that sure wouldn't cause all the cowmen in the country to come riding in here hellbent for election like these fellows are piling in," Montana answered. "It's something big. And somehow, I see grub money in it for us."

They reached the hotel. Entering, they finally aroused a sleepy-eyed, half-dressed clerk. Montana registered. Then, with instructions to the boy to remain close, he went back into the street. Although but shortly after midday the blazing sun was dimmed by clouds of dust scuffed up by galloping hoofs and driven before the whining wind. Fluffy white thunderheads were sailing up from the west.

Far more elated at the prospect of action than he would even admit to himself, and determined to have a look at this new spread, against which all Thunder

Basin apparently was massing, Montana secured a fresh horse at the stable and rode toward the stockyards below the village. Reaching them presently, he peered through the poles at the men unloading the cars shunted onto a siding. Then he crawled up to straddle a top pole.

Directly below was a jolly, fat little fellow with snow-white hair, who puffed violently each time he was compelled to move about on his flea-bitten pony. Obviously the owner of the herd — branded Crossed Sevens — he cursed and mopped his brow while his crew of ten punchers yowled and cursed at the frightened cattle.

"It's beastly hot," Montana could hear the old fellow complaining. "Get a move on you, jaspers. I'll be laid up all winter just as sure as the devil if I have to stay out in this heat much longer."

"If you'd move around a bit, Pop, instead of setting that crowbait of yours like a knot on a log you wouldn't be so hot," one of the punchers advised good-naturedly. "The fact is, I can't see the sense of you being down here. Go on uptown and cool off. You've still got that permit to hold the stuff in the yards, haven't you?"

"The one I got from the railroad official in Omaha?" the old fellow demanded testily. "You don't think I'd throw it away after going to all the trouble I did in getting it, do you? We can hold the critters here as long as we want to without monkeying with the local agent. But me going now would leave us shorthanded."

"Not if it's a cowman you're looking for," Montana put in, leaping down from the poles to land beside the startled pair.

The old fellow turned in his saddle to size him up in a swift and critical glance.

"You being?" he demanded.

"Montana Ellis."

"I'm Kirk Masterson — owner of the Crossed Sevens or Buzzard brand."

"Heard about you," Montana said.

"And I've heard about you," Masterson shot back. "Fellow by the name of Lewis was down here a while back. I used to know him years ago, in Omaha. And I never knew him to pick a man wrong. He told me of your little set-to uptown. And that you're looking for work. He gave you a fine send-off. Coming from Lewis that means — I'm needing a foreman bad. My man, who's been with me for years, took sick suddenly and died in Alliance. We've come through shorthanded."

"I'm your ramrod," Montana assured him. "I'm not the smartest fellow in the world. But I know cows. I was born on a roundup, I reckon."

"I was aiming to go uptown later and look you up, on the strength of Lewis's recommendation," Masterson admitted. "But now you're here — Course, I'm shooting blind. But I don't often go wrong on human nature. I like your looks." His keen blue eyes were sweeping over Montana critically. "I like what I heard about you calling that jasper uptown. You're hired. Shoot square and deliver the goods. You'll never regret it."

Montana stuck out his hand. Masterson took it warmly.

"It ain't just the thing to admit, but I reckon I've got a little personal grudge in this Thunder Basin ruckus," Montana said. "Nothing big, but I'm snorting to tangle with a certain gent if he gets too tough. That's one reason I want particular to tie up with your spread. I like to see a square deal. Another is, I'm needing grub money. If you care to check on me, I'm from the Yellowstone. Nephew of an old cowman up there — Nat Ellis."

"Nat Ellis?" Masterson cried. "Knew him for years. That's enough, son. You've got the job of ramrodding this spread. Get to work."

"You pull uptown and get out of the heat," Montana suggested. "Take your time, Mister —"

"Pop Masterson to the boys," the old fellow said. Then his face grew grave.

"The way you just spoke — about this Thunder Basin ruckus — you've heard something?"

"Nothing to speak of. Just gossip."

"I've got a hunch. There hasn't been enough of the natives down to the yards to look us over. 'Pears like they're either uppish or hostile. Lewis gave me a tip or two. But he was leary of talking too much. I've got a permit to stay in these yards as long as I want. I'm in favor of feeding and holding the stuff right here until the critters get seasoned a little and we nose around. I'll leave you boys some money to buy hay. I'll shag it uptown and plank myself down where it's cool. Kind of feel out the natives."

He drew forth a large roll of bills and peeled off several, which he passed over to Montana.

"I'm taking you at your face value as ramrod of this outfit," he said. "If I've picked wrong, I'm out of luck. If not, you're setting prettier than you ever dreamed. There's plenty more money where this came from, so you don't have to be niggardly with anything in this spread. This herd is just feeder stuff; we'll bring in a real one later. But now, I know you can handle the critters a heap better without me. I've been away from it too long. I'm only in your way. And just to show you my heart's in the right place I'll h'ist one for you as soon as I get uptown."

Smiling broadly, he quit the yards and started his pony on a dog trot toward the village, his body pounding the saddle, his stubby arms flapping. Montana watched him until he had dipped from sight in a ravine. Then he turned back to the punchers, who were regarding him suspiciously.

"The old jasper has a lot of faith in mankind," Montana remarked, pocketing the bills beneath his chaps.

"It's Pop's way," one of the cowboys said. "He either likes you or he don't the minute he lays eyes on you. And if he does size you up as a square-shooter, he'll give you his shirt. He's worth all kinds of money, too."

"Hope he didn't get overheated," Montana remarked. "He strikes me as a white man if there ever was one."

"They don't come any whiter on any range," the puncher agreed. "And his men scrap for him to the finish. What are you aiming to do?"

"Pop said he had a permit to hold the herd in the stockyards as long as he wanted to. So we'll feed right here. But we'll have to rustle hay. Shake a leg, jaspers. Let's shag them out."

The sun had sunk behind a barrier of sullen gray clouds when the last animal had been unloaded. Then, carefully padlocking the gates, Montana headed for the village, the men at his heels.

As he rode across the dreary sagebrush flats, which stretched to the verge of sight in every direction, their level floor gashed by ugly draws, Montana, too, now that he had so suddenly been precipitated into a position of responsibility, became prey to a vague uneasiness. Time and again during the last two hours he had peered anxiously toward the village, hopeful that some of the natives would be drawn by curiosity to the stockyards. But he had waited in vain. Not once did anyone come near. Only occasionally did he so much as sight a horseman galloping along the trail that ran to meet the sky line to the south.

A man of the West who played his hunches, he sensed the gravity of the situation. The sudden activity he had seen in Elbar, the humid August air itself seemed pregnant with some vast and ominous portent. Thunder Basin had issued a challenge in the way it had ignored the new spread. Cowboy that he was he knew that Thunder Basin was arraying itself for war!

CHAPTER
FIVE

An Evil Plot

While Montana, the new foreman of the Buzzard spread was busy unloading cattle at the stockyards, Elbar had taken on even more the appearance of a city. The Midway saloon — before which Montana had encountered Smokey Tremaine upon his arrival — was packed. Punchers gathered in knots to converse in undertones. Some stood staring thoughtfully into space, others hunched against the bar to toy with half-empty glasses. Still others sprawled over poker tables, idly thumbing a deck of cards or rattling a stack of chips. The doors had been shut against the swirling dust. The air reeked with the odor of leather and stale beer.

No one spoke save the bartender, a stubby, red-faced Irishman, who kept up a running fire of conversation as he scooted bottles and glasses with unerring aim along the polished bar.

"They don't dare do it," he rattled on garrulously. "Just you fellows wait until King Kent of the Diamond A gets here. Kent will danged soon show them where to head in, make them hunt cover. And Smokey Tremaine — Say, won't that bunch be duck soup for that hell-bending foreman of the Diamond A? Especially now since he's stowed away a few under his belt?

"That fellow Tremaine is poison both ways from Sunday when he's sober as a judge, but when he's drinking, like he is today, say, tying into a litter of coyotes with the ma around is plumb kid's play compared to this. Tremaine will eat them up guts, feathers, and all. Here, you funeral-faced rannyhans, drag your carcasses up here. See if one on the house won't cheer you up."

He paused long enough in his prattling to fill the glasses of the men who, while they came trooping up in willing, eager acceptance of his invitation, nevertheless signed for their drinks like mutes.

"Crossed Sevens — the Buzzard outfit," the bartender snorted contemptuously, when he had served the silent crew and stepped back to wipe red hands on the soiled apron tucked in the belt at his ample paunch. "Who in hell ever heard of the Buzzard outfit on this range? Or any other?" His hands dry, he fell to polishing the glasses piled high below the bar. "Probably some wild-onion spread that just grew up from nothing and never will amount to anything more than that. The cow country is full of them. Pop up from nowhere in the spring, just like wild onions. Do fine on summer range until the sun gets in its licks. Come winter they've got no feed. They're busted clean to their dewclaws. Mark my words, jaspers, this Buzzard outfit has bit off a sight bigger chunk than it can chew in Thunder Basin. Fill 'em up again — on the house. We cowmen have got to stick together if —" He broke off abruptly to face the door as a man entered importantly. "Howdy, Mister Kent."

A great, strapping fellow was Kent, with frozen steely eyes, a leathery, weather-pitted face, purple, deep-seamed, cold-set. A thin, grim mouth was domineering, suggestive of relentless determination, a ruthlessness more noticeable because of the eyes that seemed to pierce with a heartless gleam. Unlike the others, clad in denim and leather, he was flashily garbed, reflected in his silk and flannel shirt, his bangle-studded chaps, a flare for the ornate.

The bartender reached for a special bottle on the backbar, caromed it dexterously the length of the bar and brought a glass sliding up to stop neatly beside it.

"Throw that under your belt," he invited cordially. "I'll bet she was just plenty hot and disagreeable riding. Ninety in the shade here in Elbar this morning. Seems to be getting hotter right along. Come sundown, unless that storm hits, there'll be no sleeping tonight. Well, I'll be a box-kneed, spavined mule —" as a second man ducked inside to bang shut the door against the inrush of the whistling wind. "Howdy, Smokey. Thought mebbeso you'd pulled back to the ranch. What will yours be?"

Along with Kent, Tremaine, still decked out in his flashy garb, swaggered to the bar. His eyes were beady, glinting. His pock-marked, brutal face was covered with a stubble that made it swarthy. Thick, weather-cracked lips curled back like a cornered wolf's over tobacco-stained teeth. When he spoke his great sullen voice held something of a reminder of a grunting porcupine.

"Still running off at the head, you Irish bum," he threw sourly at the talkative bartender. "Never will learn to keep a dally on your tongue, will you? Make mine straight whisky and plenty of it. What you drinking there, King?"

"Special blend." King Kent slapped the dust from his shirt and hat and faced the crowd which, after muttered greetings in which respect and fear were intermingled, had fallen back to watch him with something of eager expectancy.

"Well, what have you wallopers got on your chests to shag me in from the ranch hot as it is?" he demanded.

"There's a new outfit pulled into the stockyards and is unloading two thousand head of stuff." Bob Hartzell of the T6 stepped out from the crowd to answer. "Crossed Sevens they're branded — the old Buzzard brand. Jasper by the name of Masterson owns them — Kirk Masterson. He's bought the Dunning place in the Basin, north of your Diamond A spread. It's only a six-hundred-and-forty. That means he'll run his stuff on our range and the Lord knows it's got every hoof on it now that it will feed. You being president of the County Stock Association we figured it would be best to get you in here and auger the thing. We're plumb willing and eager to back you up in anything you decide to do."

"Another damned wild-onion spread, huh?" Kent snorted disgustedly. "Getting so they're worse than drought on any man's cow range. Masterson? Masterson? You're dead sure this walloper calling himself Masterson isn't running stuff for some commission house we don't dare get funny with?"

Hartzell, a tall, angular man with little, shifty, faded eyes, a wizened, peaked face, set off by a straggling yellow mustache that drooped at the corners of a flaccid mouth, found a plug in the hip pocket of soiled overalls and twisted off a chew with snaggle teeth.

"Commission stuff, hell," he blurted out when he had worked the chew into a ball in his cheek. "He's just another one of those range spongers that have driven us crazy for the last ten years. They bring critters in here from God knows where. They manage somehow to pull them through a winter, snake poor. The brutes put on a little heft by hogging our grass in the summer. Come fall, the moochers ship the half-starved stuff and pocket every cent they can get while we foot the bill with short range. If we don't like it we can go to hell. That's the way the state and the government are treating us in backing up the homesteaders and range hogs, throwing our range open to any drifter with a flea-bit pony and lame cow.

"I claim this here Masterson has got just plenty of gall dumping that many critters onto Thunder Basin range and expecting us to turn over our feed to him without a holler. The T6, for one, isn't going to stand for it without bellyaching just long and plenty." As his anger mounted he fell to chewing faster until his lean jaws were working like those of a rabbit, his little eyes snapping hatefully. He paused to glare around at the set faces and note with smug satisfaction the nods of approval.

"There's no denying it's gally," Kent agreed, tossing off the drink the solicitous, but now thoroughly squelched, bartender had poured for him. He lifted his wide-brimmed hat to brush close-cropped gray hair back from a deeply furrowed brow. "But as you say, thanks to the interference of the state and government we can't come out any more and post No Trespassing signs on open range. Most of it is government land when you come right down to it — open to homestead entry — and we've broke our hearts trying to grow beef on it. But that's another story. Have any of you jaspers got a scheme?"

"You're danged right," Hartzell offered hotly. "Lope down to the stockyards, give this Masterson an earful, make him reload his stuff and get the hell back to where he came from with his wild-onion outfit."

Kent helped himself to another drink from the bottle, dashed it off, smacked his lips loudly, dragged forth a gaudy kerchief and dabbed his mouth.

"That might have worked ten years ago," he said, wagging his head thoughtfully, "but we've got to figure a little on the law nowadays." He turned his back to the staring crew to scrutinize himself appraisingly in the big mirror behind the bar. "It's a dead mortal cinch that six hundred and forty acres in the old Dunning place won't feed any two thousand head of critters," he mused to his image in the glass. "And there isn't a drop of water on it winter or summer. Our fences take in the springs. But there's only one thing we can do. Give them rope and let them hang themselves."

"I've got a scheme." Smokey Tremaine, who had been drinking steadily while the others talked, and whose hard face had grown even more brutal with the flush of liquor, now hoisted his chaps with his wrists and lurched around to regard the group with unconcealed contempt. "If those critters have come very far they're gaunt and wolfy as teased snakes." A crafty gleam flared up in his eyes. A crooked smile twisted his lips. He reeled away from the bar to stand on spraddled legs, the unlighted stub of a cigaret dangling from his lower lip, gloved thumbs hooked in his studded cartridge belt beside his two forty-fives. "They've got to be fed and watered right here in Elbar. Supposing a big bunch of cattle — say that five hundred head of Diamond A's we've bunched down on Powder river, for instance — was run up to the stockyards on the pretext of us going to weed out some old stuff and ship? This here Buzzard spread could be warned not to mix their critters with ours. Then just what the hell would this new friend of ours, Mister Masterson, do?"

CHAPTER
SIX

Gunplay If Necessary

A moment of silence greeted Tremaine's question. Apparently the significance of it was lost on the crowd. More apathetic now under the influence of liquor, they only regarded the foreman of the Diamond A with uncomprehending stares. Tremaine stood swaying on his feet, leering at them, antagonism, brutality in his glazed eyes.

"I'm asking you again," he demanded, thick-tongued, "just what the hell our friend, Mister Masterson, would do in a case like that?"

Still no reply. The cowboys edged in, waiting for him to continue. But obviously given to a flare for the dramatic, Tremaine chose to speak in riddles.

"I guess I don't just get your scheme," Hartzell ventured timidly after a time. "Supposing we did throw five hundred head of stuff outside the stockyards and warn Masterson not to mix his Buzzards with us?"

"He can't keep his critters under fence forever in this heat, can he?" Smokey snorted. "And just how is he, or anybody else, going to turn his stuff out of the stockyards without mixing if we've got him surrounded?"

Slowly the trick began to dawn on the groggy crew. Furtive glances passed between them.

"And if they did?" Hartzell essayed.

"I don't reckon the law Kent talks about, or anything else, could make us stand for him turning his two thousand head out when he knows they're dead certain to mix, can it?" Tremaine snapped.

"Why, they'd feed and water in the yards, of course," Hartzell countered in a tone which, while mildly argumentative, carried a note of subserviency.

"But just supposing Kent went over and told the railroad agent they weren't going to feed in the yards because the Diamond A needed those yards right away to load out?" Tremaine countered sneeringly. "Then supposing every storekeeper in Elbar ran out of hay sudden-like? And there wasn't a pound to be bought at any price in the county?"

At last the liquor-dulled crowd caught on.

"That's the boy, Smokey!" the punchers broke their long and moody silence to yell.

"Damn me, that is a scheme that's bound to get 'em," Kent cried, slapping his foreman on the back and helping himself to another generous drink from the bottle the watchful bartender kept close beside him. "Give that Masterson fair warning not to mix with our herd — then make him do it. That will furnish us the best kind of an excuse for scattering his stuff from hell to breakfast. What do you think of it, Jerry?" he demanded of the bartender who, with elbows crooked on the bar, chin braced in the palms of his hands, was hanging on to every word.

49

"That's the ticket, Mister Kent!" The bartender beamed. "And I'm saying for one you're just plenty lucky having a foreman with the head Smokey's got on him. Us cowmen can't have wild-onion spreads invading our range and eating off all our grass. Why, two thousand head —"

"Shut up your yawp, you lousy bar-swipe," Smokey cut in hatefully. "Us cowmen! You give me a pain in my innards with your raving. Us cowmen? Shake a leg filling up those glasses for the house and you won't have so much time to run off at the head. It's on me!"

The bartender jerked away to obey. Long since he had learned to heed the storm warnings. Liquor always made Tremaine more brutal. Sober he was bad enough; drunk he was a ruthless brute. And well aware of the ugly spirit whisky fired within the foreman of the Diamond A, the loquacious bartender wilted under the scathing rebuke and did meekly as he was ordered.

When the group had gulped down the new rounds of drinks, Hartzell spoke.

"This here thing of cornering the hay in Elbar might work, and then again it might not," he ventured ponderingly. "It would for sure if it wasn't for that new jasper, Whitey Hope, who bought the store down on the corner a while back. He's as bullheaded and unreasonable as his ma, who runs the restaurant — and you boys know how stubborn she is. The way we've treated him he sure hasn't got any cause to love us, either."

"Whitey Hope!" Tremaine swung around to snort. "Why, that damned counter-jumper —"

"I haven't heard of anybody hanging the Injun sign on him just the same," Hartzell had the temerity to say. "Any more than they have on his mother, or his pa before him. And from what I've seen of him, even if he is a counter-jumper, he don't buffalo worth a damn. He's got hay and I'll lay top horses to goats we'll have to buy it from him to keep him from selling it to the Buzzards or any other outfit that has the cash."

"Like hell we will," Smokey boasted thickly. "I don't cater any to that cotton-headed walloper. Never did from the day I laid eyes on him. I've just been itching for a chance to call him since he wormed in here and bought that store. I'll tell him he can't sell hay to the Buzzard spread. And I won't mince any words either. Then, if he does, he'd better go to shooting or have a fast horse and just plenty of open road out of town for I'll be —"

"What about his sister, Sally, in the restaurant, Smokey?" someone far back in the crowd cried teasingly.

"I'll handle her just like I do him, any time I want to," Smokey bawled back. "And I'm warning you all — Lay off of her. I've picked her myself."

In spite of the dangerous glint in the eyes of the drunken Tremaine, Hartzell was prone to thresh out every detail, although it was evident from the furtive manner in which he regarded the foreman of the Diamond A, that he was deathly afraid of arousing his ire. Hartzell was known as the "yes" man in Thunder Basin; a nervous, rattle-headed cowman who never thought for himself, who was willing and eager to follow any leadership and who, in his sneaking, servile way, was but putty in the hands of King Kent and Smokey Tremaine.

"All right," he conceded presently in an unctious tone. "Just suppose you handle this Whitey Hope. Once his hand is fouled the Buzzard spread can't buy a pound of hay. The Diamond A's will move in and surround the stockyards. Kent sees the agent and blocks the chances of this Masterson getting a permit to stay in the yards more than another day. There's only one thing for them to do — turn their critters out. They've been warned there'll be merry hell to pay if they mix herds. But just supposing they've got a hole card stashed somewheres that we're not on to? Or supposing they do get feed? What then?"

"Borrowing trouble again just like you always do, you lousy coward," Tremaine snarled. "It's getting so of late I hate to waste the time augering your damned fool notions with you — trying to get anything through your mullet head. But just taking the time now to try and make you understand something, supposing they have got a hole card stashed? The Buzzard spread, or any other wild-onion outfit, hasn't any business on a range without making arrangements for enough land to handle their stuff. That's an unwritten law of Rangeland, although you probably never heard about it. Kent is the big squeeze in the County Stock Association. If everything else fails we can blackball them, can't we?"

The stinging scorn in Tremaine's voice lashed the color from Hartzell's face. He slunk back crestfallen, plainly fearful of attempting a reply to the Diamond A foreman, who stood defiantly, his whole attitude one of overbearing challenge.

"That's the way out!" Kent exclaimed. "We'll blackball them if they out-smart us in any way, shape, or form. We'll bar their 'rep' from riding with the pool roundup. We'll make them put out a wagon of their own — do their own riding and gathering. We'll block them from ever shipping a single head of stuff. Don't get me wrong. We won't touch one of their critters." His mood was mockingly serious as he eyed the group. "That is — unless for roping practice or when our meat supply is low. Of course, slicks —" He shrugged and winked broadly. "Might be a little different proposition — one on which a cowman might strain a point if he was sure. If we work it right it won't take very long to bust this wild-onion spread wide open — unless they've got a bank or two behind them. Now here's just the way we'll figure . . . If they should happen to squeeze through this blockade at the stockyards, they're blackballed in Thunder Basin and their stuff is legitimate prey for every man in the country.

"Smokey," he called out as his foreman pushed away from the bar and lurched on unsteady legs toward the door, "you shag somebody down the river with word for the boys to gather up and crowd through those five hundred Diamond A's and surround the yards. Tell them to move along like all hell was after them. Then see the station agent. You," he ordered Hartzell, "see to posting the storekeepers not to sell this Buzzard outfit a pound of hay."

"Me post the storekeepers not to sell the Buzzard hay?" Hartzell almost whined. "What are you doing, aiming to pass the buck to us so if anything comes up your Diamond A spread will be setting in the clear. Are you scared Al Cousins won't stand for your —"

Kent stopped him with an explosive snort of contempt.

"Not by a damned sight!" he bawled. "Al Cousins will do just as I say. Smokey here will tend to lining up Whitey Hope. You handle the other storekeepers. They'll be for us. I was just figuring on saving Smokey for more particular work later on. There's no sense in him mixing into this penny ante stuff."

"You — mean — gunplay?" Hartzell demanded hoarsely.

"You're damned right," Smokey snarled, patting the butts of his forty-fives. "No wild-onion spread is going to run a whizzer on us and start a grub line for starving critters in Thunder Basin or my name isn't Smokey Tremaine."

He stood swaying on his feet, a savage gleam in his liquor-dulled eyes. Seconds ticked by; seconds of palpitating stillness, unbroken save for the shifting of nervous feet. Many times the crowd had seen the brutal foreman of the Diamond A in action. Twice he had faced a court on a charge of murder. Both times Kent had managed to get him off. And now Smokey Tremaine had pledged himself before them all that the Buzzard outfit never would gain a foothold in Thunder Basin. It could mean but one thing. Bloodshed!

"Another drink for the bunch on me, Jerry!" Kent broke the piercing silence in a hollow tone. "And then we'll start the ball rolling to make Mister Masterson hard to catch."

The tension snapped. Pent-up breath soughed forth. Obviously thankful for the respite, the group crowded up to the bar.

"Drink her down," Smokey yelled. "A hot shot for a hot day. To the end of another wild-onion spread on Thunder!"

Hartzell stood gripping his glass with bloodless fingers.

"I'm against the Buzzard outfit," he said in a voice high-pitched, quavering with nervousness. "But I'm saying here and now, the T6 will be no party to murder!"

In a single stride Tremaine was before him.

"Drink her down — and like her," he snarled. "Drink to the end of the Buzzard spread — one way or another. Drink or I'll pour it down your throat!"

Hartzell cast one fearful look at the grim-set faces about him. Then he swallowed the fiery liquid in a single gulp.

Tremaine whirled, with a throaty chuckle reeled from the saloon.

"I'll post the station agent," he flung back from the door. "And if any of you see that strange jasper who got mouthy this noon just tip him off I'm gunnin' for him."

CHAPTER SEVEN

Unexpected Help

While even in the short time he had been in Elbar, Montana sensed something of the hostility in which the Buzzard outfit was held, he was scarcely prepared for the frigid reception he got from the first two storekeepers he approached in his search for hay.

"We haven't got any," was the curt reply of both, who glared at him for an instant, then turned back to their work to ignore him completely.

By the time he reached the door of the third and last store a slow anger had been aroused by the unfriendliness. Youth though he was, Montana had faced opposition before. The laughter died in his blue-gray eyes, which grew hard and cold. His lean, tanned jaws bulged with the pressure of set teeth. With a word to his men to wait for him, he jerked open the door and stepped into the store.

"A ton of hay delivered to the stock —"

He stopped to gaze at the storekeeper in blank amazement. Save for a shock of hair bleached almost white by prairie sun — and which was lighter than Montana's own sandy thatch — and mild blue eyes, it might have been himself to whom he was talking. Never before had he encountered a man who bore him such a striking resemblance. Their bodies could have been cast from the same mold. The fellow had the loose-hipped, easy grace of a cowboy. His face was pleasant, bore the stamp of youth — the same carefree, reckless youth that impressed all who met Montana.

And if Montana noticed the resemblance it was no less obvious that the storekeeper too, had noted it, for he stared in unconcealed surprise. There came to Montana a flash of wonder if this resemblance had been what Smokey Tremaine had noticed; if this could account for the gleam of puzzled recognition in the puncher's eyes? Yet the Diamond A foreman also had seemed to recognize the boy.

"Well I'll be damned if I ever knew I was twins before," the storekeeper blurted out. "But I either am or I'm seeing things. If you'll trade your gray eyes for my blue ones, and your sandy hair for my white layout I reckon you'd be me and I'd be you, wouldn't I?"

The manner of the fellow was so cordial, his smile so winning, that Montana felt himself being drawn to him irresistibly.

"Reckon we're about as near doubles as human beings get." He grinned. "And I'm hoping to know you better. Me, I'm a stranger in Thunder Basin. But I don't aim to be for very long."

Instantly the storekeeper's smile faded. A worried look flashed into his eyes.

"Oh," he said quickly, "you belong to the Buzzard spread?"

"Foreman," Montana returned. "And I want hay."

"Sorry." The youth turned back to resume his interrupted task of sorting case goods. "I haven't any."

"Isn't there a place in town handles hay?" Montana asked. "Aren't there any cows in this country? Or horses?"

"Lots of them."

"What do they feed them?"

"Hay."

"Where can a feller get some, then?"

"I don't know."

"Listen, jasper." Montana leaned against the counter to size up the light-haired youth with cool speculation. "You're lying to me. The other storekeepers in this town might have gotten away with it, but you can't. You're too much like me — a poor liar. You've got hay."

The storekeeper spun about.

"You're right, feller," he returned coldly. "I have got hay — lots of it. But it isn't for sale. Mebbeso you'll like that better." He started around the counter with the slow, cautious movement of a stalking cat, his eyes never leaving the face of Montana, who straightened up to stand easily, thumbs hooked in his cartridge belt. "I was lying. But I don't aim to be told so by any stranger — even if he could pass for my double." A few paces from Montana he halted.

Completely at a loss to understand the fellow's sudden hostility which, it seemed, was not so much the result of his accusation as a pent-up fury touched off by raw nerves, Montana regarded him coolly.

"Listen, jasper," he said presently in a voice that had become soft and persuasive, "I'm not here looking for a row. I'm looking for hay. If you aren't a liar, after claiming you didn't have any hay then admitting you did have, I'm willing to apologize. But now that I know you've got it I'm going to have it if I have to —"

"To what?" cut in the white-haired youth, meeting his gaze with eyes in which there was not so much as a flicker of fear. "To what, jasper? If you figure to come into Elbar and bull your way through you're going to find out mighty quick that you've tied into the wrong bunch. You're up against a hard proposition — you and your Buzzard spread. You can't buffalo me and if you'll take a fool's advice you'll pack your critters into those cars and shag your freight right back to where you came from."

"You mean skin out like a yaller dog just because a few lying jaspers r'ar up and get hostile?" Montana demanded softly but with biting scorn. "Hell, feller, you don't know me — nor the Buzzard spread. We don't run worth a damn. But I don't get your play. You sure aren't in the store business for your health. Yet you've got hay and won't sell it. What's the joke?"

"I've got orders not to sell you any hay, if that's a joke," the light-haired youth blurted out. "I hate it, jasper." Friendliness of a sudden had replaced the belligerent note in his voice. "I know what you're up against. I used to follow cows myself — over on the Snake where they have real punchers instead of lying, sneaking tinhorns. And I know what hungry critters are. But I've got to make a living in this town. They —"

"Who are they?" Montana asked, although it took but a glance along the crowded street to know. "What are you talking about?"

"All of them," the white-haired youth cried. "The minute I came to this tomtit of creation they call Elbar, they tried to hang the Injun sign on me. They didn't do it. I'm not scared of them. To hell with them. But they're my bread and butter. Smokey Tremaine —"

"Who's he?" Montana asked only to keep conversation going.

"Foreman of the Diamond A — the big gut spread on Thunder range. He's bad, tough, dirty — the kind that will plug a walloper where his galluses cross — a two-gun man. I'm sorry, jasper. Plumb. I'd sell you hay, but —"

"I don't quite get the drift yet," Montana encouraged. "What has Smokey Tremaine got to do with you selling me hay?"

"Smokey hates my guts. Because he can't buffalo me, and he's in town today drunk, drunk and hunting trouble. He warned me not to sell you hay. I'm not scared of him, understand — not a damned bit. But I've got to think of my business."

The light of understanding flashed into Montana's eyes.

"So that's it, huh?" he mused grimly. "Tremaine has warned you storekeepers against selling hay to the Buzzard outfit. We'll see about that later. What is your name, feller?"

"Whitey Hope."

"Mine is Montana Ellis. I'm not much on bluffing or scrapping. And I reckon you, being almost my double, aren't either. But I'm telling you plain, Whitey, now that you've admitted having hay you're going to sell it to me or —"

"Or what?" To Montana it seemed that mention of their resemblance had set the barest trace of a smile to hovering on the lips of the youth. "Or what, jasper?"

"Or I'm going to take it away from you," Montana finished coolly. "You aren't monkeying with any wild-onion spread, Whitey. We're cowhands. We've got the cash and we've got the critters. And we'll have the range, too, if they get funny. Now show me that hay."

The white-haired youth shrugged. Montana watched him closely. But he saw no evidence of fear. In fact, the mild blue eyes seemed to be laughing at him.

"And supposing I won't?" Whitey countered. "Then just what do doubles do?"

Montana was positive now that the youth was laughing at him. Scarcely before he realized it his hand had fallen to his gun.

"You'll sell it to me or, like I said, I'll take it away from you! That's what this double will do."

Whitey stepped back a pace. A smile worked its way slowly over his face. But instead of going for the forty-five within easy reach on the counter he stuck out his hand.

"Put her there, jasper!" he grinned. "You're acting just like I would if I had hungry critters. You're right, any walloper who has as homely a mug as mine, like you have, can buy my hay. I'm not scared of that gun of

61

yours — nor nobody else's. I'm a cowhand, a bronc peeler. I went into the store business after I hit a lucky streak and unloaded my homestead for cash. But my feet are itching, itching to feel steel. To hell with the store business! To hell with Elbar! I got fifty ton of hay on hand. It's yours, jasper, yours and the Buzzard's. The hellions around here have ridden me, boycotted me, raised hell with me as long as they are going to. I've had to swallow it because I was playing a lone hand on a hostile range. I've seen other spreads move in like yours is doing; but they were all yaller, buffaloed from the jump and moved out.

"You're different, jasper. You'd shoot for that hay. I like the way you tote your iron — like the ornery squint in those eyes of yours when you're sore. I like everything about you — even your face that is as homely as mine. My store isn't worth a tinker's damn when I sell you that hay. But here she sets, jasper. The Buzzard gets her for cost — on one condition — You give me a riding job. Then if the Diamond A, or any of the rest of them, try to tell me what to do they'll find me setting where I don't have to take it — and snorting to tie into them. What do you say? Is it a go?"

Montana heard the outburst in an amaze too swift to hide. With the instinct of a Westerner who early learns to read human nature in the eyes of men, he watched the light-haired youth closely, striving to see beyond his mild blue eyes and know the true character of this cool yet nervous man, who bore such a striking resemblance to himself. And what he saw sent his fingers edging back along his belt from his gun. The strange impelling force that first had drawn him to the storekeeper again took hold upon him. A wave of gladness that somehow he had won the fellow's friendship instead of his enmity swept over him. Here was a man of his own kind, a man whom he knew he could trust, a fearless friend in whom he could place the utmost confidence.

With a quick movement he took the extended hand.

"They sure must have ridden you powerful hard to make you blow up thisaway, Whitey," he said. "And I admire your guts for kicking over the traces and showing fight. I'll guarantee you don't lose anything on the deal. From now on you're riding for the Buzzard. As for the store — I'm new with the spread myself." Quickly he related how he had ridden into Elbar, his set-to with Tremaine and of his line-up with the Buzzard. "But I think the Old Man will see my way. Let's understand each other. We'll stick together, us two, until hell freezes over, huh, feller? I'm sorry I even made a move toward my gun — against my double."

"Sorry, hell!" Whitey flashed warmly. "I'm glad — plumb glad. It showed me you were the jasper I've been waiting to hook up with. A man who will stand up for his rights, not a back-shooting, four-flushing hellion like Tremaine or Kent or Hartzell. We're too near doubles to scrap. We've got to team up. Who knows, the way we look alike might come in handy on this range before the ruckus is settled." His mood changed. His face grew lean and serious. The worried look came back into his eyes.

"We've got to move fast. Tremaine has posted the storekeepers not to sell you any hay. We've beat him there because I can furnish you with plenty. But that isn't all Tremaine has done. He's moving a herd of Diamond A's in to block you in the yards. They're going to warn you not to mix, then make you do it and stampede your stuff from hell to breakfast. I'll get the hay to you if I have to shoot my way through. Turn your stuff onto the flats quick! We'll feed outside and guard them. Then if they want to fight I reckon we can oblige them, can't we?"

"You're damned right we'll scrap." Wheeling abruptly, Montana quit the store and rejoined his men, who were waiting impatiently. In a few words he explained the situation. With muttered curses they wheeled their horses and raced for the stockyards.

"It's a hell of a time to hold a herd, jaspers," Montana said when the cattle had been turned from the yards and bunched in a great bend of Tongue river some half mile below. "But we're into it now, and the Buzzard outfit don't turn back. With Pop's permission there's a five-dollar increase in every man's pay — scrapping money. We're here to stay. Shag that sleepy cook out of the caboose. Hook onto that mess wagon and snake it down. Let's get a fire started. Quick as the hay gets here we'll feed. Then I'll find Pop and wise him up to why we had to move. We figured to come onto this range peaceful. But if they want to fight, damn 'em, we'll fight them to a standstill!"

CHAPTER
EIGHT

Outlaw Poker

The sultry August day, in which so much had occurred with such startling rapidity, was drawing to a close when Montana had finished feeding part of the hay which, true to his word, Whitey Hope in some way had managed to smuggle to the bawling brutes in the Tongue river bottoms. Then, having placed a double guard, the new foreman started for the village in search of Pop Masterson and to have a look in on the youngster at the hotel.

His mission in Thunder Basin was to deliver a letter to Al Cousins. Yet here he was, within a few short hours one of the central figures in the thick of range war. To turn aside now was to show yellow. To take the boy, complete his mission and pull out was — His teeth clicked grimly on the thought. There would be time later to deliver the letter — later when he had again encountered Smokey Tremaine —

He found himself staunchly defending Whitey for his revolt against the Thunder Basin clan; admiring him for the reckless courage he had displayed in running the gantlet with the hay. Behind Whitey's outbreak he could realize something of the bitterness the former bronc peeler had been forced to endure in Elbar. And he thrilled to the thought that this man, who had dared defy the Buzzard's foes, was his friend; felt secure in the knowledge that Whitey Hope was with him now, accepted by the men — as he, too, had been accepted — who recognized in the cool assurance and fearlessness a cowboy born to the range.

Montana broke off his musing as he rode across the railroad tracks and into the village, the huddled buildings looming like great hulks in the swiftly falling twilight. Here and there a coal-oil lamp sent forth feeble rays which failed utterly to pierce the gloom and became instead only thin fingers of light in a vast and ominous dusk.

Lifting his horse with the rowels, he loped up the street to pull rein before the Elbar Hotel.

Clem met him at the door, anxiety in his eyes.

"Gosh, pard," the boy exclaimed. "I sure was scared something had happened."

"It has," Montana assured him. "We've landed a job already — foreman of a new spread. But come along, let's put on the feed bag."

The boy joined him quickly. Leaving his horse, the two strode up the street, presently to encounter Whitey Hope.

"Just looking for you, Montana," said the youth, who had laid aside his "store" clothes for the flannel shirt and batwing chaps of the range.

"Talk while we're eating," was Montana's brief word. "Where's a good place?"

"That place we ate dinner," Clem put in.

"Kind of stuck on that girl, aren't you?" Montana teased.

"Did you ever see her, mister?" Clem demanded of Whitey as they entered Mother Hope's Café.

The girl, Sally, came forward smilingly.

"Well, yes, I have met them," Whitey smiled, waving to the woman in the kitchen and chucking the girl familiarly under the chin. "You see, Sally — meet Montana Ellis and —"

"She already knows us. And likes us," Clem said.

"You're lucky," Whitey smiled. "Because if Sally likes you —"

"Does she like you too, mister?" the boy demanded.

"I hope so. Do you, Sally?"

"I sure do," she smiled. "I love him."

The boy's eyes widened.

"Gosh, Montana, that's too bad," he blurted out. "I'd kind of hoped that —" He stopped short at the panic in Montana's eyes.

"Sisters are supposed to like their brothers, aren't they?" Whitey's words broke the swiftly growing tension.

"Is she your sister?" Clem gasped.

"Nothing surer than that."

"That's different." Clem's relief was obvious.

When they had ordered, Whitey took Montana to the kitchen where he was introduced to Mrs. Hope, a large motherly woman to whom he was drawn instantly. Montana stood by while Whitey related the story of their meeting, how he had sold Montana the hay and accepted a job as a rider with the Buzzard spread.

67

"I can't take it in the store business, Ma," he blurted out. "I thought I could — I stuck for you — but when Tremaine goes to dictating who I can sell my own goods to, it's time for me to do something about it."

"Your pa was like that," Mrs. Hope said. "And I don't blame you. That Tremaine is dirty. I hope things pan out. But I'm afraid you two have got a hard row to hoe on Thunder."

They went back to the lunch counter presently. Little was said during the meal, Whitey speaking from time to time to his sister and answering questions put to him by his mother. Montana, plainly ill at ease before the girl, was content to remain silent. Clem made no effort to conceal the fact that he was completely taken with Sally.

The meal finished, Montana sent Whitey back to camp, returned Clem to the hotel, where he saw him safely in bed, then mounting his horse, he rode directly to the Midway saloon. Dismounting, he tied his pony to the hitchrail, along with a score of other horses, and entered.

The big resort was packed with punchers. But by now their mood had changed. Liquor long since had routed the silence of the hours before. Paying no heed to the tipsy mob, Montana elbowed his way about looking for Masterson. After several minutes of futile search he had almost reached the conclusion that the cowman was not there when suddenly a burst of laughter, from a group around a poker table in the farthest corner of the room, came to his ears. Thinking perhaps to locate Masterson among them, and always a willing spectator to a poker game, he pushed his way toward the table. Presently he gained a point where he could see the players, some ten in number hunched over their cards.

While in the wan light shed by the flickering pendant lamps their faces were so deeply shadowed as to be scarcely distinguishable, he knew by their seamed and sun-blackened necks, by the wide-brimmed hats — pulled low over their brows to shield their eyes — and by the spur rowels jangling from time to time against the rungs of their chairs that they were cowmen fresh from the range. And another thing he noted. At the hip of every man was a forty-five, which jutted up above the rim of the table, within easy reach of the gnarled fingers that gripped their cards.

But after a few moments it was not so much the men themselves who held his attention. It was the boisterous fun they seemed to be deriving from the game. It struck him as singular for cowmen to play poker thus when it was ordinarily their custom to play the game silently, thoughtfully, with deadly earnestness.

"I'll bust her for a critter," came a rough voice, thick with liquor that caused Montana to start. Although he could not see the speaker the voice was that of Smokey Tremaine. "Who the hell isn't in? Ante up you jaspers, if you're aiming to buy cards in this game. Cows are cheap on Thunder."

Puzzled by the strange manner of opening a jackpot in Elbar, and wondering what sort of men were these who could gamble with cattle instead of chips, Montana attempted to crowd closer only to be jostled back by others who were watching the game with breathless interest.

Roaring with laughter at the opener, the entire group of players stayed with the bet. Nor did it seem to do other than increase their drunken glee when Tremaine stood pat on the draw and bet five more critters. Scarcely believing his ears, Montana gave up in his effort to push nearer and stood straining to hear if the others would stay with the heavy bet. But apparently the wager did not phase them, for they only howled the louder and each raised in turn against the pat hand.

"Let's see," one of the group remarked with mock seriousness. "At eight dollars a head, five steers would be worth forty dollars. Hell, that isn't any bet in this man's game. I've still got fifty critters left of my share of the herd. If they can top that eight-dollar market they're worth four hundred bucks. I'll just hike you those fifty critters, Smokey, and take a look at that bob-tailed flush you played pat!"

"They sure aren't scared to bet 'em high, wide, and handsome in these parts, are they?" Montana remarked to a tipsy puncher at his side.

"Hell, no." The fellow grinned. "But they would be if it was their own cows they were playing for. It's easy to bet when it isn't any skin off your shins whether you win or lose."

More perplexed than ever by the reply, Montana went back to watching the game just as Tremaine who had stood pat, gave vent to an outburst of oaths and threw down his cards.

"I'm cleaned of critters," he growled, pushing back his chair while the others roared with delight. "Hell! And once I owned nigh onto a thousand head." He got to his feet to stand swaying drunkenly. "Go ahead, you jaspers. Play your heads off."

Prey by now to a consuming curiosity, Montana was on the point of putting another question to the man beside him when suddenly he caught sight of Pop Masterson directly behind Tremaine. He started toward the owner of the Buzzard spread only to halt as he caught Pop's voice raised in anger.

"You fellows may think you are having a lot of fun at my expense," the old cowman cried. "But if you do, you're crazy."

"Like hell we are," threw back Tremaine, who now whirled to face Masterson, his broad back toward Montana. "Blackballed critters are anybody's meat on Thunder range."

"We'll see about that too," Masterson retorted. "Any time you fellows think you can play poker for my stuff you've got another think a-coming."

Still Montana could not get head or tail to the thing, although one word crashed on his brain. Blackballed! To be blackballed on any range was the worst disaster that could befall a cowman. It meant that he could not gather his cattle unless he did it himself, for no pool roundup would handle them. If he did succeed in getting them bunched they could not be shipped from the county for they were under a cloud as black as quarantine. Yet what right had Tremaine to mention blackballing in reply to Pop Masterson? It was usually

71

the procedure against rustlers whose herds were known to include animals belonging to other outfits. But there could be no such suspicion directed against the Buzzard spread. Still, in the face of the underhanded opposition they already had encountered, Montana knew that it was not beyond the Buzzard's foes to attempt a blackball in their efforts to intimidate them and keep them from gaining a foothold on Thunder range. Yet never a man to jump at conclusions, Montana held himself in check until he could obtain a better understanding of the whole affair.

"Well, we did play poker for your stuff," Tremaine returned snarlingly, to explain to Montana in a flash the unusual merriment and wild bets of the game. "And I lost my split in them. But wait until these other jaspers get through. Then we'll see who owns the Buzzard stuff — you or them."

"You're talking through your hat," Masterson said with biting scorn. "It's the liquor you've drunk boasting. If there is any blackballing to do it won't be by a bunch of drunks around a saloon. It will be your County Stock Association. And they'll have to show cause, and plenty of it, ever to blackball the Buzzard spread from this range or any other."

"I'd like to know who the County Stock Association is if it isn't us," Smokey sneered. "Danged nigh every member of the Association is playing for your stuff here and now. Most of the critters on this range are represented here at this table. And when we say your Buzzard stuff is blackballed that is just what we mean. We told you how things stood when you came single-footing in here this afternoon. We gave you a chance to pull your freight. But you got tough and mouthy, tried to shove things down our throats and make us like it."

He lurched around to face the players, who had paused in their game to listen to the apparent renewal of the altercation.

"Play them up, jaspers!" Tremaine roared maudlinly. "Those Buzzard critters will die of old age anyhow before they ever get shipped out of Thunder Basin. We might just as well go to splitting them. What don't die of old age will starve plumb to death, because the outfit hasn't any range."

"Maybe we haven't much range," Pop continued the argument in a weary tone. "But we are willing to buy. You fellows don't own all Thunder Basin. It's mostly government land; most of it is open to homestead entry right now even though it is under your fences. I saw to that before I ever thought of moving in. What's the idea of acting this way? I haven't done anything to hurt you."

"Your just being here is an insult," shouted the drunken Tremaine, again turning his back on the nerve-taut Montana. "We've told you a dozen times that Thunder Basin can't support any more stuff. That's why we offered you eight dollars a head for them. But you wouldn't talk turkey at our figure, even after we told you you were blackballed. You got your old neck bowed and went hostile. So we just decided you didn't know enough about cows to run them. That's why we divided them up and played for them. The

County Stock Association will get them anyhow in the long run."

"I won't stand for your —" Pop began furiously.

"You've got to, jasper!" Smokey cut him short. "Got to, because there isn't anything else for you to do. If you'd only look at it sensible you'd see we did you a favor in taking those critters off your hands. You'd have to keep them under fence on that Dunning place you say you bought. It's only a six-hundred-forty. Wouldn't feed a flock of cottontails. Why, there isn't even water on it. But there you would have stayed, jasper, because if you ever moved a hoof out onto the range we'd of done a damned sight worse to you than we're doing now. And when you even think of homesteading the pasture land we've got under fence you're just breeding yourself a bunch of hell you'll wish you never had run into."

"But you don't understand," Pop expostulated. "I'm —"

"We don't care a damn who you are," Tremaine interrupted again, sneeringly. "You'll wonder who you are yourself before we get through with you. We're not fooling. We mean business. If we hadn't of taken those critters away from you we had you sewed up so tight anyway you'd have been squealing like a stuck pig pronto."

"Sewed up?" Pop asked anxiously. "How?"

"Never mind how." Tremaine's words ended in a burst of laughter. "You'd have damned soon found out, wouldn't he, fellers?"

74

"But boys," Pop persisted. "I've got money to buy places. That's what I figured on doing — buying more land. I'm not going to homestead your pastures. I'm no nester. I'm here to work with you, help you, You aren't giving me a square deal. I haven't hurt you. If I do, then raise hell about it. I tell you I'm —"

"And I say we don't care a damn who you are," Smokey grated. "You moved onto Thunder range without an invitation. That's enough to make us against you and your lousy little wild-onion spread. We're warning you for the last time — you shag yourself back to where you came from or we'll —"

CHAPTER
NINE

Merciless Killing

Montana waited to hear no more. He pushed through the group and planted himself in front of Tremaine.

"Hold on a minute, jasper," he said in a tone which, for all its softness, still carried to every part of the saloon to quiet the boisterous crew and set booted feet to shifting uneasily. "You're taking a little too much of a load on your own shoulders to my way of thinking. There's a few things for you to try and get through that big head of yours quick. In the first place the Buzzard outfit isn't any wild-onion spread. In the second place it isn't moving off Thunder range.

"As for your betting the Buzzard critters at poker you're either just plain fool or trying to hang the Injun sign on somebody. The two thousand head Pop Masterson brought with him is only feeder stuff. When he gets ready he's going to move a real bunch of cattle in here."

He paused to sweep the crowd with a coldly glittering eye.

"I came to this town on business — nothing whatever to do with the Buzzard spread. I stayed on account of you, Tremaine. Now, damn you, if you're feeling hostile you pick any fight you've got with me."

Again his eyes bored into the little beady ones of the foreman of the Diamond A.

"So it's you again?" Smokey blurted out, sobered somewhat by Montana's sudden appearance and visibly nonplused at his fearless challenge. "Just what the hell business have you got butting in here?"

"I happen to be the new foreman of this Buzzard spread," Montana shot back. "Tied up with them a-purpose to force a square deal. I'm the jasper who is going to have just plenty to say about you collecting those poker stakes you've been playing for. I'm wise to your breed, Tremaine; you're the walloper running up the Diamond A herd to blockade us in the yards; the smart jasper who tried to keep us from buying hay by intimidating the storekeepers. But get this, feller, we're already out of the yards — out and fed in spite of you!"

"That lousy Whitey Hope!" Tremaine exploded, flying into a rage which until now had found an outlet in the contempt and sarcasm he had forced Masterson to endure. "Shag down there some of you boys. Give that counter-jumper the damnedest chapping a man ever got. Ride him out of town on a rail. I ought to have plugged him in the first place."

"Whitey Hope's a friend of mine," Montana warned in a voice now little above a whisper. He turned slightly to halt several of the erstwhile poker players who, obviously eager of an opportunity to leave, had seized upon Tremaine's suggestion, thrown down their hands, leaped up, and were crowding toward the door. "You're too late to do any chapping, or rail-riding either to Whitey Hope, fellers," he said without raising his voice. "The Buzzard spread has bought him out — hay and everything." He shot a quick glance at Masterson to get his reaction to the announcement. The old man was fairly beaming. Sure now of his ground, Montana rushed on. "There's a law to stop you from stepping foot inside that store. What's more, Whitey Hope is now riding for the Buzzard spread. A scrap with him means a scrap with every man in our outfit."

He swung back to face Tremaine squarely, leaving the others gaping at him in open-mouthed amazement.

"You're just about the caliber I figured you, Tremaine," he said scornfully. "A walloper ready to devil a feller as old as Pop Masterson — and offering him his choice of taking eight dollars a head or losing his critters at poker. It sure shows the guts you've got.

"And that hay deal. That was another dirty play, Tremaine. But you're the one who got caught by it if anybody did. Our stuff is in the river bottoms. And while I think of it, I want to warn you that when you move those Diamond A's up you want to be sure and not let them mix with us or we'll scatter them from hell to breakfast, like you figured to scatter our critters. You might have bluffed folks on this range for a long spell, Tremaine. But you can't bluff us."

An ominous silence by now had settled down over the big saloon. Save for the rasping breath of the tipsy onlookers, the tinkle of spur rowels and the swish of the bartender's towel no sound broke the gripping stillness. Smokey and Montana stood framed in the flickering light, motionless as stone, muscles taut, gazes locked. Both faces were expressionless, yet a slow pale shade was driving the flush of liquor from Tremaine's pitted cheeks. His gloved fingers, hooked in his studded cartridge belt, had the advantage in the distance they had to travel to his guns. But obviously the recollection of Montana's speedy draw of a few hours before was all too vivid. The crowd stared in wonder. Again the strange cowboy had dared defy Smokey Tremaine. And they waited with fearful expectancy for the outcome.

Someone moved. A chair crashed to the floor. Smokey started. Aside from a jerk of straining muscles, Montana gave no sign that he even heard. The man who had risen from the poker table was big King Kent.

With amazing calm Pop Masterson felt the tension grow. His sixty years in the West were pregnant with the recollections of fatal gunplay. In days long past — before he had laid away his own forty-five forever — it too had exacted its toll of human life. Yet it occurred to him as he watched that never had he seen eyes so utterly devoid of fear as the blue-gray ones of Montana, who was smiling into the Diamond A foreman's bloodless face.

Sizing up the situation with a precision born of many desperate encounters where one false move meant death, when he spoke Pop's voice was little more than a whisper, yet it seemed to boom through the room. The deadly tension snapped.

"Come along, Montana," he urged gently. "I've tried to tell them who I am, but they won't listen. There'll be other ways to settle this thing."

Montana dared a glance at him. But before he could reply Kent found his voice.

"No there won't," he bawled. "I told you when you first came in here that I was King Kent, owner of the Diamond A and president of the County Stock Association. You're up against it, jasper — no range, no water. There's only one way for you to settle it. This poker game may seem like a joke to you; but it just goes to show how high your critters rate with us. And the Association is ready to back us up in anything we do. Now you'll either sell at our price or you'll get the hell out of the country!"

Masterson started to sputter a reply. But Montana stopped him.

"Let me do the talking, Pop," he said. "You've been away from this kind of wolf too long. They're hard — or think they are." His tone was careless, yet it teemed with stinging scorn. He wheeled on Kent, careful however, to keep Tremaine well within his range of vision. "The Buzzard outfit is here to stay, jasper. Neither you nor your whole Association can scare us off. We figured on moving in peaceful. If we can't come that way we're coming any old way we can!" He seized hold of Masterson's arm and jerked him back as the old cowman hurled his hat savagely to the floor and lunged toward Kent, his white hair bristling, his face aflame with anger.

"You're too old, Pop," Montana cautioned. "There was a day when you could've et the two of them up. Go on over to the hotel now and cool off. When things quiet down —"

"Things aren't going to quiet down!" Kent thundered. "They're going to get worse — a heap worse — till you've got your bellies full of range stealing and —"

The rest of his words were lost to Montana who was struggling to hold the fuming Masterson in check. With main force he shoved the old fellow toward the door.

"Wait a minute, jasper!" Tremaine bawled. "We're not through with you yet by a hell of a ways. You don't need to run away."

"Run away!" Montana whirled to bite off the words. "Run away! Why — you white-livered four-flusher you never saw the day anything or anybody would run away from you. You, the kind of a jasper who tries to buffalo storekeepers into not selling hay to hungry critters. A jasper who tries to throw the fear of the Lord into a man old enough to be his father. And you're just the caliber who never shoots till the other man's back is turned. I've got you pegged. Now four-flush and be damned. Play poker for our stuff if you get any fun out of it. Then try to collect what you win if you feel lucky. Get going, Pop!"

Again he started the blustering old fellow toward the door. And again Tremaine hurled a stinging taunt after them.

Before Montana could reply Kent shouted, "Remember, you're blackballed from every roundup in the county. You'll run your own wagon and gather your own stuff. You'll never ship a head out of this county. The Association will —"

"Blackball and be damned!" Montana shot back coldly. "When the time comes to ship, we'll ship, and don't you forget it. As for us gathering our own stuff, from the looks of that jasper" — indicating Tremaine — "we aren't so dead anxious to have your pool wagons handle it. We're willing even now to forget the whole thing, play with you, shoot square with you, give you the best of it if you'll come down off your high horses. But stick to straight poker and don't start any freeze-out games with Buzzard stuff; because you're going to get the worst of it in the long run."

"Get the worst of it!" Tremaine howled. "Get the worst of it from a damned lousy bunch of —"

"We may be four-flushers to your way of thinking," Montana cut him short, "but you'll find out we take what is coming to us."

"And you'll get that, too!" Smokey bawled. "You —"

"Careful," Montana warned softly, his face set, colorless, his lips braced in a thin line across his teeth. "You can think those things if you want to; but don't say them out loud. Get going, Pop!"

His tone sent the crowd edging farther into the sheltering gloom outside the rim of light. Masterson opened his mouth to protest. That protest was never voiced. Three shots cracked one on another. The reverberations crashed down deafeningly on the tense and motionless group. Spirals of acrid blue smoke drifted lazily toward the ceiling.

Smokey Tremaine swayed slightly. One of the two Colts he had jerked from his holsters — the left, Montana noted in surprise — was smoking when it

82

clattered to the floor. Tremaine's knees buckled. His other gun dropped from limp fingers. He pitched headlong across the poker table!

Montana's eyes swept the dumfounded crowd. Kent, too, had a gun clutched in his hand. And another man — a stranger whom, until now, he had scarcely noticed — was sheathing a forty-five. A low moan brought him about. Pop Masterson threw out his arms and crumpled in a heap.

"You —" Montana shouted hoarsely, holstering his own hot-barreled Colt and clutching for the wounded cowman. "You lousy —" He dropped to his knees beside the prostrate man. "If Pop is hurt bad this range hasn't ever seen any hell like it is going to. Water, bartender!" He raised the snow-white head in his arms. "Pop! Pop! Where are you hit?"

A soft light drove the pain from the old cowman's eyes as they fluttered open.

"You did your best, Montana," he panted. "I didn't figure they'd shoot a man who didn't even have a gun." His voice sank to a whisper. He fought gamely for breath. Montana leaned closer to catch his words. But, the effort was too great. Only a gurgling sound issued from pain-locked lips.

From the corner of his eye Montana saw the man, Kent, holster his own gun, pick up Tremaine's, ram them into the foreman's holsters, throw an arm about the groaning fellow, lift him from the poker table and half carry, half drag him toward the back door.

"Hold on there!" Montana cried. "If Pop dies that drunken lobo will swing from the nearest tree in Thunder Basin."

Kent's only answer was to double his speed. Shifting Masterson's head in his arms, Montana drew and fired. A warning bullet — a bullet that ripped through the door just as Kent threw Smokey outside, leaped after him and banged it shut behind them.

Montana had no time to think of pursuit. For at that moment Pop again found his voice, husky and weak though it was.

"Reckon the jig is up with me, Montana," the old fellow faltered. "I don't know much about you — But you've showed me you deal from the top. I haven't any kin — no one to carry on for me. If you want to —"

"I sure do, Pop," Montana flashed. "I want to stick here until I clean out this wolf den — Make these backshooters —"

The old man attempted a grim smile that ended in a twinge of pain.

"Stick then, Montana. Right here in Thunder Basin. There's a will back in Omaha — leaves all my stuff to my foreman who is with me when I cash in. I figured the other jasper in Alliance — But it's too late to change it now — I know you'll fight — like I'd want you to fight. Get yourself a good partner — One you can trust —" He clutched at his chest in a desperate effort to hang on.

"I've already got him, Pop," Montana said. "The truest pardner ever I had except — Whitey's his name, Whitey Hope. He'll stick to me till hell freezes over."

"And you've got another pard," came a voice from above him. "Another pard who will play the game with you. From this day on Bob Hartzell of the T6, is with you."

Montana glanced up quickly to meet the eyes of the third man he had noticed holstering his Colt immediately after the gunplay.

"Thanks, jasper," he muttered. "I reckon I'll need friends if I'm going to fight this damned underhanded gang."

"Fight 'em," Pop gasped. "Fight 'em to the last ditch. You've got the winning hand. You'll see what I mean by my papers back in Omaha. It's a bad break now. But — clean out the whole works — Get Kent first. You'll understand when you see the will, the papers — And I know you'll do it. Wire Bert Jones in Omaha. His address is in my pocket. I want to be buried in Omaha — I — So long!" His voice trailed off to a sob. He shuddered and straightened out.

Montana sat for a moment without moving. Then he laid the white head down gently and got to his feet.

"I reckon this is the first draw in Thunder Basin," he muttered, a new hardness in his voice. "It was against me. But it won't be the last one. You jaspers —" He swept the mute punchers with eyes that now were glazed with a terrible light. "You'd best be picking your sides — because no man can be neutral. To think men would get so low they'd kill that white-haired old feller," he muttered brokenly. "But they'll pay — just plenty."

Then he was himself again, his emotion in check.

"Some of you get the coroner and the sheriff!" he commanded. "The rest of you — get out!"

Still stunned by the swift-moving tragedy they had witnessed the men slunk from the saloon, leaving Montana and the bartender gazing down at the still figure of Pop Masterson.

"Poor old Pop," Montana repeated, dropping again to his knees to take the snow-white head in his arms. "Your first day in Elbar — Like it's mine. They got you. But they didn't get me. They've showed their hands. Now, damn them, they'll play them as they stand — to the finish!"

CHAPTER
TEN

Clue to a Killer

Long after the others had left, Montana knelt beside the body of Pop Masterson, stunned by the tragedy that had burst with such appalling suddenness about him, prey to chaotic impulses that cascaded through his brain to fire him with passion; red, blinding passion.

With a masterful effort he succeeded in getting some control over himself. In the pocket of Pop's coat he found some letters, a notebook in which were the addresses he had mentioned; then he started to rise to his feet. Purely by chance he encountered a small hard object beneath the coat. He fingered it idly for a moment. Then curiosity got the better of him. Lifting the coat, he groped under it until his fingers came in contact with the object imbedded in Pop's clothing. Working it loose, he pulled it forth. It was the bullet that had brought Pop down. A hard-nosed bullet encased in a copper jacket and the end of which had been niched! Its size, he imagined, would indicate that it had been fired from a forty-five. Apparently it had passed clear through Masterson's body but had so far spent itself that it had failed to pierce the coat.

Instantly Montana was alert to the value of his discovery. The pellet of lead was damning evidence of guilt. Few men used copper-jacketed bullets; fewer niched them. He had heard that the niche kept the bullet from glancing, forced it to drill a straight hole when an unniched bullet would deviate and follow the line of least resistance. It was a secret of gunmen who shot to kill and never wound their victims. Yet, he reasoned, hostile as the Thunder Basin clan had proved itself only luck would ever give him a chance to examine the cartridges in their guns.

He got to his feet to stand gazing at the bullet, which lay in the palm of his hand. Thought of the grim tragedy the harmless-looking pellet had caused again set the scalding blood of passion to pounding through his veins. But he was quickly master of himself, his rage submerged in the lucid thoughts that began arranging themselves in his brain. After all, he decided, niched though it was, the bullet would do him no good. He had all the evidence he needed. Smokey Tremaine had killed Pop Masterson. There had been three distinct shots. He had fired the one that sent Tremaine down. And Tremaine had fired the other two — one each from the brace of forty-fives he had whipped from his holsters.

He walked over to the stove, resolved to rid himself of the bullet which ever would be a reminder of the tragedy.

"What are you aiming to do, jasper?" a voice inquired at his elbow.

Montana whirled to face the little bartender who had come up quickly behind him.

"Isn't that a bullet you've got there?" the fellow demanded before Montana could reply.

"Yes. The one that dropped Pop. Went clean through him and lodged in his clothes. It's niched."

"What are you aiming to do with it?" the bartender repeated.

"Throw it in the stove. It isn't any good now."

"The hell it ain't," the bartender burst out excitedly. "It's niched, huh? Don't throw it away, jasper. It might prove who killed the old feller."

"Prove who killed him?" Montana growled. "That don't have to be proved. Tremaine did that killing."

"If you ever prove Smokey Tremaine did it you'll do more than has ever been done in Elbar before," the bartender said, laying a hand on Montana's arm. "You save that bullet. Some day it might come in handy. And jasper —" He hesitated a moment, gazing into Montana's eyes. "I was against you when you hit this town. I was with Kent and Tremaine. I heard this frame-up about the blockade, the blackballing. But since I've seen you and that good old feller they plugged, I just want you to know that Irish Jerry is for the Buzzard spread. And if there is anything I can ever do for you, just tip me the wink." He offered his hand in a simple gesture of friendship.

Montana gripped it warmly.

"Thanks, Jerry," he said huskily. "You're the kind of a friend I'm looking for. Another like Whitey Hope. And I'll keep this niched bullet —"

"Under your hat," the bartender cautioned, placing a warning finger on his lips. "And watch out for another frame-up." He moved swiftly back behind the bar. Montana wiped off the bullet, dropped it into his pocket and threw himself into a chair to resume his endless chain of thought.

The arrival shortly of the sheriff — a hatchet-faced old Westerner with gray hair and a harassed expression on his weather-whipped countenance — and the coroner, a shifty-eyed individual in a frock coat, who resembled more a tinhorn gambler than a representative of the law — cut short his retrospection. He watched them dully as they set the men who had accompanied them to lifting the body of Pop and carrying it away.

Then the coroner was beside him.

"Jerry says you're the Buzzard foreman," he was saying in a gruff, jerky voice. "You did some shooting yourself, I hear. You just trot along with us, feller. We'll see if you can come into a peaceful town like Elbar and start hell like this. We're going to hold the inquest now."

With a mighty effort Montana conquered the hot anger that flared up within him. Something in the coroner's unfriendly tone, the manner in which he had managed to shift responsibility for the affair from Tremaine and Kent to Masterson and himself, warned him to silence. Getting to his feet he left the saloon and plunged into the unlighted street, followed by the sheriff and coroner.

At a small frame building below, the sheriff, to Montana's surprise, left them. The coroner opened a door and stepped back for Montana to enter. Once inside, the cowboy looked around. Short as had been the time since the affray, already there was a score or more men assembled. Yet, he noted, neither Tremaine nor Kent was present. Wondering, he held his tongue and took a seat.

The impaneling of a jury, none of whom Montana knew, was a matter of routine. Then, in a manner that suggested the whole affair was distasteful to him and he was eager to be finished with it, the coroner started the taking of testimony. Everyone smoked, laughed, and talked at once. Utterly disgusted with the procedure, which he quickly saw was nothing but a farce, a travesty on justice which he was powerless to prevent, Montana sat mute and motionless.

Nor was he asked to testify. A few of the now sober onlookers gave their version of the affair as they had witnessed it through liquor-glazed eyes. That was all. Neither Tremaine nor Kent put in an appearance. The bartender was not called. Before Montana believed the inquest to be well under way the jury withdrew to return almost immediately with its report.

"We, the jury, find that Kirk Masterson came to his death as the result of a gunshot wound inflicted by a party unknown!"

The slow anger that had been smoldering within Montana since first he had challenged Smokey Tremaine flared out of bounds. He leaped to his feet.

"Killed by a party unknown," he scoffed in the same soft tone that had set the same tipsy bunch edging back in the Midway. "Why, you lying coyotes, you saw

Smokey Tremaine shoot Pop Masterson down in cold blood."

"There is no testimony to prove that Tremaine did this killing," the coroner observed in a tone of judicial thought. "You, being the jasper who picked the scrap and wounded Smokey naturally would blame him. But this inquest isn't the place to unload a lot of personal spite. If you can prove Smokey did it we're willing to hear you. If you can't, then you'd best keep your mouth shut. There are a lot of Tremaine's friends here; and I'm not so sure the sheriff is through with you yet, either."

"There were three distinct shots," Montana held his rage in check to point out coolly. "I fired one of them. Tremaine had two guns. He shot Pop Masterson with one and took a pot shot at me with the other."

"Is that so?" the coroner sneered. "Well, I only saw one exploded shell in Smokey's gun — in the left one."

"It's a damned lie!" Montana blurted out, although hazily recalling that he had been conscious at the time of the gunplay that only one of Tremaine's forty-fives — the left one — had been smoking. "Tremaine fired two shots. I fired one. I can prove it by my gun here." Breaking the chamber of his forty-five he offered it for inspection, only to stop and stare blankly. Instead of one exploded cartridge there were two in his gun! Then suddenly he remembered. He had sent a second shot ripping through the door as Kent dragged the wounded Tremaine outside. "I dropped Tremaine with the first shot — then I fired at him again —"

"Did anyone hear this jasper shoot twice at Smokey?" the coroner interrupted.

Everyone shook their heads.

"That settles it," the coroner said. "You haven't proved anything by Smokey having two guns. The fact is, you're only incriminating —"

"Kent had his gun too," Montana put in hotly. "And that feller, Hartzell —"

"Well, which one of you shot Masterson then?" The coroner yawned wearily. "You're the man with two exploded cartridges in his gun. Here, Hartzell!" he ordered the T6 man, who had not testified but who had paid strict attention to the proceedings. "Just to satisfy this, let's have a look at your gun." Without a word, Bob Hartzell passed over his forty-five. The chamber was full of unexploded cartridges.

"I never said Hartzell did it," Montana flared. "I said he had his gun out. He's the only one of your tribe that has acted like a white man. Him and Jerry, the bartender. You said you saw Tremaine's guns. I want to see them." Convinced by the strange twist in the affair that the niched, copper-jacketed bullet he had found in Masterson's clothing — and which had it not been for the bartender he would have thrown away — would place the guilt, he played his last trump.

"Smokey has his guns," the coroner said. "There was no need of me keeping them. He —"

"Tremaine and Kent saw you before I sent for you, didn't they?" Montana accused.

"I'm a doctor," the coroner admitted plainly before he could check himself. "I fixed Smokey's arm."

"And fixed this inquest, that's what he did," Montana shot back. "Fixed it just like he and Kent have fixed everything else on this range. Where is Tremaine now?"

"How should I know?" the coroner snarled.

"Isn't it customary to make it your business to find out where a suspect in a murder is?" Montana demanded.

"I questioned Smokey — examined his guns when I fixed up his arm where you shot him. I'm running this inquest, not you."

"And a hell of a fine job you're doing," Montana snorted disgustedly. "Every man who saw that shooting ought to be hauled in here and made to testify to the truth. You had no business letting Tremaine and Kent leave. Tremaine killed Pop Masterson and you know it!"

"Unless you can prove it the verdict of this jury, that Masterson came to his death at the hands of a party unknown, stands!" the coroner shouted angrily. "Your gun has got the only two exploded cartridges in it I've seen."

"You mean to intimate that I shot Pop Masterson?" Montana asked with almost a croon in his voice.

"We don't know you; stranger things than that have happened."

Montana bounded across the room.

"Say that again and I'll bend this forty-five double over your worthless head! I've run into longhorns before, but I never in my life tied up with such a bunch of lying, four-flushing hypocrites as you jaspers. I demand the arrest of both Tremaine and Kent."

"For what?"

"For the murder of Kirk Masterson."

"Arrest King Kent?" the coroner exclaimed. "Why, it would be the biggest fool move you could make. He owns half the town and county. You've got nothing on him — or Smokey either. If you're smart you'll let this verdict ride. Then, if you can get proof —"

"Proof, hell," Montana muttered. "You don't want proof. If you did you'd be hunting some yourself. That's what you're paid for — to find clues." Thought of the niched bullet popped into his mind. "You haven't even looked for the bullet."

"I have," the coroner jerked out — nervously, Montana thought. "I probed for that bullet before I started the inquest. It went clean through. As long as we haven't got it I reckon it won't cut no ice."

"Mebbe not," Montana conceded grimly. "But I'm repeating, you arrest Tremaine and Kent or —"

"Or what?" the coroner demanded frozenly.

"Or —" Turning, Montana studied the faces about him. Not one of them was friendly save perhaps the sneaking one of Bob Hartzell.

"You win, jaspers," he said presently in a deadly quiet tone. "The deck is stacked against me — again. We'll let your verdict ride for now. But get this, and get it straight. If you represent the law in Elbar it's time some of us were taking it into our own hands. No matter what you decided, Pop Masterson is dead — shot down in that saloon. And I'm going to bring the man who did it to justice." He wheeled and started for the door.

"Hold on!" ordered the coroner. "We aren't through with you yet."

Montana's only answer was to bang the door shut behind him.

Then Montana was outside in the dimly lighted street. The wind, whining in from the greasewood flats, cooled his hot face, the scalding blood of anger boiling through his veins. Gone now was all thought of quitting the Basin. Forgotten for the moment was his mission in coming to Elbar. One thing hammered above all else in his mind. He would fight the thing to the bitter end — bring Smokey Tremaine and King Kent to justice!

Routing out a sleepy-eyed station agent, he sent several telegrams to addresses he found in Pop Masterson's pocket. Notifying the man, Bert Jones, Pop had mentioned with his dying breath, and completing arrangements for the return of Masterson's body to Omaha for burial, he left the station and went to the hotel. There he assured himself that the boy was safe and sleeping soundly. Then going back to the Midway he secured his mount, rode it to the livery barn, exchanged it for his own horse, by now somewhat rested after putting into Elbar, and loped across the tracks in the direction of camp. Far up the river a storm was lashing the horizon, vivid streaks of lightning, distant, grumbling thunder. Out of the far dark of the moonless night came the bark of a coyote, followed by a long and quavering wail that blended with the wind whining through the draws. Somehow the dismal sound found answer in the loneliness that lay heavy upon him.

A short way from the Buzzard camp he jerked from his lethargy and pulled his pony to its haunches. Out of the gloom ahead suddenly came a sound — a sound not unlike the rumble of the distant thunder. But Montana knew it was not thunder. To his trained ear it carried a more ominous meaning than the mere growling of a storm.

"It's the herd," he muttered grimly. "And they're running like hell!"

He lifted his horse in a gravel-flinging lunge. It snorted savagely, leaped away in the direction from whence came the sound.

CHAPTER ELEVEN

Stampede

How long he pounded through the darkness Montana never knew, nor did he care. The reckless pace of his horse seemed to ease his violent emotions. He was only vaguely aware that from a rumble the sound of running cattle had grown in volume until it had become a steady hum, like that of a great planing mill.

Past the smoldering embers of the campfire he raced. In a single glance he saw that the men were not in their bedrolls, still piled near the mess wagon. A few snorting horses in the rope corral — the remnant of the cavvy — told him plainer than anything else that the Buzzard punchers were on the job. His thoughts flew to Whitey Hope. Whitey's was the foresight that had held the cavvy in an emergency; he was the cause of the men being on duty. He was a top hand, indeed, well worthy of the trust that had been imposed in him.

Rounding the wagon, a shapeless bulk in the darkness, Montana again gave his horse the rowels. It thundered on, taking the gullies in great muscle-straining leaps, miraculously maintaining a footing in the brush, ever pulling and fighting against the taut reins. Louder and louder grew the noise of hammering hoofs ahead.

A mile or more from camp some impelling force drew his gaze back over his shoulder. The pent-up anger within him flared into a consuming rage that for a moment blinded him. A curse left his lips. He jerked his horse savagely to its haunches to stare at a finger of fire that suddenly had sprung up. Fanned by the wind it mounted higher and higher until it became a dazzling, writhing pillar in the Stygian heavens. Came a great burst of flame, a shower of sparks like a gigantic pyrotechnic display, then a rolling cloud of smoke even blacker than the sky beyond.

"Oil!" he cried in dispair. "They've drenched the wagon, bedrolls and hay with oil and fired them!" His teeth clicked grimly. "But it's too late to stop it now. If we can mill the critters and save them we'll be lucky. I reckon this is some more of the work of Smokey Tremaine —"

He waited a moment longer, then wheeling his mount he thundered along after the stampeding herd, the sound of which, in the brief seconds of delay, had died almost to a throb on the distant night air.

Clumps of brush and rocks flew by with amazing speed beneath the hoofs of his lather-smeared horse — a chimera of hazy, indistinct objects which loomed stark and ominous for an instant beside him, then sped away to become a part of the ebon void. Once again the steady hum began to increase in volume. Inch by inch his straining pony crept up on the running lags which, although undistinguishable, still gave to the darkness an undulating movement that was sinister.

Then he had closed the gap and was abreast of the column. The wind stung his cheeks, brought tears to his eyes. But he paid no heed. Dangerous as it might be, his place was at the head of the running cattle which were lumbering along like a river at flood stage, sweeping before them everything that dared resist the devastating advance.

More by sense than by sound, Montana became aware of a horse blowing beside him.

"Who's there?" he shouted at the top of his voice to make himself heard above the turmoil.

"Whitey Hope," came back the answer. "That you, Montana?"

For the first time in hours the sound of a voice filled Montana with hope.

"Yes, Whitey," he yelled. "What happened?"

Out of the darkness loomed a figure.

"I don't know," Hope cried. "Knowing what we were up against instead of letting the men roll in, I kept the whole crew on guard — even the cook. I held the cavvy and had the horses saddled. Of a sudden the critters quit the bedground like they'd seen a haunt. Quicker than you could bat an eye they were running. We did our best to hold them. But it wasn't any use. Once I thought I heard other cattle bellering — I wasn't sure, though. We shagged along after them. But we didn't have any more chance of stopping them than a snowball in hell. It makes it worse because they're on strange range and they're headed for the river rapids.

Been storming up the river for an hour — Afraid of a flood. But we did our best, Montana."

"I know you did, Whitey," Montana said earnestly. "But a feller's best don't amount to much against the snakes we're tying into. They killed Pop Masterson."

"What?" Whitey cried incredulously. "Who did it?"

"The coroner's jury said a party unknown," Montana answered grimly. "But it was either Smokey Tremaine or King Kent. They both had their guns out. So did a feller by the name of Hartzell."

"Hartzell! What about him?"

"He had his gun out," Montana returned. "But he's the only one in the bunch who was white enough to offer his friendship. Him and Jerry the —"

"Listen, Montana." Whitey roweled his snorting mount closer and leaned over in his saddle. "I don't like that Hartzell jasper. He's the one man on the whole range who has treated me white. But I don't like him. He's got a snakey eye — He's yaller — He's scared to call his soul his own when Smokey is around. But when you come right down to it, I've heard he's the crack shot of the whole range. He —" He broke off suddenly as he chanced to glance back over his shoulder. "Montana!" he cried. "The camp is afire!"

"It's gone by now, I reckon," Montana told him bitterly. "Some more of Tremaine's work probably. He killed our boss, fixed the inquest and burned our camp. And I'll bet my last dollar it was him and his gang that stampeded our herd with those Diamond A's they moved up to block us in the yards. But I got in one good lick at them. I winged Smokey Tremaine."

101

"Winged Smokey!" Whitey exclaimed exultantly. "Good for you. I knew I wasn't picking any bob-tailed flush to draw to when I tied up with you. Winged Smokey! It's a pity you didn't kill him. He's the one who is stirring up all this hell. Him and old King Kent. They've given us a jolt, too, pard, but they haven't got us whipped yet, have they?"

"You damned know it, they haven't," Montana flashed back. "And until they have —"

"They'd better double their own guard," Whitey finished. "Listen!"

Montana strained for the sound that his companion had heard. Presently he caught it above the bedlam about him. The crash and boom of turbulent water.

"The river!" he cried hoarsely. "Rapids. Isn't there somewhere we can cross, Whitey?"

"Back a ways. Not down here. And we never can turn them now. Reckon after all the other trouble it's good-by to the critters. But we'll do our damnedest, Montana."

Particles of earth pelted Montana in the face as Whitey gave his horse its head and roweled away. Montana too, urged his mount to greater speed. Slowly they crept up on the lumbering column. Out came their Colts to belch jets of flame into the gloom. But the angry barks were but puny pops, all but drowned in the uproar. Then of a sudden the river boomed directly ahead. Montana's heart sank. There was little hope now of stemming the frenzied rush of the animals flying on, with no sense of direction, no heed of impending doom, a blinded, hurtling mass, amenable only to

102

the whim of the panting brutes thundering at their head.

Side by side Montana and Whitey threw themselves into the terror-stricken mass. By main strength and daring they succeeded in turning the leaders. Around and around they flew, their ponies slipping dangerously, now falling on their knees to bump along a few paces, then springing up to race on at redoubled speed. It was deadly, dangerous work. But the two gave no thought to the risk. They only knew that to mill the maddened brutes would break the backbone of the stampede.

"They're coming our way!" Montana shouted. "Don't let them bust now, Whitey!"

His exultant cry went unanswered. He cast a glance over his shoulder into the darkness. Apparently Whitey had taken some other course for no longer could Montana hear the blowing of his horse. But he dared not stop to investigate. Kicking, cursing, fighting his unwilling pony, he strove with might and main, with belching Colt and throat-slitting yells, to mill the crazed brutes. Once he thought he would succeed. But hope died as it was born. The animals broke wildly about him. He barely had time to gain the outer edge of the torrent as it swept past in a new burst of speed. Many times the hand of death hovered over him as his pony was sucked into the vortex of merciless hoofs. Each time some miracle saved him.

A raucous bawl came roaring out of the blackness ahead — a bawl half-human, half-bestial, far different from the defiant bellowing of the other hundreds. In it was terror; stark terror of inevitable death. Instantly Montana knew what had happened. One of the leaders had reached the brink of the river; had hurtled off the bluff into the darkness.

Whipped, beaten, conscious of a sense of utter, hopeless defeat, he rode to safety, climbed down from his horse, and threw himself full-length on the ground. Still the cattle thundered on. Man that he was it drove him to the verge of tears. This new tragedy at the moment seemed to spell ruin to the Buzzard's chances of securing a foothold on Thunder range. The pounding of hoofs were the drums of destiny, beating a dirge to his hopes. To his mind flashed the pledges he had made to the dying Masterson; his defiance of Tremaine, his threats to beat the cattlemen of Thunder Basin at their own game. Those threats all seemed inane and puerile now; the mere boasting of a child about to be broken on the wheel of fate.

Still the cattle poured by, running to their doom in the raging torrent. Each terrifying bawl that rent the air tore at his heart. Little did he expect ever again to see but a remnant of the great herd.

After a seemingly endless period of time a gradual cessation of the tumult brought him to his senses. The few bawls that reached his straining ears beat faint and piteously above the taunting crash of the victorious river. A great wave of loneliness swept over him. For the moment he wished that he had gone on about his business, seen Al Cousins as he had intended, turned over the letter to him, and then with the boy returned to Montana. But in the few passing hours he had become too deeply enmeshed; even delivery of that letter seemed far away at the moment.

He thought of Whitey, of the Buzzard men. Strange he had seen nothing of them. He wondered what had become of them, if they had gone down beneath the merciless hoofs. The fear momentarily took his mind from his own predicament, seemed to steady his jumping nerves. He sprang to his feet to stand for a moment rubbing the pain from his joints and peering about in the darkness.

Then he mounted and started out to locate Whitey and the other men. On and on he rode, his horse snorting and shying violently away from a fallen critter. He paused from time to time to shout for Whitey. But no answer came out of the night save the steadily increasing roar of the flooded river, the bleating of brutes still struggling for their lives in the turbulent stream.

After an infinity of time he began to realize the utter hopelessness of searching for his companion until the Stygian darkness lifted and dawn should reveal what lay about him. Much as he hated the thought of delay, dreaded the torment of uncertainty, he finally abandoned the futile hunt for Whitey and his men. Dismounting again, he set out to pass the time walking about.

Hours dragged by with maddening slowness. The tumult about him gradually died to a few pitiful bellows. The thunder of hoofs ceased entirely, but the roar of the raging river increased. The darkness thickened until he was hemmed in completely, unable to see even his pony in the ebon void that enveloped him. Occasionally, as he walked, he leaped back as a weary critter started up from under his feet. Yet he had small hope that the animals were other than the drags, which by reason of their very slowness, had escaped the death of the hard-running brutes in the lead of the stampede.

As quickly as it was light enough, Montana mounted and started anew his search for Whitey and the missing punchers. But now, as during the night, his hunt was in vain. He saw nothing but small bunches of cattle, lying about chewing their cuds contentedly, or struggling to their feet at the approach of his horse. The number of brutes he could see surprised him, although he shuddered to think of the countless others that had perished in the water.

Making his way to the bank of the river he swung down and sprawled full length to peer over. The point to which the leaders had led the herd was a sheer bluff that dropped away some thirty feet to the water below. The bodies of several of the cattle still swirled about in the deep, foam-crested pools beneath him. Others had been washed up on a narrow shelf. Still others, cripples, moaned and groaned on the jutting rock of the rapids a short distance below.

After several minutes spent in an idle and lonely survey he remounted and again took up the search for Whitey. Yet it was not until the sun had tipped the horizon to rout the creeping shadows from the flats and flame down upon the dreary scene that he sighted

106

Whitey. The cowboy was stretched full-length on the ground, his horse standing guard above his motionless form.

CHAPTER
TWELVE

The Toss of a Coin

Roweling to the side of the prostrate man, Montana threw himself from his horse and lifted Whitey's head in his arms. A faint pulse told him quickly that the cowboy was alive. With frantic haste he felt for broken bones. He found none. But it was not until he had examined the puncher a second time, and with greater care, and rolled him completely over that he succeeded in locating his injury — a large discolored bruise on the temple where Whitey had struck the ground with a violence that had rendered him unconscious.

Half carrying, half dragging him to the bluff above the river, Montana searched about until he found a cow trail winding to the water's edge. Making his way down it he filled his hat with water. Returning he set to work bathing the bruise and Whitey's colorless face. For a considerable time he rubbed the puncher's wrists briskly, then, pulling off his boots, chafed his ankles.

Presently his efforts were rewarded with a slight show of life. Soaking his kerchief in water, he bandaged Whitey's forehead. Making a pillow of his coat and stretching the towheaded puncher out comfortably, he waited anxiously beside him. But Whitey's return to consciousness was slow, so slow that Montana, having exhausted his knowledge of first-aid measures, was on the point of starting back to Elbar for medical aid when, of a sudden, the cowboy's eyes fluttered open.

"Where am I?" Whitey muttered weakly.

"Down and out along with the rest of us, I reckon," Montana said grimly. "Your horse must have fallen with you. Lucky you didn't cash in altogether from the looks of the bump you got on your temple. But I can't find any busted bones. You'll be all right in a little while, outside of a rip-snorting headache probably. I'd begun to think you never were coming to."

"I remember now!" Whitey cried hoarsely, struggling to rise. "We were trying to mill those running Buzzards. My horse fell right on the outer edge of the stampede. Seemed like a ton of brick flew up to meet me." He fingered the painful bruise on his temple gingerly and nursed his throbbing head. "But I reckon I'm not busted up any. Give me a lift." With Montana's help he lurched to his feet to stand swaying dizzily. Then he attempted to take a step which presently, with a great effort, he succeeded in doing.

"Nope," he said gamely, despite the pain that whitened his lips, "no bones busted." His gaze flew to the river. "Did it —"

"It got a good many of the critters," Montana said, reading the question in his eyes. "I didn't try to take a tally. But the whole river is littered with carcasses. These few" — he pointed to the staring brutes within

109

range of their vision — "are what is left of the Buzzard spread, I guess. The rest of them are either dead or scattered from hell to breakfast." A cold smile came to hover for an instant on his drawn lips. "A fine beginning on a new and hostile range, isn't it?"

Slowly Whitey's gaze moved back along the trail. As far as he could see the ground was dotted with carcasses of critters that had gone down in the mad rush.

"It isn't just what a feller would call encouraging," he remarked soberly. "But then again, I reckon it could have been worse. Buck up, Montana. There's an old saying that 'while there's life there's hope.' And we aren't dead yet by a devil of a ways." He sat flat down on the ground and started pulling on his boots. "We might raise a little stink on this range yet. You can't never tell."

He waited a moment for Montana to answer. When he did not, he glanced up. Montana had walked away a short distance to face the infant sun, which was swimming up over the rim of the desolate plains in a sea of metal brilliance. Presently he turned back to Whitey.

"Where are the boys?" he demanded in a hard, metallic voice.

A startled look flashed into Whitey's eyes. His gaze whipped out anxiously over the flats.

"Hell, I haven't even thought of them. They left camp the same time I did. I supposed they'd report to you with daylight. You don't reckon they —"

"It isn't probable they all went down in the stampede," Montana put in thoughtfully. "More likely they laid down on the job, pulled their freight back to camp when they saw they couldn't stop the critters."

"In that case they would have tied up with the jaspers who fired the camp," Whitey pointed out. "But I didn't hear any shooting. They'll show up all right. Reckon they're of age and can take care of themselves." Limping over to his horse he set to work straightening the saddle, which had turned underneath the patient animal's belly.

"The way they've dropped from sight worries me," Montana mused, joining him. "What do you say we take a *pasear* back yonder, look over what's left of the camp and see if we can uncover anything."

"You'll get your foot into it if you do," Whitey warned quickly. "That is just what Tremaine wants you to do. You'd play right into his hand, because you can make up your mind he's got some more devilment planned by now. Our best bet is to gather what critters we can and head straight for the Dunning place."

"How far is it and what direction is it in?" Montana asked.

"About five miles down the river. We can wait there for the men — or work out of there. Then —" He stopped abruptly to stare at one of the brutes they had killed in their attempt to halt the stampede.

"Montana," he muttered grimly, "you were right about what started our Buzzards to running. It was

111

some more of Tremaine's work. We're in for hell now. See here!"

Montana looked at the animal to which he was pointing. Instead of the Buzzard brand he expected to see, a big Diamond A was burned on its upturned shoulder. Moving quickly to the other dead animals on the bank of the river he set to work examining them. No less than a dozen were Diamond A's.

Presently he straightened up to meet Whitey's gaze.

"Reckon this shows where Tremaine was while I was at the inquest," he observed. "Him and his men moved the Diamond A's up to the yards intending to surround us. Instead of that they met us in the dark. Our herds mixed. We killed Diamond A's trying to stop the stampede."

"And we're due for merry hell now." Whitey emitted a low whistle. "King Kent and Smokey Tremaine will play this to a fare-you-well."

"Let them play it," Montana flared. "Killing steers isn't half as bad as killing Masterson. And they've still got that to answer for."

"You don't know this breed like I do," Whitey said. "You're framed, Montana — framed hard. We're playing a lone hand, you and me. They've got the cowmen and the Stock Association behind them. When King Kent cracks the whip everybody jumps in Thunder Basin."

"Isn't there a square shooter in this country?" Montana demanded. "What about this Al Cousins? He owns some of the Diamond A. Does he know about all this hell Kent raises? Does he stand for it?"

"Mebbeso, mebbe not," Whitey answered. "Some say yes, some say no. Nobody knows. Nobody ever hears about him, Kent does all the blowing. If Al does know about it and backs it up, it's strange, for he's a fine feller. But we'd best be shagging it. If we hang around much longer we'll get caught with these steers. And let me tell you if we are it's going mighty hard with us."

"I've got some things I've got to do," Montana said stubbornly. "First I've got a letter that has to be delivered to Al Cousins."

"A letter to Al Cousins?" Whitey shot him a quick inscrutable look. "Anything to do with the Buzzard?"

"No. It's what brought me into this country before I ever heard of the Buzzard. Don't even know what it's about. But I've got to deliver it right away in spite of hell and high water. Then there's my little pard in Elbar; damn them, they'd better not lay a finger on that kid."

"Well, whatever we do we've got to use horse sense with it," Whitey counseled. "Once they catch you with these dead critters and get you behind bars, where you can't fight back or help yourself, they'll prove anything against you. I know it galls like hell to run, but it's up to us to run to cover, feller."

"I reckon you're right, Whitey." Montana swung onto his horse. "A jasper would stand a damned poor show once those coyotes got him in jail." He shifted sidewise in his saddle to look out across the flats. "I hate like the devil to skin out without first looking up the boys and explaining. But it's a cinch they're not hurt or we'd be able to see something of them or their horses around." He touched his pony with the rowels. "We might just as well round up what Buzzards we can and head them for the ranch. If the boys haven't showed up by that time we can scout for them. Then I'll slide into Elbar, get the boy and deliver this letter to Cousins."

"What are you going to do with that kid after you get him?" Whitey demanded.

"Why, take him down to the Dunning place — and —"

"And bring him up dodging the law like we're going to have to do until we get the Buzzard's gathered?" Whitey snorted. "That's a fine way to raise a kid; teaching him to be a lawbreaker, a jail dodger."

"But I've got the little shaver now," Montana argued. "He's the finest little —"

"Then give him a break. I've got a scheme. Sally wants to finish her nursing course in Omaha. Why not let her take the boy with her and put him in school till things settle down here."

"That's not a bad idea," Montana said ponderingly. "There's some business she can do for me in Omaha, too." Quickly he related to Whitey what the dying Masterson had told him of a will and his papers. "I don't know just what it will mean to us," he finished, "but Sal — your sister can find out and post us. What are we going to use for money? I'm cleaned slick as a frog's tooth."

114

"I've still got the money you paid me for the hay," Whitey said. "And I had a little besides — plenty to have Sally pull out with the boy."

"I reckon from the way Pop spoke there'll be some money somewhere to run the spread," Montana said. "And probably pay wages. Your plan sounds good. You get word to Sal — your sister. Let's gather these critters, and get going."

Whitey's answer was to drag himself stiffly into the saddle and start on a circle around the herd. Putting the cripples they found out of their misery, prodding the dog-tired brutes and getting them bunched required some time. When they had the cattle rounded up the two fell in side by side. Montana recounted the events from his departure from the stockyards to find Masterson, the night before, until he had ridden back to find the herd stampeding.

"The hellions!" Whitey exclaimed when Montana told him of the poker game in which the Thunder Basin cowmen had wagered Buzzard cattle. "They sure took a lot for granted, betting our stuff, didn't they? And they blackballed us, huh? Well, I reckon we'll have something to say about both those deals, won't we? But tell me more about Masterson."

Montana related the details of the killing and subsequent happenings at the inquest, which brought repeated curses from the cowboy. But he had no time to tell him of the bullet he had taken from Pop's clothes, for Whitey drew rein suddenly and wheeled to watch several riders who had bobbed up out of a ravine far to the right and were coming toward them at a gallop.

"It will probably be our men," Montana observed, also pulling up to watch the approaching group. "But how in hell they got way over there is more than I can figure."

"It isn't our men, Montana," Whitey observed. "It's those damned Diamond A jaspers. And we're in for hell. Now listen — We're pards — There isn't a bit of use of us both getting into this mix-up, because it's a dead mortal cinch they'll either have us arrested when they find these dead Diamond A steers or they'll crack down on us. One of us has got to stay clear to care for the Buzzard herd. You go on to the Dunning place. I'll stall them until you make your getaway. Then you can help me from under cover."

"Like hell I will," Montana flared. "You go. Let me talk to them."

"It's your duty — to Masterson and these cattle," Whitey argued. "All our hell isn't over by a long way. Get going."

"If anybody goes, you will," Montana repeated stubbornly. "I'm not running from those lobos."

"Let's flip a coin to see who goes or stays," Whitey suggested. "Heads I go, tails you go. Are you on?"

"Flip her high," Montana ordered as the cowboy drew forth a coin and covered it with his hand.

"Haven't got time," Whitey hedged, keeping an anxious eye on the horsemen. "This is good enough."

"All right. What is she?"

"Tails," Whitey announced, uncovering the coin. "It's your move, cowboy. Head down the river — and ride like hell. If they get me you can start work. Mebbeso break into jail."

"You didn't flip that coin," Montana accused hotly. "You can't badger me. Throw it over again."

"Somebody's got to stay in the open and somebody's got to stay under cover," Whitey snapped. "Somebody's got to get that kid before they devil him to death — turn him over to Sally and get her started for Omaha with him. If you think you can do that —"

There was stark panic in the gaze Montana turned upon him.

"I thought so," Whitey chuckled. "So you skin out and I tend to the details. They'd have you in jail before you even got started in Elbar. Me, they've got nothing on me but these steers, and I can swear you did it. I'll handle the boy — turn him over to Mother and Sally — Say!" He exploded, "We look enough alike to be doubles. We both noticed it. We'll just never be seen together from now on. I'll make out like you're dead in the rapids yonder. You be Whitey Hope — I'll be Whitey Hope. Deliver your letter to Cousins if you want. Do any damned thing — but do it fast. We'll keep in touch at the Dunning place —"

"It might work." Montana lifted his pony with the rowels. "It's worth trying — But if anything happens to you, Whitey, I'll feel like a coward the rest of my life. Get the boy lined up and meet me at the Dunning place as quick as you can."

117

"Ride, jasper," Whitey grinned after him as he disappeared over the river bluff, then whirled his horse to face the oncoming riders, who presently came up over a hogback and galloped down upon him. "I framed you with the flip of that coin, but I haven't a thing to lose. And I'd just as leave crack down on Tremaine or Kent now as any time. It's bound to come sooner or later."

CHAPTER
THIRTEEN

Hiding From the Law

Montana had been gone but a short time when the horsemen, ten in number, galloped close enough for Whitey to recognize them. In the lead of the party rode Kent, his long legs stiff as rails, his huge body braced against the cantle of his saddle. Beside him loped Smokey Tremaine, standing in his stirrups to ease the bandaged arm from the jolting motion of his horse.

Then came the sheriff, sight of whom set Whitey's nerves to strumming, although he could not suppress a chuckle at thought of the manner in which he had tricked Montana into making his timely getaway. Behind the officer were several others whom he knew to be Diamond A punchers — and two T6 men. Came to him a flash of wonder at the presence of the latter, especially in view of what Montana had told him of Hartzell's proffered friendship. Yet he had no time to ponder the thing.

"Oh, it's you, is it?" Kent snarled, pulling rein in front of the youth.

Whitey met his glare fearlessly and with no outward show of emotion.

"Who did you think it was?" he asked impudently. "The King of England?"

"None of your lip, jasper," Kent flared. "We thought you were that Buzzard killer, Montana. We've come to have a showdown with him. Where is he?"

Whitey sized up the crowd with cool speculation.

"Montana?" he repeated in perplexity. "What do you want him for?"

"Lots of things," Kent growled. "Chief among them being for the murder of Kirk Masterson!"

"For the murder of Masterson?" Whitey gasped.

"Montana killed Masterson last night in the Midway saloon," Kent bawled. "Shot him down in cold blood. There were three shots fired. Tremaine shot once — at Montana and missed. Montana fired the other two shots. One at Smokey and one at Masterson."

"He must be powerful quick on the trigger to shoot twice while two-gun Tremaine yonder is unlimbering and only shooting once," Whitey observed sarcastically. "And by the looks of that arm Smokey is toting in a sling, Montana must be even better at scoring a bull's-eye than he is fast." He ignored the ugly glance Tremaine cast him, his mind busy pondering the full import of Kent's accusation. That Montana, his new-found friend, who to him had appeared so wholesome and trustworthy, could have killed his employer seemed the height of improbability. Yet — Instantly he hated himself for even thinking of such a thing. No matter what they said, Montana was innocent.

"Of course, they held an inquest. The coroner looked at Montana's gun, didn't he?" Whitey inquired lazily.

"Sure," Kent snorted. "And if the damned fool coroner had of had any sense he'd of arrested Montana then and there because there were two exploded cartridges in his gun. This county is going to have a new coroner on the strength of this deal, you can bet your sweet life. But we haven't time to sit here augering all day. I can see by the way you are stalling that you've seen Montana. You tell us where he is or we'll take you for aiding and abetting."

Although Whitey made no reply his mind was working swiftly. He shot a glance at Kent. Then his gaze flew to Tremaine. But if the waiting men thought by the slight surge of color into his cheeks that he was on the point of revealing Montana's whereabouts they quickly realized their mistake. For a cold hard light glinted in his eyes as they centered on Tremaine.

"A few other things have come up since you jaspers played poker for the Buzzard stuff," Whitey said slowly. "And I reckon —"

"That proves you've seen him," Kent bawled. "That killer told you that —"

"And I reckon as long as you accuse him of killing Masterson you might just as well blame him for those other things, too," Whitey went on, ignoring the interruption. "The burning of the Buzzard camp, for instance." He had the satisfaction of seeing Kent start guiltily. "Considering all the hell your Thunder Basin gang has raised with the Buzzard it strikes me that it was one of you, not Montana who plugged Masterson.

What did you take a sneak for? Where did you go after the killing?" he fired point-blank at Tremaine. "How does it come you weren't held for the inquest?"

"None of your damned business." The Diamond A foreman's lips curled scornfully.

"Well, I'll make it some," Whitey said with maddening calm. "It won't do you any good to get tough with me, Tremaine. I've showed you time and again that you can't buffalo me. And when your gang accuses Montana of killing Masterson you're barking up the wrong tree. You've got two forty-fives. Did you show them both?"

"He didn't have to," the sheriff chipped in. "Tremaine only shot with one gun — the left. He showed me the exploded cartridge."

"Why didn't you make him show you his right gun?" Whitey persisted. "He's a two-gun man — or claims to be."

"I'll run my own business," the sheriff blazed. "Right now we're after that Montana. We know you've seen him. And you better be telling where he is. I've got all his men in jail."

"All his men in jail?" Whitey blurted out. "What for?"

"For driving the Buzzard herd into the Diamond A last night and stampeding our stuff, that's what for," Kent answered. "We'll show this damned —" He broke off to give vent to a violent oath as his gaze chanced to fall on one of the dead steers. "And you've killed Diamond A critters to boot! I'll —"

122

"You'll choke to death if you don't quit bellering," Whitey cautioned dryly.

"You — You —" Kent ranted. "You'll go to jail. Where is Montana? Quick!" He started for his gun. Before he could jerk it from its holster Whitey had the crew covered and was backing his horse away.

"Not so fast," the youth warned coolly. "If I go to jail it will be for killing either you, Kent, or that snake-eye, Tremaine. You've made life hell for me ever since I hit Elbar. Now it's going to be my turn for a while." His eyes were blazing, his finger trembling on the trigger.

"You're so dead anxious for a showdown, Kent, let's have one, now. When you say our men stampeded your Diamond A's you're a liar. It was just the other way around. You stampeded our stuff. Did it deliberately, just like Tremaine bragged he would when he warned me yesterday not to sell the Buzzard a spear of hay. If we had any officers in this county instead of cowardly snakes" — he shot a withering glance at the sheriff, who bristled with indignation — "they'd have sent you and Tremaine over the road long ago. But you've got this jasper, who calls himself a sheriff, buffaloed so hard he'll eat out of your hand. If anybody but you had accused Montana of killing Masterson I might have listened. But damn you, Kent, you or Smokey Tremaine did that killing and you know you did. You framed the inquest to make a getaway. And you've framed this sheriff."

He paused for a breath, a deadly terrible light in his eyes.

"You're damned right we killed Diamond A's — Because they were leading the stampede. And the only regret I have is that we didn't kill more of them. But you've evened things up a-plenty. Burned our camp and arrested our men when we needed them the worst. And these Diamond A's we downed won't anywhere near pay for the Buzzards you ran into the river, you dirty —"

"I've heard all I'm going to," Kent thundered. "You can't say those things to me. You killed my critters and you're going to pay for it. You mixed herds on purpose to do it. Round up those cattle, sheriff. There are Diamond A's among them. And there are dead Diamond A's here too — shot for spite. We've got to stop this kind of business. The law is on our side. I'll attach this herd of Buzzards to pay for the stuff I've lost."

"Why don't you let the feller who won them in that poker game at Elbar take them?" Whitey taunted. "As long as you have made your brags about them being blackballed why don't you buy them from your lousy Stock Association for eight dollars a head like you offered Masterson? Don't go to planning to attach these critters, Kent, when you've already figured every other way you can to get them without rustling. But let me tell you that's the only way you or your Stock Association ever will get them — rustle them. I'm working for the Buzzard spread; and I'd like to see any Diamond A jasper who ever lived, or any four-flushing sheriff either, try and take one of them. Stay back, sheriff!" he warned, making a gesture with his forty-five as the officer roweled forward, his face contorted with fury. "I'm not in a mind to kill an officer of the law — but I will if I have to to protect this herd."

"We haven't any scrap with you, Whitey," Smokey put in craftily. "Put up your gun. It's Montana we want. I tell you he killed Masterson."

"You're a dirty liar, Tremaine," Whitey said between clenched teeth. "You never saw the day you could tell the truth — about anything. Like hell I'll stash my gun, you back-shooting lobo. You or King Kent killed Masterson. You and King Kent blackballed the Buzzard, framed the inquest, and bought off this sheriff. You and King Kent fired those wagons and had our men arrested. You and King Kent mixed those Diamond A's into our herd and stampeded them. You and King Kent ribbed up that poker game for our stuff to buffalo poor old Masterson, thinking you could scare him off. Now, damn you, if you aren't both yeller clean to your socks, let's see you even look like you want to take a single Buzzard critter!"

"You're under arrest," the sheriff bellowed. "You can't bluff us with big talk like that. Where's Montana? Spill your guts, jasper."

Prey to a consuming rage which, now that it finally had burst its bounds, was sweeping him on recklessly and blinding him to reason, Whitey was on the point of blurting out the truth and defying them in their attempts to capture his friend.

"Montana is dead!" he found himself announcing sadly.

"Dead?" the group echoed incredulously. "How?"

"When your Diamond A's stampeded the Buzzards, Montana tried to mill them." Whitey blinked back an imaginary tear. "His horse fell over the cliff yonder in the dark. The poor devil went into the rapids during the high water. I've looked since daylight — but I don't reckon we'll ever find a trace of his body."

"Damned good riddance," Tremaine snarled. "Just saves us the trouble of swinging him. And you," he hurled at Whitey, "you'd better back down while you're all together. I've kept my mouth shut so far. But the sheriff says you're under arrest. And you are."

With a quick movement that brought a twinge of pain he shifted his crippled arm. One gloved hand swooped down, up. But the forty-five gripped in his fingers never spoke. For at that instant Whitey Hope fired. With a hoarse bawl Tremain's horse dropped, pinning its hapless rider's leg beneath it.

Pandemonium broke loose. Curses, snorts, shouts rent the air. But no man attempted to go for his gun. Whitey sat his mount calmly surveying the crew.

"I'm riding, jaspers," he announced. "Riding away and deserting this herd because I can't hold it against such odds. They're scattered from hell to breakfast, just like you figured. But mark my words — don't touch a one of them, because I'll get three Diamond A's for every missing Buzzard and my meat supply to boot!"

"Five hundred dollars to the feller who plugs him!" Kent cried. "From this day on you're a hunted man, Hope — a fugitive with a price on your head. You could have been one of us; now it's too late. You threw in with that Montana. And it's a lucky break for him that his horse saved us the trouble of stringing him up."

"I'd rather be a fugitive than one of your gang any day," Whitey threw back. "If Montana hadn't died he'd have made Thunder Basin a living hell for you. But he's gone, so it's up to me. And remember, Kent — three Diamond A's for every missing Buzzard and my meat supply to boot! You've put a price on my head. But before anybody collects it there'll be a bullet through yours. And yours," he spat at Tremaine, still stretched on the ground beside his struggling horse. "I'm going now. Don't try to follow me, because I'm itching to get the first one of you who bats an eye."

He started his horse backing away, his gun sweeping the thoroughly cowed crew. And he timed his escape well. Barely from range, Tremaine began bellowing for help. The punchers dismounted to ear down the horse and aid the cursing Smokey. Whitey wheeled his pony, gave it the rowels and raced into the brakes of Tongue River.

CHAPTER
FOURTEEN

Baiting a Trap

Days lengthened into weeks, weeks into months. Thunder Basin took on the garb of fall; endless buff prairies, graying sage, multi-colored splashes where the frost of crisply cold nights had touched the quivering leaves of aspens at the water holes. Came Indian summer to cast its lazy, hazy spell over the region, distorting the hogbacks, veiling the distant box buttes and turning the horizons into floating, undulating seas of pearl.

Then, almost overnight, came winter, bitter, savage winter that lashed the country with Arctic fury. Freezing winds stripped the rustling leaves from the cottonwoods, screaming on to leave them gnarled and barren and lifeless things, standing lonely vigil along the washes and ravines. Blizzards snarled and tore across the flats, driving half-frozen cattle to shelter in coulees and beneath cutbanks.

March blew itself out in a burst of withering cold, leaving behind a world banked high with drifts of snow that defied the onslaughts of the rains of a raw and furious April. The illimitable sweep of prairie was a dull white expanse, its surface level, unbroken save for jutting rocks or the frost-nipped helms of greasewood and sage. A cold, rain-laden wind howled day and night, crusting the humped backs of the half-starved cattle with ice, driving them deeper into the shelter of the brakes where they huddled, spent and shivering, or, with the optimism of range stock, pawed the snow hopefully for a stray morsel of frozen, matted grass. The bony hand of death hovered above Thunder Basin, dotting the dreary wastes with carcasses and tightening across staring ribs the hides of the fittest of the brutes that managed to survive the fury of the elements.

April, too, dragged to a sullen, soggy end, taking with it the last spear of hay, which even while it had lasted, had proved utterly inadequate to satisfy the pitifully few animals lucky enough to come within range of the frost-rimmed eyes of the line riders.

Then, in a dying gasp, the wind cleared the sky of clouds and howled its own requiem. A blistering sun burst forth to start rivulets of melted snow down the hogbacks, fill the water holes to overflowing and send Tongue river on a rampage. Harassed cattlemen heaved sighs of relief and abandoned their pitchforks for skinning knives and throw ropes to begin scouting the bogholes that claimed a heavy toll among the cattle, which, once in their treacherous mire, had not the strength to help themselves. The prairie carpet changed from white to green. The wind came back to howl and whine. But now it was slow and hot and spicy with the tang of blistered sage and fennel.

Ranchers, who, but a scant month before had cursed the snow and cold, now eyed the tumbleweeds rolling lazily across the flats with worry-wrinkled brows. The whirlwinds that spun about like miniature tornadoes filled them with apprehension.

June came. The heat grew stifling. The sun glared down brassily to cure the greening grass. Again the prairie carpet changed its hue. But now it was buff; the vegetation on its vast expanse seared and withered. The whining winds became like sickening breaths from the mouth of a blast furnace. Great, ugly fissures were opened in the gumbo by the sun that sucked the moisture from the water holes, leaving them but tepid, brackish pools infested with vermin. Flies and gnats swarmed in clouds against the flaming heavens. Range stock milled frantically to escape the merciless heat and the endless pests that buzzed at their heads and heels or lay in sheets along their necks. Summer, it seemed, had set out to prove itself mightier than winter, the lingering death it wrought through drought more terrible than the ravages of snow and cold.

And if the terrific heat had turned Thunder Basin into an inferno it had done but half of what it had accomplished in the village of Elbar. The big supply wagons no longer rumbled in from the ranches to load back with provisions. Business was stagnant. The town was in a torpor. Scarcely a soul ventured onto its streets during the broiling days. A few cattlemen, who could spare the time, or who already had seen their herds wiped out, passed idle hours within the saloons.

From that night when Montana had ridden out of Elbar, after having made arrangements for returning Pop Masterson's body to Omaha for burial, nothing had been heard of him. That he had died in the turbulent waters of Tongue river, along with the scores of Buzzard cattle, everyone now accepted as a fact.

The boy, Clem White, had disappeared from Elbar as mysteriously as had Montana himself. Sally Hope also had gone. Some said the boy had gone with her while she finished her nursing course in Omaha. No one knew for certain. Whitey had seen to that. No one cared save possibly Tremaine, who made no secret of his fondness for the pretty sister of Whitey Hope and who, in his periodic drunken sprees, had boasted of his intention to marry her.

As for Whitey Hope, punchers from time to time told of sighting him on the range, but he had always disappeared as if by magic when they reached the spot where they had seen him. On several occasions passing cowboys also had reported signs of life about the Dunning place. But never had they been able to satisfy themselves that the occupant was Whitey. Where he lived or how he existed was still another mystery.

It did not occur to the busybodies in Elbar to peer through the thick coating of dust on the windows of Whitey's abandoned store. For if they had they would have seen not shelves stocked with provisions but empty shelves, stripped of canned goods under cover of darkness by the new *segundo* of the Buzzard spread.

Absorbed as it was with its own troubles, Elbar in the passing weeks forgot Whitey Hope. A few things only it remembered — one thing in particular. Whitey Hope, whom Elbar had come to know as a hotheaded youth, utterly devoid of fear, had made his threats against the

131

Diamond A. If he lived, some day, Elbar knew, he would claim his revenge.

The investigation into the death of Pop Masterson ended with the sham inquest Montana had attended. Thanks to Kent and Tremaine all Elbar became convinced that Montana himself had done the killing and few there were who did not think he had received his just dues in drowning.

Smokey Tremaine's arm healed quickly. In the span of a few short weeks he was swaggering about, bullying everyone as he had attempted to bully Montana and Whitey Hope. While most of rangeland swallowed the abuse in silence it secretly gloated over the tales of how both Montana and Whitey had made Tremaine back down and cherished a hope that one or the other of them some day might return to rid the Basin of the brutal foreman of the Diamond A.

The Buzzard punchers, including the cook, who, as Kent had told Whitey, had been arrested the night of the stampede, were arraigned the following morning on a trumped-up charge of having "deliberately and with malicious intent stampeded, scattered, slain, and otherwise harmed five hundred Diamond A cattle." At first the men — who until then had had no direct dealings with Kent and Tremaine — were prone to take the matter as a joke. But they quickly realized that any justice would miscarry in Elbar. And when Kent finally came to them with a proposition to dismiss the charges provided they left the country they seized upon the chance and disappeared forthwith.

The Buzzard cattle were scattered to the four winds. Half-starved, straggling bunches roamed Thunder Basin, yet the main herd had vanished. Whether or not it had succumbed to the rigorous weather no one knew. Nor did they care. The remaining brutes supplied many a rancher with meat and offered excellent roping practice for frolicsome cowboys.

Despite his threat to attach the herd, it was so difficult to pull the Diamond A's through the bitter winter and spring that Kent let it be noised about that he would let the matter drop rather than burden himself with more stock and would leave the final disposition of the blackballed stragglers to the County Stock Association.

Then came the pool roundup. Before the middle of June "reps" from every outfit on the range, with the exception of the Buzzard, began putting into the Diamond A, driving before them their cavvy strings. Soon the big ranch was crowded with punchers. The bunkhouses were filled to overflowing. Bedrolls and paraphernalia littered the yard. Dust rose in suffocating blankets from the corrals where the work of topping off new mounts to fill out the strings was being rushed. Saddles, bridles, and blankets were inspected, boots oiled, kinks stretched from new ropes, odd jobs of mending attended to, duffel bags stuffed, soogins sorted. The blistering days were an endless round of action. The close and sultry nights were filled with laughter, song, and the rattle of poker chips.

When all the neighboring outfits were represented, Kent called the punchers together for final instructions.

133

"Concerning the Buzzards," he said in conclusion, "you all know they've been blackballed. The slicks, of course, go to the Stock Association. The grown stuff does too, for that matter, but a steer might come in handy now and then for fresh meat; and they're always good for trying out your ropes. But we don't want any Buzzards in the day herd. Let them be until the Association decides what it is going to do with them. It will do that as quick as it can and get them off the range just like they were strays. So remember, for the time being, we haven't any business monkeying with any critter packing the Buzzard brand."

At dawn the following morning the roundup crew, in the charge of Smokey Tremaine, and, strangely, accompanied by both Kent and Bob Hartzell of the T6, moved away from the Diamond A and struck down Tongue river. Ahead thundered the cavvy, pitching, snorting, kicking, threatening to bolt while the sleepy-eyed horse "jingler" dozed in his saddle and let them run. Behind came the bed and mess wagon, driven by a grumbling cook and on which the night wrangler, between jolts, tried vainly to make up for the sleep he knew he would lose before the roundup swung about and put back into the home ranch.

Through the blazing heat of the day they rode, finally to make camp far down the river. Supper over, the punchers sprawled on the bedrolls around the campfire, smoking and talking. With the crack of dawn they were up and gone on circle. Piloted by a puncher astride a bawling, pitching bronc, the wagon careened along the cow trails and across the sagebrush toward the noon camp. The big pool calf roundup of Thunder Basin was under way!

Then on the third night a strange thing happened. A man rode boldly into camp. At sight of him Tremaine, seated cross-legged near the fire, leaped to his feet and would have whipped out his forty-five had not King Kent stopped him.

"What do you want — Whitey Hope?" Kent demanded, peering through the flickering light at the cowboy who seemed to have grown a trifle stouter and more wrinkled since he had dropped from sight after the stampede.

"A job," the puncher answered in an exceedingly quiet and unperturbed tone, Kent thought.

"You'll get a job," the cowman snorted. "A job busting rock. As long as you're here I reckon you'll stay. We haven't forgotten your bluffs back yonder at the river the day Montana was killed. And if you'll recklect there is still that five hundred dollars I offered on your head."

"I've got a proposition, Kent," Whitey said in the same cool careless tone that puzzled the cowman. "If you'll let me talk to you alone for a minute we'll see if we can dicker."

Grudgingly Kent detached himself from the group and followed the youth into the shadows, careful however to keep his hand on his gun. Tremaine and Hartzell stood peering after them, and while Whitey never once gave them so much as a glance he could feel their eyes boring into his back.

135

"I made a mistake, Kent," Whitey said when the two were out of earshot of the others. "I can see it now. I wasn't trying to help Montana in particular. But Tremaine had made life so miserable for me I just blew up."

"Coming to your senses, huh?" Kent sneered. "I thought you would sooner or later. But that isn't what you had on your mind to risk riding into this camp."

"You're right," Whitey admitted. "When Masterson died, charge of the Buzzards went to Montana. When Montana died, charge of the critters naturally fell on me. Me being the only one of the spread left on Thunder. It's been a long spell now since the Buzzards moved in and I haven't been able to get head or tail to who owns them — if anybody does — or anything about them. They are scattered bad. I've stuck with what I could find of them as long as I can without wages. I'm getting sick and tired of it.

"A pile of the stuff is winterkilled. The rest is — the Lord knows where. I haven't got the men to gather them. And anyhow they're blackballed. I haven't even a place to run them under fence except the Dunning place. I'm up against it properly. I can't buck a strong cowman like you any longer."

"Now you're beginning to talk like you aren't all plumb loco," Kent observed, a crafty note in his voice. "I could have told you all that before. But no, you knew it all."

"I'll admit that I've been hotheaded and shortsighted," Whitey agreed with unbelievable meekness. "But here is my proposition. As near as I can find out those

Buzzards don't belong to anybody. There isn't one chance in a thousand that anybody ever will claim them. I can't gather them alone. The Diamond A is the only outfit running enough men to do it. Suppose you give me a job — just an ordinary riding job. Then supposing, without saying a word to anybody, not even Tremaine or Hartzell, you start re-working those Buzzards into Diamond A's. It will re-run dead easy. No trick at all."

"Rustle!" Kent exploded. "If that's your proposition you might just as well not mention it. The Diamond A has never rustled yet."

"All right," Whitey said, gathering up his reins. "If that is the way you feel about it. Just let Hartzell and the rest of the ranchers knock them off from under your nose. That's what Hartzell came along with the wagon for. Course, I reckon it would be rustling in a way. Then again, when those critters are eating the grass that your stuff ought to have, and nobody owns them, you ought to have a right to pick them up; at least enough to pay for your feed bill. The shape the range is in, you haven't enough feed for yourself, let alone for a herd that doesn't seem to belong to anybody."

It was obvious to the sharp-eyed cowboy that Kent was swayed by the argument, although he gave no outward indication of it other than a slight puckering of his brows.

"No," he said briefly. "I can't do it. The Diamond A does not rustle. But —" The crafty gleam deepened in his eyes. "I'm willing to let bygones be bygones with

137

you and forget. Hunt you up a bedroll and report to Smokey for guard. You can work for me — but don't ever fool yourself that you can pull any monkey business."

"Thanks," Whitey muttered. "I'll watch my knitting."

"Be sure you do," Kent returned impatiently. "Just hit the ball for us and we're willing to shoot square with you. But remember, King Kent turned your proposition to rustle those Buzzards down cold. Now go talk to Smokey."

CHAPTER
FIFTEEN

Rough-String Rider

Whitey rode directly to the campfire to halt his pony in the gloom just beyond the circle of flickering light. Once he glanced back at Kent, who stood where he had left him, staring into the blackness of the night. And a cold grim smile came to rest for a moment on Whitey's lips.

"Tremaine," he said quietly, "Kent just gave me a job riding for the Diamond A. Told me to report to you. Can you stake me to a bedroll?"

"I'll give you a job," Tremaine snarled, moving away from the fire. "I haven't forgotten you killed my horse and damned nigh got me crushed to death the morning back yonder after Montana cashed in. And I haven't forgotten your big talk, either. Damn you, you've got a lot of guts to be asking for a job after that play. I'll see you in hell before you'll ever ride with a wagon I'm ramrodding. You —"

"Smokey?" The voice of Kent interrupted from out of the gloom. "Come here a minute."

Eyeing the unperturbed Whitey balefully, the flickering firelight accentuating the sinister gleam in his black eyes, Tremaine strode over to join Kent. They talked for a moment in lowered tones. Then Tremaine came striding back.

"There's a bedroll yonder," he growled. "Crawl in. You take the graveyard watch. And damn you," he came close to glower at the cowboy, "you'd better toe the scratch, for the first break you make you're plumb out of the picture. You get that?"

Whitey's only answer was to dismount, lead his pony off a short distance, hobble it, drag the saddle from its back and disappear into the darkness in search of a bedroll.

A cooling breath of air had sprung up when Whitey rolled out to stand his guard. A myriad of stars of startling brilliance glowed in the ebon void a moonless night had flung across the heavens. Sagebrush and greasewood loomed like hideous monsters of a nightmare. A silence as vast as that found in chambers of the dead lay on the flats; a silence broken only by the long-drawn, contented sighs of cud-chewing cattle on bedground, the distant *yip, yip,* of coyotes and the thin, shrill noise of crickets. It was a world at peace after the scorching heat of the day.

Saddling his pony, Whitey rode forth whistling, a far different Whitey than had come into the roundup camp and humbled himself for the sake of work, far different from the Whitey who had shot Tremaine's horse out from under him and defied the crew to do its worst.

"The poor damned fools," he muttered under his breath as he rounded the herd. "Kent fell for that gag a heap easier than I figured he would. No, he won't rustle! I should say not. But I notice he called Smokey right over and they augered plenty after he'd toned the walloper down and I'd hit the hay. All right, Mister Kent," he chuckled, twisting in his saddle to stare back at the camp, "don't forget what Whitey Hope told you — three Diamond A's for every Buzzard and our meat supply to boot!"

The first tinge of dawn in a flawless sky — which gave promise of another blistering day — found the punchers pulling on their dew-damp boots. Even before the cook had summoned them to their breakfast, Kent and Tremaine, Whitey noted, already were up and in a deep conference over by the rope corral. He sauntered toward them.

"Whitey," Kent said as he came up, "about that proposition you made last night — I don't want any mistake, understand. I'll have no part of it. It wouldn't be honest." He paused to give effect to his words. Smokey turned away with a shrug. Whitey met the rancher's gaze without batting an eye. "We don't want anything to do with those Buzzards. Now you understand?"

"Sure," Whitey said. "That's what I figured last night."

"I just wanted to be certain," Kent reiterated. "Our men have strict orders not to touch a head of Buzzard stuff on circle. And when you're out just bear that in mind. Don't pick up a single Buzzard! No man can say King Kent ever took a critter that didn't belong to him."

"Yes, sir," Whitey replied. "Have you got a spare string for me?"

"Smokey will fix you out with one," Kent returned. "And you just remember what I told you, don't pick up a single Buzzard."

He turned on his heel and strode away toward the mess wagon. Whitey watched after him until he had rejoined Tremaine and together they strolled away in the opposite direction.

"The lying old fourflusher," Whitey snorted to himself. "The first thing he did was to talk my proposition over with Smokey. But I notice they're not letting Hartzell in on the deal."

Breakfast over, Whitey sought out Tremaine with a request for a string.

"Did you ever do any riding?" Smokey sneered.

"A little," Whitey answered. "If you've got any braying, long-eared stuff among those crowbaits branded Diamond A, I might manage to tromp one down."

The insolent reply took Tremaine's breath away. Czar of the pool roundup that he was, it was something new to have a man in the outfit dare to answer him thus. Anger darkened his tanned cheeks. But the furious glint in his eyes gave way quickly to a malicious gleam.

"Just for that you'll ride the rough string," he snarled. "When those snake-eyes get through with you I reckon you won't be so mouthy; and you won't find any mules among them either." He swung on his heel and started away.

Whitey stared after him, a smile tugging at the corners of his mouth.

"It's funny a new hand would draw the rough string when you don't even know whether he can ride or not," he threw after Tremaine. "Do you give a jasper a decent burial if his horse bucks him down and tromps him to death?"

The careless tone brought Smokey about.

"Not you, jasper," he sneered. "You're coyote meat as far as I'm concerned." His gaze whipped on to the men in the corral. "They've got a rope on Black Spirit there now — the meanest hellion in your string — in any string. Climb aboard and let's see him buck the part clean out of your hair."

Whitey turned to look at a big bay horse the men were fighting to ear down in the rope corral.

"I'm scared you've framed me, Smokey," he said meekly. "That horse isn't anybody's fool."

"I'll say he isn't." Tremaine grinned maliciously. "And if you top him you're a bronc peeler from who laid the chunk. The other two up ahead of you — Well," he shrugged significantly.

"Did anybody ever ride him?" Whitey inquired.

"Nobody but me," Tremaine boasted. "Toss this bronc snapper's saddle on him, fellers!" he yelled to the men in the corral. "We might just as well peg him for a four-flusher now as anytime."

Without a word Whitey walked over to watch the saddling of the bronc. Tremaine came grinning behind. When the sweating men finally had succeeded in getting the saddle onto the brute, Whitey himself cinched it up.

"Has he got any eyes?" the puncher asked suddenly of Tremaine.

"Sure he's got eyes," came the surprised answer. "Why?"

Whitey swung into the saddle.

"Because I always get an eye with my rowels the first jump," he threw back. "Turn him loose, jaspers, and get a bucket of water. There's going to be one bad horse minus an eye pronto!"

"You gouge that horse's eye out and I'll —" Tremaine began only to stop and leap to safety as Whitey came out of the rope corral aboard Black Spirit. The brute let forth a bellow of rage, threaded its nose between its fetlocks, bowed itself like a hairpin and hit the ground with an impact that brought a groan from both man and horse.

Straight through the camp the outlaw pitched, bawling like a foghorn, kicking over the Dutch oven, scattering the cooking utensils, sending the embers of the campfire flying after the cursing cook who ducked behind the mess wagon, then bolting across the flats to pitch from sight in a draw. But apparently Whitey Hope had been there before. And much to Tremaine's surprise and disgust, he rode back some thirty minutes later, the thoroughly whipped outlaw bathed in lather but docile and eager to do the bidding of the human leech that had bucked it down and raked its blood from its shoulder and rump.

"You didn't gouge out an eye, did you?" Tremaine snarled. "If you did —"

144

"Hell, no," Whitey grinned. "He didn't pitch hard enough for me to connect with his eye. Much obliged for this rough string, Smokey. I always like a horse with life. I reckon if this one is a fair sample the others ought to be danged fine riding."

A roar of laughter went up from the watching punchers. Tremaine flushed angrily and strode away.

Days passed. Blistering hot days with countless flies and gnats that goaded the gaunt cattle to a frenzy. Searing, scorching days that set man and beast to scouring the country for water and shade. Yet water there was none save the greenish, insect-laden pools that stunk along the parched bed of the river. When the thirsty, bawling brutes did get a whiff of the tepid water, stampedes were narrowly averted.

The mornings on circle were not so hard on the men, who loped out in the cool of dawn, a snappy new horse with a hump in its back and fighting the bit, beneath them. But as the blazing sun rose higher in the heavens and the heat increased, they began to wilt. Then even conversation became an effort.

Working the day herd in the sweltering heat and dust of the afternoon was enough to test the mettle of any man. But through it all Whitey, by now — to the chagrin of Tremaine — complete master of the rough string, held up his end. While they could not but admire his horsemanship, the Diamond A punchers, still smarting under the taunts he had forced them to swallow the morning after the Buzzard stampede, and remembering the threats he had made, regarded him with suspicion and had little to do with him.

Not so Smokey Tremaine. The wagon boss loaded him with useless labors. Whitey seemed not to mind. He did his work without complaint, although his keen-edged tongue kept Smokey in a constant fit of temper.

CHAPTER
SIXTEEN

Strange Roundup

Then one morning on circle, after he had been with the pool roundup crew for a week, Whitey Hope ran onto several wild Diamond A's. Try as he would to bunch them, the fly-crazed brutes persisted in breaking. He soon had his horse in a lather in his attempt to gather them, but they finally broke away from him completely and started off across the flats. Determined to overtake them, or play out his horse trying, he started in pursuit.

Coming onto a hogback, he pulled rein suddenly, dragged his pony back from sight in the jutting rimrock, dismounted and dropped on all fours. Directly below in a ravine were Smokey Tremaine and King Kent driving a small herd of cattle.

"It isn't often a fellow sees the boss and the foreman riding circle," he mused to himself, sprawling out on his belly to watch. "They ought to be down around the noon camp somewhere. It's funny, with all the men they hire, they still haven't enough to handle their stuff."

Curious to know what the two were about, he worked his way stealthily along the hogback to a thicket of greasewood near the end of the draw down which the two were headed. There he concealed himself, waited motionless. The bunch of cattle came on slowly. Then the brutes were directly beneath him. He started at sight of the brands. Buzzards! With an effort he held back the laughter that crowded to his lips, managed somehow to lie quietly until the two had passed on with the herd.

"The damned thieving wallopers," he chuckled as he crawled back to his horse. "Oh, no, King Kent won't rustle." Pulling his pony from sight on the other side of the rimrock, he swung into the saddle. "I reckon my little scheme is working out just like I figured it would. He wouldn't trust me to go in cahoots with him. But he put it up to Smokey. Those two are going to steal the Buzzard ragged; after giving the men orders not to pick up a single head. Well, I'll just nip their little game right now." With not so much as a look at the pick-ups he himself had been trailing, he whirled his horse and roweled away in the direction opposite to that which the two had taken.

The blazing sun crossed the zenith, started its downward course. The cook, still nursing a grudge against Whitey for wrecking his outfit the morning Black Spirit had pitched through camp, held dinner an hour for the puncher. Then, cursing savagely, he threw it out and washed up the dishes.

The panting punchers worked the day herd on the flats above Tongue river without Whitey. The alkali dust stirred up by pounding hoofs rolled away into the flaming sky to settle back in a suffocating blanket, powdering the perspiring crew from head to foot and

148

glistening in the stubble on their grimy faces. Nervous, high-strung cutting ponies were bathed in lather. Ropers missed a throw to sit for several seconds in their saddles, cursing. Then they coiled their lariats and threw again. A bawling calf would run to the end of the rope, crash in a somersault and blat raucously as it was snaked up beside the branding-fire.

There the half-naked wrestlers would seize hold of the brute. But the sun had sapped their strength. They were forced to grapple with it where ordinarily they would have upset it in a twinkling and pounced upon it. The voice of the tallyman was thick and hoarse. The iron man bent over his chip fire, face blistered, streaming perspiration. When he started with an iron he moved with faltering steps. The branders, too, took the cherry-hot irons mechanically, and slapped the brand on any old way to have done with it.

Lower and lower sank the brassy sun to shroud the prairies in dancing, shimmering waves of heat. Still no Whitey. Tremaine cursed and threatened. Kent joined him with vehemence. The weazel-faced Hartzell, more or less a pariah, held his tongue.

It was almost evening when Whitey finally did show up with a small bunch of cattle and his horse splattered with foam. Smokey saw him coming and met him with a stream of oaths. In characteristic manner the cowboy waited until the wagon boss had cursed himself out before he spoke.

"These critters were wilder than jacks," Whitey offered apologetically. "They put in the whole day looking for something to get scared at; and they found just plenty — their own shadows mostly. But I stuck with them, brought them in. I figured that was what I was riding circle for."

"Of course it's what you're riding circle for," Tremaine snarled. "But if you aren't cowhand enough to gather a lousy little bunch like this in a whole day I'll get somebody who is."

"Do you reckon you could have done any better with them running from heel flies?" Whitey demanded.

"They don't look to me like they've run," Smokey threw back. "They're not sweating — I mean —"

"Did you ever see a critter sweat?" Whitey shot in, giving Tremaine no chance to finish. "If you do find one sweating excepting on the flanks and behind the ears let me know, will you. I want it for a museum. It would take the honor away from the blood-sweating —" He dismounted, turned his back on the furious Tremaine to begin unsaddling his horse.

Now the waiting punchers were certain the ever-nearing crisis between the two had come. But to their amazement Tremaine again swallowed his rage and strode away. Thus the thing passed with Whitey, as usual, the victor. But the whole crew knew that Smokey was but biding his time. And from then on it was apparent that he had set out with new determination to force the cowboy to start for his gun. But while the men expected the blow to fall that evening they were doomed to disappointment. Whitey idled about, seemingly oblivious to the nerve-racking tension. Smokey spent his time talking with Kent, or in sullen silence.

150

Nor had his disposition improved by morning. He swilled his steaming coffee and wolfed his food. Kent, too, looked like a thundercloud. Ever careful not to roil either of the two until they had breakfasted, the punchers ate in silence. When he had finished, Kent threw his plate and cup at the feet of the startled cook, arose, and strode angrily toward the rope corrals. Tremaine followed shortly. Hartzell, his eyes plainly showing his curiosity, sat and stared.

"What the hell is eating those two?" demanded one of the men in an undertone. "They've been augering ever since they got up."

"You'll find out plenty soon enough," another answered. "Neither one of the gents are the kind to keep anything to themselves very long. Reckon it is going to pop right now!" as Kent wheeled suddenly and started to retrace his steps.

"Who all was on guard last night?" Kent demanded of Smokey as they came within earshot.

"Charley and Riley and Whitey. He was on the graveyard watch."

"Whitey," Kent said in a loud voice. "Did you see anything suspicious on your guard last night?"

"Nope." Whitey helped himself to another cup of coffee. "Critters plumb peaceful. Unusually so. Tuckered out with the heat probably. Not even a coyote yipped. Why? Something missing?"

Kent and Tremaine exchanged quick glances.

"Well —" Kent checked himself abruptly.

"Well, what?" Whitey encouraged.

"Somebody is working in this herd!" Kent blurted out.

"Rustlers!" The word ran in a whisper around the group.

"What makes you think so?" Whitey alone had the temerity to ask. "Missed any stuff?"

"Yes." Kent snapped off the word.

"Diamond A's?"

Again Kent and Tremaine exchanged quick glances, but neither spoke.

"It wasn't on my guard. Nothing surer than that," Whitey announced. "I'll stake the ace every head of Diamond A's that I took over are out there on the flat right now."

"Diamond A's aren't the only brands in this herd," Kent shot out. "There are T6's and —"

"There's everything on Thunder Basin except Buzzards when you come right down to that," Whitey cut in. "But I'm saying to you that there isn't a single head of the brands we're handling missing. Of course, you weren't looking for other stuff, were you?" He captured Kent's gaze for a moment, held it.

"You're damned right there are no Buzzards in our herd!" the cowman flared up. "And it will be tough on the jasper who runs any in, too." For an instant longer he stared at Whitey as though trying to read the cowboy's thoughts. But Whitey's eyes were as expressionless as his face, although the barest trace of a smile seemed to be struggling at the corners of his mouth.

152

"You don't need to pick me out to stare at when you caution against picking up Buzzards," he amazed Kent and the whole crew by saying. "I'm working for the Diamond A. I'm not gathering Buzzards. But supposing — just supposing a man did get one of those blackballed critters by mistake. What would the penalty be?" The question was put in a tone of serious interest. Yet it brought a dull flush to the faces of Kent and Tremaine.

"I'll kill the jasper who picks up a Buzzard," Tremaine snarled before Kent had a chance to reply. "Get that, walloper? I'll kill the jasper who brings a Buzzard critter into this herd."

Whitey got to his feet, slapped the dust from his chaps, straightened the cartridge belt at his waist and sauntered away toward the rope corral. His whole attitude was defiant, his deliberate, studied movements an impudent challenge.

Tremaine chewed his lips with rage. Once his gloved hands slid toward his guns. Whitey whirled at the instant to face him, his own thumbs resting easily in his cartridge belt. The punchers stared in blank amazement. Incredulous as it seemed, Whitey Hope again had defied Smokey Tremaine and gotten away with it!

But they had no time to ponder the unbelievable thing for Smokey wheeled on them savagely, cursing them for wasting time over their meals and threatening to discharge them all if they did not start out on circle earlier in the morning. His fury lashed them to action. They left their eating to secure their mounts and ride away. The looks they cast at Tremaine were black with

153

hatred. For the first time there was open admiration in the glances they gave the unperturbed and grinning Whitey.

But once away from camp, Whitey dropped his nonchalant air. Instead of continuing with his companion circle rider on the route he had been allotted, he gave some excuse for falling behind. Dismounting quickly, he dropped into a ravine. There he lay in the stifling heat, watching the camp through the shimmering waves of heat that rose from the flats like rays from a griddle.

After the wagons had been loaded and had started their careening course down the river toward the noon camp, two riders mounted and rode back on the trail along which the roundup had moved the day before. When they had dropped from sight over a hogback, Whitey swung up, circled the camp site and took in after them. Always he kept a safe distance behind them to escape detection, although at times he was close enough to see them gesticulating wildly in their talk. And their gestures brought a broad grin to his lips.

By mid-forenoon the two had picked up several head of cattle, which they threw into a deep draw. Each prowling range bunch was worked and the cut driven on, bunched together. By noonday the pair had gathered some twenty head. As quickly as they had started for camp, Whitey galloped to the critters they had left behind in the ravine. As he had expected they were Buzzards!

"Oh, no, King Kent won't rustle," he mused aloud, eyeing the animals, which lifted their heads from their

154

grazing at his approach, snorted and ran off a short distance to stare inquisitively. "I should say not!"

Having satisfied himself as to what the two were about, Whitey turned back and loped across the flats. Some time later, he rejoined his companion circle rider and helped him in with the drive.

Days passed thus. The monotonous drag of circle riding, working the herd, bedding down the thirsty brutes, trying to sleep out under the stars that glowed white hot in a seething heaven — which even darkness failed to cool — reduced the punchers to automatons. Tremaine became even more brutal and surly than before. Hartzell had little or nothing to say; in fact, absented himself as much as possible from the camp, which had become little more than a melting pot of rebellion.

King Kent seemed suddenly to have lost all control of himself. He was constantly prowling about among the men, firing at them questions they did not understand and heaping abuse upon their heads until they were all on the point of quitting.

"It's the heat," one of the punchers remarked one morning as he watched Kent, pacing nervously back and forth between the camp and the rope corral. "The heat's got him; and the drought is playing hell with his calf crop. Old Kent isn't sitting so well, you know. That last deal of Smokey's cost him heavy. They say he had to slap another mortgage on the Diamond A to get Tremaine out of it."

"What deal was that?" Whitey, who chanced to be near, inquired casually.

The man shot him a withering glance and fell silent. But he had said enough to arouse suspicion. Whitey met him later on circle a few miles from the camp.

"That crack you made about Kent being down to bedrock and having to put more paper on his ranch to get Tremaine out of a scrape?" he asked carelessly. "You were referring to that Masterson deal, weren't you?"

"I haven't forgotten you were against us in that play, jasper." The puncher eyed him coldly. "I don't trust you overmuch. What is it to you what I mean?"

"Just curiosity, I reckon," Whitey returned good-naturedly. "I didn't mean to be prying. But as long as I'm working for the Diamond A I'd like to know how sure my check was. I got a tip from a jasper a while back about a good job coming up during beef roundup. I figured if I could get a few of you fellows, who know Kent's financial standing, to stick with me we'd give him the go-by this fall and throw in with a real spread."

The man pricked up his ears.

"Are you telling me straight?" he demanded. "Or are you talking through your hat?"

"I don't reckon I'd be making cracks like that if I couldn't back them up, would I?" Whitey shot back. "Of course, I'm telling you straight. If King Kent is getting cornered by this drought and isn't going to be able to pay wages, come fall, I know where a bunch of real cowhands can bed down at a sizable increase with an outfit that has plenty of money."

"What spread is it?" the puncher asked.

"I asked you a question," Whitey evaded. "You told me it was none of my business. I didn't care a damn

156

about an answer to it, because I reckon it wasn't any of my business. But I'm not trading information with any jasper who isn't plumb willing to trade with me."

"What was it you wanted to know?" the cowboy asked in a more civil tone.

"What is eating King Kent? I understand you and Tremaine have been having trouble; I figured you might have caught on to something."

"Damn Tremaine," the puncher blurted out. "Everybody has trouble with him. You seem to be the only one who has hung the Injun sign on him. I'll tell you what is eating Kent — and Smokey too. Kent's down to bedrock. I've got a hunch he's pulled a lot of his dirty tricks without his partner, Al Cousins, knowing about it. And old Al isn't a man to stand for much — if he gets wise.

"Tremaine did that Masterson killing, sure as the devil. Although he has always stuck to it that he didn't. But the coroner got a wad of dough out of it just the same; and I reckon the sheriff and the county attorney's palms were greased a-plenty to drop things the way they did.

"The whole rotten deal was laid on that Montana jasper. And it's just the luck Kent and Tremaine always play in, that Montana up and got killed. That settled things as far as they were concerned — wiped their slates plumb clean, thanks to the crooked officers in Elbar.

"But there's a report going around that before Kent learned about Montana he slapped more paper on the ranch to get ready cash."

"Strange he could do that without Cousins's consent," Whitey mused.

"There's a joker somewhere," the puncher said. "But the talk that's going the rounds must have some foundation. There's a rumor that some commission house in Omaha has got Kent cornered; that he's come to a point where he can't turn any way. Then this drought is cutting the calf crop down to nothing. I overheard him telling Smokey the other morning that unless the commission house would extend his paper with the payment of a little interest money that he'd be cleaned out slicker than a whistle come fall shipping time."

"So that's what's worrying him?" Whitey observed. "But it's a danged funny setup, how Cousins comes into it. But it seems there's something else, too."

"There is," the puncher said. "But I can't get head nor tail to it. I'm riding with Smokey the other day, dozing. Kent loped up. They go to augering, me acting like I'm too near asleep to notice. Kent begins cussing and telling Smokey that somebody is rustling from him. Smokey says he knows it and he's gunning for the jaspers.

"Now I turns that over in my head. I'm plumb educated on this Diamond A stuff. And likewise I know the T6's and the rest of them. I'm working the herd and I'm danged sure there aren't any of our critters missing. Course, it's no secret that somebody has been stealing the Diamond A ragged for months; detectives have tried to get the low-down. No results. But right now I can't see where there's a critter missing from the day herd." He shifted sidewise in his saddle to stare at Whitey.

"It's got me guessing, feller. We've about decided the worry and the heat are too much for Kent — and Tremaine, too. I've heard tell of a jasper getting a bee in his bonnet like this rustling one of King's and going plumb loco in hot weather with it."

"There are no Diamond A's missing," Whitey said definitely. "Well, so long, jasper. When the time is ripe I'll spring this job with another spread on you. But keep it under your hat."

He roweled away, leaving the puncher gazing after him, a puzzled expression on his face.

CHAPTER
SEVENTEEN

A Surprising Threat

By the first week in July the heat had become almost unbearable in Thunder Basin. Each day was the same — dawn lifting along the rim of the prairies in a burst of flame. Mirages sprang up on the sagebrush flats, great undulating lakes of water that drove the sweltering men almost to the point of madness. The heat waves shimmering upward from the prairies blinded them. Dust scuffed up by the leaden hoofs of the bawling, thirsty cattle hung over the flats in a choking blanket, filling the eyes and noses of the weary cowboys, powdering their grimy, sweat-streaked faces with glistening particles of alkali and gyp and making breath itself an effort.

Day after day they rode their circles and worked the day herd grimly, doggedly. Gone long since was their laughter and song. They did their tasks mechanically, half dead with heat and thirst. Their nerves were raw and jumpy, dangerously near the snapping point. They grew surly, stubborn, resentful. Fights, which but for timely interference might have ended tragically, sprang up over trifles. Such was the hair-trigger temper of the crew that even the abusive Tremaine ceased his persecution to avoid a clash. But not so King Kent. His biting tongue kept the camp in a constant turmoil. He dared not turn his back for fear some of the cowboys, prey to the reckless impulses that had taken hold upon them, would drop him in his tracks.

Then, after an endless period of heat, thirst, flies, and trouble, the wagon swung around and started back up Tongue river in the direction of the Diamond A ranch. Hopeful of rest and water, the men shook off their apathy and began to liven up. The cows and bleating calves, too, seemed to know that somewhere ahead lay rest and feed.

When the camp was but a few hours' drive from the Diamond A the climax came. It was at breakfast time. The cowboys were seated cross-legged on the ground, eating. Since dawn King Kent and Smokey Tremaine had been engaged in heated conversation on a hogback overlooking the bedground. When, finally, they started toward the camp it was evident from their angry strides that some new blow was about to fall.

"The roundup is over, jaspers," Kent announced as he came up. "Tomorrow we will be home. So we're going to thresh out some things here and now. We've had a rustler with us. He has stolen us ragged all during the roundup. One among you has been doing that stealing. I'm going to start at the head of the list. And I'm telling you, you'd better come clean. Who did that rustling?"

A dead hush fell on the men. Frightened glances flew between them. They cast furtive looks at Kent, who stood, thumbs hooked in his cartridge belt, face merciless and brutal. Behind him hovered Tremaine, his lips twisted in a snarl. Not a puncher dared to move — save one. Whitey Hope, who that morning had been singularly quiet, so engrossed in his meal he had scarcely glanced up. But now he got to his feet to eye the pair coldly.

"You say there has been rustling, Kent?" he inquired casually. "What has been stolen?"

"Critters!" the cowman bawled. "What did you think?"

"Were they slicks?" the cowboy asked.

"Partly."

"Diamond A's?"

"No!"

"T6's?"

"No!"

"Bridle Bits?"

"No!"

"Car Links?"

"No!"

"Then what the hell has it been?"

Kent flew into a rage.

"The jasper who did it knows!" he thundered. "And he'd better come clean. We've got our suspicions who did it. Whitey Hope, you'd better tell!"

From that point on things happened with such an amazing speed the men never were just sure what did occur. A soft crooning sound issued from between the cowboy's set lips. He sent a cup of hot coffee flying as he leaped back. His hand fluttered down and up.

Clutched in nerveless fingers was his forty-five to menace both Kent and Tremaine.

"All right, jaspers," he said in a voice that was deadly in its coolness. "As long as Kent wants me to tell what has been happening, I'll sure do it. There is stuff missing from the night herd. It disappeared on the graveyard watch. It was —"

"Say it and I'll kill you," Tremaine roared.

"With me holding the edge?" the cowboy taunted softly. "Why you back-shooting — You've tried it before, and failed." Something in the tone, brought every man to his feet to stand tense.

"I told you I'd tell what stuff was missing. You asked for it. They're Buzzards!"

"You're a liar!" Kent bawled. "You can't make rustlers out of us."

"No? I've got your number Kent — you and Tremaine. You were slick. But not slick enough. That proposition of you gathering those Buzzards was sprung on you knowing you would fall for it hook, line, and sinker. And you did, Kent, better than was even figured. You gave your men orders not to pick up a Buzzard. Why? So you and Tremaine could pick them up yourselves! You've branded the slicks and run over some of the she-stuff brands. You threw them into the night herd under cover of darkness!"

"You lie!" Kent bellowed, starting to back away. "I'll — I'll —"

"You'll stand and take it," the cowboy cried, sending a bullet to lick up a furrow of dust at the feet of the

163

two. "I'm r'aring to shoot — and I'll get both of you if you make one move toward those guns of yours."

"Show me any Buzzards!" Kent roared. "Prove what you're saying. If there is a Buzzard in this herd I'll —"

"You'd win the money on a bet like that, jasper," the puncher returned cooly. "Because there aren't any. We saw to that. We rustled them out of the herd on the graveyard guard as fast as you threw them in."

"You're a liar!" Kent cried. "You never left the herd. We watched you night after night."

"Right again. I never did leave the herd. I knew you were watching. But the Buzzards were cut back just the same. You and Tremaine were followed every day on circle, and the bunches you gathered spotted. You were watched when you threw them into the night herd."

"You couldn't of done it alone, you lying four-flusher," Kent screamed, losing all control of himself. "Even if they were there you couldn't have done it alone."

"So that's what's been chewing on you?" the cowboy smiled grimly. "That's what has been keeping you in a sweat and a stew? You knew the stolen stuff was being stolen again as fast as it went into the herd. But smart as you think you are, you couldn't just figure out how. Well, I'll tell you, jasper. I had help — help of one of the best men this range has ever seen. Whitey Hope!"

"Whitey Hope?" Kent blinked "Why, you idiot, you're loco! You're Whitey Hope."

"Just for the time being," the cowboy grinned. "If you'd have had any sense you'd have seen through this play. But I picked you for a big-headed ass; and you're

164

double that. I'm Whitey's build, I've got light hair. But his eyes are blue. Take a look at mine, jasper. They're gray.

"You jailed the Buzzard men, scared them off the range. We didn't dare come out in the open. You can't fight snakes in the open. Besides, you were too many for us — too crooked. We didn't have the men to gather the Buzzards. So we let you gather them. You and Tremaine and Hartzell there. And we took three Diamond A's for every Buzzard you'd stolen. They're over there now in the reserve. On pasture, Kent, feeding and drinking and doing fine. And Whitey is with them."

"You're crazy!" Kent bellowed. "Drop him, one of you jaspers, quick. Whitey has gone off his head in this heat. He'll kill somebody."

"Oh, no, Whitey Hope isn't off his head. He's riding herd on a nice bunch of Buzzards forty miles from here."

"But I gave a job to Whitey Hope." A hoarse note deadened Kent's voice.

"Sure, you did. And Whitey has been here working day after day. And then again —"

"Who are you?" Kent gasped.

"Montana Ellis." The puncher ripped off his hat. "And it took a hell of a supply of flour to make my hair look as white as Whitey's. But I did it, jasper, did it because I knew you were too damned blind to see anything. Whitey worked days. I stood his guard at night while he cut out the spotted critters."

165

"I thought you were dead!" Kent choked, cringing as though before a ghost. "You were drowned that — that night."

"The night you stampeded our stuff and burned our camp," Montana lashed out. "Not by a hell of a sight, I wasn't. I was down at the Dunning place feeding myself. It was only one of Whitey's tricks. You had us cornered. We were outlaws in the eye of the law, thanks to you. You'd framed us in Elbar. We figured a dead man could do more against you crooks than we could in the open."

He stopped to sweep the dumfounded faces about him. The grin broadened at sight of the incredulity in their eyes.

"Now we're two hundred Buzzards short, Kent. That is the number lost in the river during the stampede. We'll just take Diamond A's to make up the difference. Thanks for gathering our stuff. I've hung the Injun sign on both you and Tremaine. You're jail bait the second your sheriff ever tries to serve that phony warrant for me. And whether or not he does you're heading for the pen just as soon as I get one more thing done I've set out to do." He backed away toward his horse, climbed into the saddle, his gun still bearing down upon them menacingly. Once Kent, his face working with apoplectic fury, tried to speak. Again the Colt spoke, again to slice a furrow in the dirt beside him.

"That other thing I'm going to uncover," Montana was saying as he jerked his horse backward out of range. "That is who killed Pop Masterson. When I get the lowdown sewed up so tight you can't pit your money against it, I'm coming for you, Kent — you and Tremaine." He whirled his horse and was gone into a dry ravine.

CHAPTER
EIGHTEEN

Secret Message

Word of the sudden appearance of Montana in the Diamond A roundup crew threw Thunder Basin into a ferment of excitement. And word of the challenge the cowboy — long since thought dead — had hurled at King Kent and Smokey Tremaine, set the region to buzzing with apprehension.

In the maze of events that followed swiftly one on another the citizens could scarcely keep up with the rumors. The sheriff, against Kent's orders it was whispered, started on the trail of Montana, still wanted on a false charge of murdering Masterson. Scarcely had he ridden out of town when Sally Hope returned from Omaha. And with her was the boy, Clem White, a bright-eyed youngster presenting an entirely different appearance in his new "store" clothes.

A lone cowboy met the evening train as it ground to a halt at Elbar. Some who glimpsed him in the twilight dusk said it was the girl's brother, Whitey Hope. Others said it was Montana himself. No one knew. Nobody cared to investigate. And for that reason the scene at the station went unobserved by prying eyes. The cowboy had ridden into Elbar and down the street with never a challenge. He led a spare horse, saddled, fitted with new trappings — spangled leather to delight the heart of any youngster. Swinging down at the station, he tied his horses and nervously paced the deserted platform.

As the train rolled in and stopped he started along the coaches. Presently he sighted the girl, garbed in a chic suit that brought out every line of her trim figure. Once she had assisted the youngster to alight, she spied him, came forward on a run to throw herself into his arms and kiss him. She clung to him for an instant before she tore herself away with a startled little cry. A sputtering sound came from the man.

"I'm pleased to see you home, Miss Sally," he blurted out.

"Oh," she said, the gloom hiding the flush of her blazing face. "I thought you were — Whitey. My, how you two look alike. I'm sorry —"

"Sorry?" Clem cried, seizing hold of the cowboy's arm and clinging to him. "Gosh, Montana, you kissed Sally."

"Hush, Clem," Sally reprimanded. "Didn't Whitey or —"

"Whitey's tied up with the stock," Montana apologized. "I told your ma I'd meet you. Besides, I was kind of anxious to see Button, here. I've sure missed —"

"Oh!" The girl picked up her suitcase and started along the platform.

"I'll tote it," Montana urged, falling in beside her. "Then Clem and I will light out for the ranch. You don't need to get huffy just because —"

169

"I'm not," she snapped. "And I can handle my own suitcase." She seized the boy and kissed him. "I suppose you're going with — with your friend now," she said. "I know he'll take good care of you. Don't forget to wash your teeth. Your brush is in your grip."

"But I want to thank you for tending to that business for me in Omaha," Montana protested. "Getting those papers and all. And looking out for Button. It was mighty fine of you —"

"That was no trouble at all," she said tartly, starting away to leave him standing staring at her.

"Wouldn't that beat you?" Montana muttered to the youngster, who was enjoying the procedure hugely. "I guess I don't understand women."

"I guess you don't," Clem said. "Especially women like Sally. She's in a class by herself, Montana. But gosh, she kissed you. I should think —"

"Shut up. Give me your grip. Get moving," Montana snapped. "The horses are right behind the depot."

The boy fell in beside him. The preoccupied Montana scarcely noticed the exclamations of delight from Clem as he discovered and swung into his brand new saddle. Nor did he speak as they rode out of town, although he did pull rein at the tracks and gaze back until a trim little figure with a suitcase had disappeared into Mother Hope's Café.

"The dangedest thing ever I heard of," Montana mused aloud as they headed out onto the open flats toward the Dunning place. "Just because of a mistake and a girl kisses the wrong man —"

"You liked it, didn't you?" Clem taunted.

170

Montana made no reply. The boy's words had struck home. He had liked it, far more than he would admit to himself. To receive a kiss intended for another was what rankled. She had thought —

"Well, it won't take us long to clean up, now," he said shortly, tearing his mind from the meeting. "Tomorrow we'll light out together and deliver that letter to Al Cousins. Then there's one more thing. Quick as we get that settled up we'll get out of this danged Thunder Basin."

"What's wrong with Thunder Basin?" Clem asked. "Gosh, I've been looking forward to coming back and staying here. Just because Sally got a little mad isn't going to drive you —"

"My leaving Thunder Basin has nothing to do with Miss Hope," Montana growled. "I'd intended to go as quick as we could without showing yaller anyhow."

Silence fell between them as the ponies picked their way across the flats, drenched now with a silver haze from a great full moon that was starting its climb above the eastern horizon.

And again silence settled down upon the rumors and gossiping tongues in Thunder Basin, the panting citizens marking time until the next big event, the annual Diamond A rodeo, to break the monotony of life in the seared and withered country. Then finally after days of blazing heat that wilted man and beast, rodeo day dawned.

The sun lifting along the rim of the greasewood in a fling of vivid color, found the Two Montanas, united again, riding out in Thunder Basin bound at last to deliver the letter to Al Cousins. The morning was glorious and calm, forerunner of a typical prairie day when man feels his insignificance in the hugeness of nature. To the north, deceptively near, the Big Horn mountains reared their snow-crowned helms into a mass of fleecy white clouds. To the south, east, and west the flats stretched away, hazy and indistinct through their veil of purple. Box buttes and divides stood out like etchings, their outline growing dimmer with distance until they melted into the deeper purple of the horizon. Here and there a bull pawed dust and bawled his challenge to prowling range herds. Rabbits scurried away to belly down on their holes, ready to duck to cover. Meadowlarks teetered in the tops of the sagebrush, whistling their gayest. Far overhead a hawk wheeled lazily in the flawless heavens.

In silence the Two Montanas rode, their ponies pushing mile after mile behind them with amazing ease, each seemingly content with his own thoughts, the boy's admiring gaze always fixed on the cowboy. But Big Montana was sunk in thought that took no notice of time or distance, although his steel-gray eyes were ever whipping the flats. Constantly recurring thought of the girl as he had seen her at the train had affected him strangely. Sally Hope — Sally Hope. He had had little time to think of her during the winter months. But now — that kiss — the short moment she had been in his arms — Sally Hope. Even her name seemed to ring to the tread of his pony on the brittle, dry earth.

172

"You kind of took a shine to Sally after that kiss, didn't you, Montana?" The boy's voice jerked the cowboy from his retrospection. He looked down at the youngster who was smiling up at him. In spite of himself he flushed, for even at the moment thought of the girl was uppermost in his mind.

"What makes you think that, Button?" Montana asked.

"Oh, just the way you still get tongue-tied when she speaks. And the way you kept looking at her at the depot after she kissed you. She sure is pretty, isn't she, Montana?"

"She sure is. But I never noticed that I —"

"Too bad we ain't got a sister, or something, like her, us Two Montanas, ain't it?" The youngster sighed. "Gosh, she was great to me in Omaha. She'd be a regular pal. Look how she told me to brush my teeth regular; and you bet I'm doing it, too."

"She's mighty thoughtful," Montana said feelingly.

"Then why don't you do something about it?"

The demand for a moment upset Montana's calm.

"What do you mean, do something about it?"

"Why, marry her — or — something. She sure likes you. You could see it in her eyes. Even after she kissed you and got all fussed about it. She was just sort of peeking at you. I was watching her. And every time I caught her looking at you she got redder. Once in Omaha she — she winked at me."

"Winked at you," Montana blurted out. "Why, you doggoned little flirt! I've got half a mind to trounce you for —"

"For seeing a pretty gal likes you when you can't even see it yourself?" Clem countered, the heavy seriousness of his voice almost laughable. "And that kiss — Montana, she liked that kiss."

That ended the conversation. Again they fell silent as their ponies moved across the blistered flats. But childish as were the boy's words something of a thrill ran through the cowboy.

Past midday Big Montana drew rein on the rim of a hogback to twist a cigaret. Directly below, a crowd of people packed the grassy hillsides surrounding a natural amphitheater. As they watched, a calf sped from a chute to go dashing away, a rider thundering beside it, swinging a loop. The rope whipped out. The calf somersaulted in a blatting heap. Instantly the rider was from his saddle to hog-tie it, throw up his hands in signal that the brute was fast, then run to stop his horse which, with bridle reins trailing, was dragging the little animal across the bowl.

"This here will be the Diamond A rodeo, buddy," Montana told the quiet boy. "If it hadn't been for wanting to get this letter delivered pronto I'd have entered. Then again we'll like as not locate Cousins right here. Now we're here I've got half a notion to —"

"Can you ride, too?" Little Montana asked, watching his companion with eyes still wide with admiration.

"No big thing — but we might stir up some fun. Might be such a thing we could find Cousins and not have to go on to the Diamond A."

Roweling their ponies forward, to the delight of the boy, they were soon crowding the reluctant brutes

174

through the milling crowds. Presently they sighted the judges' stand and made for it.

"What are the chances of entering the pitching contests?" Montana inquired, riding up to the group and swinging down.

One of the number whirled at sound of his voice. Montana jerked straight, rigid. His hand flashed down to rest near the butt of his forty-five. For the first time since he had ridden away from the roundup camp on Tongue river he was face to face with Smokey Tremaine! But now the Diamond A foreman was careful to keep his own hands away from his guns. And again as he sighted the boy, into his eyes flared the unfathomable light of recognition that had puzzled Montana the day of his arrival in Elbar.

"What's that kid's name?" Smokey demanded. "Where did he bob up from again? I thought —"

"Seeing as how you are asking decently now instead of trying to bull your way through and throw a scare into somebody, like you did the first time you saw us, I don't see any reason for not telling you," Montana said. "This is my pard, Little Montana. We're the Two Montanas, Tremaine."

A look that Montana could have sworn was relief flashed across the big puncher's face.

"So you're aiming to enter the pitching contests?" He changed the subject abruptly. "Claim to be an exhibition rider, huh?"

"I don't recollect expressing any such claim," Montana retorted. "But I have bucked down about as many snake-eyes as the next fellow."

"You don't need to get hostile," Smokey flared up. "You weren't invited, you know."

"I supposed jaspers with the entrance fee could ride at any rodeo," Montana threw back, his gray eyes snapping along the crowd of onlookers which, after the manner of crowds, ever sensing trouble, had edged up from nowhere. "I didn't know you didn't want new blood. I reckon that is so there won't be any chance of you not playing whole hog with the prize money."

Hot anger leaped into Tremaine's eyes. He, too, swept the group about them. The furtive glances that met his gaze were evidence of the fear in which they held him. But behind that fear also was discernible another light — a ray of sympathy for Montana, who again dared flaunt the lion of the Tongue on his own stamping ground. Some there were in the crowd who had witnessed the other meetings of the two; others knew of them. Word travels with the speed of fire in sparsely settled rangeland.

"You're plumb welcome to enter the pitching contests as far as I'm concerned." Smokey was sneering. "But you'll find bucking down these twelve-hundred-pound Tongue river horses isn't the same as topping off the Injun ponies they call horses in Montana. It takes real men to ride these hellions. A real bronc stamper who can stay till the cows come home and tromp the devils to a standstill." While he was speaking, his gaze was riveted upon Montana. But now suspicion had replaced the light of uncertain recognition in those glittering eyes.

176

"So Whitey told me after he bucked down your rough string," Montana shrugged.

"I'm the champion buster of this country," Tremaine boasted.

"Shucks," Montana said, "that being the case I don't see any reason for me to be leary of Tongue river horses."

Smokey bristled.

"Enter him," he yelled to an arena judge riding by. "I'll learn him what real riding is." He set himself, gloved thumbs in his cartridge belt, the butt of a cigaret dangling from his lips. His hostile attitude seemed to invite trouble. But apparently Montana had no intention of becoming embroiled in a new fracas, for, with a smile he motioned to the boy. Together they led their horses away to a corral. Tying them, they returned to the judges' stand, where Montana passed over his entrance fee and a number was pinned onto his back. Smokey watched him for a moment, then, with a contemptuous snort, sauntered away.

The hillsides that sloped up gently from the natural amphitheater were a blaze of color; a bedlam of noise rolled away to batter to whispers far back in the somber reaches of the Big Horns. Young girls uttered piping little screams of delight. Hero-worshiping boys danced around wildly. Mothers cast aside their dignity and cried themselves hoarse. Staid husbands and business-men — who had shut up shop in the surrounding towns — tossed into the air their high-crowned wide-brimmed hats. It was a boisterous throng, keyed to the highest pitch. But rodeo crowds were by no means new to Montana. Nor did he have time to enjoy the picturesque setting, for a stubby, bow-legged man of drawn, weather-beaten countenance and snow-white hair hobbled up to scrutinize him sharply from faded blue eyes.

"Are you from Crowe?" he asked presently in an undertone.

Determined, after his meeting with Tremaine, to hold his tongue and keep his ears open until he was sure of his ground, Montana made no reply. He sized up the newcomer. For all the suspicion and mistrust in the man's gaze there was something likeable about him, some incomprehensible thing that won Montana's confidence.

"The sheriff got my letter?" the old fellow asked.

Scenting new trouble, instantly Montana was on his guard. Not until then did he recognize the name, Crowe. It was the name of the sheriff who held the warrant for his arrest, but who, strangely, had not to his knowledge — since his warning to Kent on the roundup — made any particular effort to serve it. The name, he now recalled, was signed to the reward notice for Three Finger DeHaven the herder had pointed out to him the day of his arrival in Elbar. Apparently this old man was on the lookout for someone from the office of the sheriff, Jim Crowe. Montana sought to feel him out.

"I'm a bronc peeler," he said shortly.

"I see, I see," the stranger surprised him by saying. "You don't want to know me openly. So you're the new rider?"

"I reckon I'm a rider, but —"

"I'm Al Cousins," the old man confided abruptly.

Montana eyed him sharply.

"Al Cousins?" he repeated. "Then you're sure the gent I'm looking for. I've got —"

"I know, I know," the cowman interrupted, edging closer. "And here is the letter I wrote the sheriff about." After a careful survey, which showed no prying eyes upon them, he passed over a crumpled piece of paper. Scarcely knowing what to do, Montana took it reluctantly.

Cousins: We've got a tip you're dickering to get another detective in here. We're warning you for the last time we won't stand any more monkey business. If another pussyfoot comes in here we'll get you and him too.

The Gang.

The warning, written in a cramped hand, was almost illegible. It occurred to Montana that anyone, no matter how poor a writer, must have used the left hand to produce such a scrawl.

"That gang has made life hell for me for years," Cousins was saying in a voice scarcely above a hoarse whisper. "They have rustled me ragged. Nobody has ever got sight of them. But we can go into that later. I reckon it is best that you act like you don't know me. There will be a dance at the ranch tonight after the rodeo; I'll meet you behind the barn at the Diamond A when the dancing gets started. But keep a dally on your tongue. Nobody is in on this but you and me. I'm going —" He broke off to glance at Tremaine who was sauntering past. "Where are you from?" he asked loudly for the benefit of the swaggering foreman.

Expecting a momentary explosion, again on the point of attempting to reveal his mission, Montana checked himself quickly and took the cue.

"Montana," he answered carelessly.

"And your name?"

"Montana."

Cousins started. "I've heard of you," he said. "I —"

"I reckon you have — just plenty," Montana stopped him. "But just the same I'm Montana." He pulled the shy boy from behind him. "And this is my buddy, Little Montana. Shake hands with Mister Cousins, buddy."

A happy gleam shot into Cousins's faded eyes at sight of the embarrassed youngster. "I'm right pleased to know you, Little Montana," he said, shaking hands with the lad, then dropping an arm about his shoulder. "I've got a warm spot in my heart for kids. We'll be pals. You stick around with me and we'll see this show from start to finish. Have you ever ridden exhibition before?" he asked Montana.

"Third at Calgary last year," the cowboy answered.

"Hell's bells! Then you must be a real rider."

"No big thing," Montana corrected modestly. "I just don't draw no color line. But what I'm trying to tell you is that I came —"

"We'll discuss that later," Cousins cut him short again. "You and this little kid have made a hit with me. For ten years I've been trying to win a Diamond A rodeo — good-natured sport among ourselves, you know," he offered quickly. Too quickly, Montana thought. "But Smokey Tremaine, my foreman, is wolf poison on a bronc. Do you think you could buck him down?"

Montana shifted to watch Tremaine, who was idling about now within earshot.

"I'm not much of a hand to brag," Montana admitted frankly. "But I've met Tremaine, and it sure would give me a heap of pleasure to try and buck him down."

Tremaine started. Once it seemed as though the gloved hands, always hovering near the butts of his forty-fives, were going down. But again something checked their course. With a contemptuous shrug he wheeled and strode away.

"Ride for me," Cousins urged. "We can talk about the other tonight."

"It's jake with me," Montana said. "Money talks no matter how I get it. On the hurricane deck of a bronc or any other way."

"Fine!" Cousins exclaimed. "I'll fix everything for you. My side has enough points in the other contests so that if we can win in the bronc-busting I'll win this show hands down. And —" he sidled closer, "if we should there won't be anything too good for you. I'll take care of your pard. Come on, sonny." He hooked his arm through that of the boy and hobbled away to confer with the judges.

Montana stood staring after them. He had taken an instant liking to the old fellow. There was something

181

appealing about him; something that impelled friend-ship, sympathy.

Then through his mind started a flood of questions. The frame-up against the Buzzard. The killing of Masterson. Did Cousins know of this? Had he been a party to Kent's crookedness? It seemed impossible, as he watched the limping old fellow with the friendly eyes, that the rancher even knew of the attempted intimidation, the blackballing of the Buzzards on Thunder. But how could he keep from knowing? And, with Kent for a partner, how could he keep from being a party to the thing?

His mind flew on to the letter. In view of what already had occurred, and the possibility of a new explosion at any moment, he already half regretted ever coming to the Basin to deliver the letter, which as yet he had had no opportunity to mention. That Cousins had mistaken him for some detective from the sheriff's office struck a semi-comical chord with him. He, Montana, the avowed enemy of the Diamond A playing the role of a detective! When they met that night he would have a chance to explain, set Cousins right, and find out if the kind-faced old rancher had had a part in —

His restrospection was cut short by the lusty bawl of the announcer.

"Ladies and gents! The next and last event is the pitching contest for a five-hundred-dollar purse and the championship of Tongue river. We have five entries. From these we will select three winners to ride off in the finals a month from today to see who gets a whirl at

182

the world championship next summer at Cheyenne. Montana, who has gained quite a reputation in Thunder Basin in the past few months, riding for Al Cousins, is slated to make his bow and open the fireworks out of Chute Number One on Foghorn!"

Mention of his name, Montana was aware, sent a whistle of expectancy through the huge crowd. But he was into the thing now; there was no turning back. He started for the corrals, suddenly conscious of scores of eyes fastened upon him and which left him far more fearful than the outlaws bawling and battling the hostlers in the chutes.

As he strode for the corrals, his gaze swept the brimming sea of faces; the loneliness of the thing chilled him — the unfriendliness. Not a single face that he recognized outside of Tremaine, who stood just off the stand leering at him. For a moment he wished for Whitey, but Whitey was back at the Dunning place caring for the cattle — Whitey the steadfast, Whitey his one friend in all Thunder Basin. If Whitey knew that he had actually been foolhardy enough to stop at the rodeo for the only reason, he now admitted to himself, to pit himself against Tremaine, Whitey would have called him no end of a fool. But —

"Stash your gun with the judges during the ride," Smokey bawled.

Nerves brought Montana to a dead halt. He jerked about.

"I'll stash mine when yours come off," he rasped out in a voice that struck him with its high-pitched unnaturalness.

"Have it your own way," Smokey retorted, unbuckling his studded belt with its two holstered forty-fives and passing it over to a judge. "We're about even now."

In three swift strides Montana was before him. With a quick movement he slipped his gun from its holster, passed it over. Then he straightened up. But the blazing retort that flashed to his lips was never uttered. For suddenly his eyes had found someone he recognized. Beside Tremaine stood Sally Hope. A trim little figure in a modish, tailored suit, her face glowing with color and excitement. And she was smiling at him, smiling with a dazzling brilliance that set his head to whirling. He caught but a glimpse of her before his eyes fell. With a muttered word and a bow he spun about and passed on.

Tremaine said something. From the corner of his eyes Montana saw the girl flush angrily and move away from the puncher's side. But he had no chance to follow the urge that surged up within him. The announcer was paging the field for him. He broke into an awkward trot for the chutes.

CHAPTER
NINETEEN

Near Tragedy

Montana! The name buzzed on every lip. The man who had dared go for his gun in Elbar against Smokey Tremaine. The man who had dared defy King Kent and Tremaine and show up in the Diamond A roundup camp posing as Whitey Hope. The man whom some in Thunder Basin still believed dead, a victim of the rapids of the Tongue during the Buzzard stampede.

Montana!

The name brought to their feet every man, woman, and child, crowding for a glimpse at this cowboy whose daring exploits had made history in Thunder Basin. The packed mass of humanity on the hillsides swayed and screamed in the excitement of the moment, sight of the puncher who had risen to something of a hero in the eyes of the range folk.

Well down toward the rim of the bowl, Little Montana leaped up and down with excitement, while Al Cousins watched him with a strangely happy light in his faded eyes. King Kent fell to pacing about, his nervously working hands belying the smug assurance in the smile that twisted his weather-cracked lips. The instant Kent had heard of Montana's arrival he had started out in search of the sheriff. But he had made no great effort to locate him, in fact, had been somewhat relieved to discover that the officer was in Elbar, unable to attend the rodeo.

But it was the boy who was getting the thrill out of the spectacle. Although his few years had been spent on a ranch, never before had he seen a rodeo with its blare and color. The snorting, striking horses being dragged along, shaking their heads savagely, forehoofs plowing furrows in the earth, or trying to climb the narrow chutes to battle the men strung out on the poles above, fired him with excitement. The moaning of the long-horned steers, the terrified blats of the calves, the constant whirl of action, threw his mind into a turmoil.

He waited eagerly, fearfully, for Montana to come out. But the hoarse bawls, the crash of angry hoofs on timber and the thick clouds of dust swirling up from the chutes clearly explained the delay. For all the overwhelming odds against him, Foghorn was putting up the fight for his life against the saddle that was being cinched beneath his belly with a grappling hook, against the bucking-strap that was being drawn tight about his flanks.

Of a sudden a burst of applause arose, swelled in a crescendo tumult. Little Montana seized hold of Cousins's arm and raised himself on tiptoes just as the heavy gate of the chute swung wide.

For a breathless second a horse — a huge, broad-rumped black — crouched in the chute

186

quivering with terror. Then it wheeled and bolted forth, lunging away into space to land like a stone-crusher in front, stiff-legged, double-barreled behind.

In a flash it was gone into the air again, its nose threaded between its fetlocks, its great body bowed like a horseshoe — on the curve of which sat the grim-faced Montana — its rump twisting, its tail swishing an angry accompaniment to its bawls of rage.

Little Montana watched with awful fascination. A pitching horse was no novelty to him. Since he could remember he had seen the strings broken out for the roundups, had heard the taunts, the occasional scream of a cowboy badly hurt at the dangerous work. But then it had been but ranch routine, a part of the day's work; and the men who had ridden were hard-faced, cursing punchers who spared neither man nor beast — men with hearts as wicked as the outlaws they rode.

But now it was different — the noise, the color, the excitement. And aboard that bawling outlaw was the one human who had taken the trouble to show him kindness — the one thing in all his life upon which he could center his childish love.

The "thumpity, thumpity" of the brute's clipping hoofs as they hammered the ground were no louder than the cracks of Montana's body as he lurched about in the saddle, scratching the outlaw from shoulder to rump, his spurs singing along its ribs almost to meet behind the cantle, his dime-thin rowels matted with hair and dripping blood.

The crowd went wild. Men leaped about, slapping one another on the backs. Women screamed hysterically. Of all the thundering hundreds the man aboard the lunging, bawling horse seemed the least excited.

Then the brute, blood flying from its flaring nostrils and mouth, was swapping ends, sunfishing until it seemed to lie on its side in midair, landing on legs stiff as crowbars, teetering for an instant and catapulting away to repeat the grueling, dizzy performance, bawls as raucous and penetrating as the bellow of a foghorn rumbling from its throat.

With tears of excitement trickling down his cheeks, Little Montana watched the grim and deadly battle between man and horse. Of a sudden a great groan set his nerves to strumming. The crowd was surging forward. Men were shouting hoarsely. Women's screams took on a different note. Terror rose up about him. He clung frantically to Cousins's arm to be dragged along.

"What's the matter?" he managed to choke out, although within him he knew the cause of the cold terror that clutched at his throat, the sudden sluicing roar of his own blood in his ears.

"That jasper is hurt," someone was bawling. Little Montana caught his words out of the awful sickness of fear. "That horse fell right in the middle of him — He's pinned down. God, why don't somebody —" Little Montana's faculties seemed to halt. His senses were reeling. Stark terror possessed him. All the strangeness, excitement he had experienced centered in one breathless moment. He was choking, clawing frantically at his throat, which suddenly seemed closed to breath.

Then the jostling crowd before him parted. Through great clouds of dust he caught a glimpse of gray on the ground. Above it a patch of black whipped about savagely.

"Pick him up! Pick him up!" The horrified crowd all seemed to find their voices at once.

"Hazers! Hazers!" The hoarse shout rose deafeningly.

Little Montana strained to see. The patch of gray had taken form. It was the shirt, the dusty garb of Montana beneath the black outlaw upon which men had pounced in an attempt to ear down.

"Give the horse a break!" A voice suddenly rose above the uproar to crash on Little Montana's drumming ears. "What the hell is this, a frame-up? Let him make his ride or disqualify him!"

Came a momentary silence. Then hisses and catcalls met the shout. At that instant Little Montana got a glimpse of the speaker. His swarthy face was twisted furiously as he cursed the hazers away from the floundering outlaw. It was Smokey Tremaine. And — Little Montana's blood seemed suddenly to freeze in his veins — just beside the hulking figure of Tremaine — who suddenly rose up as an ogre, a hideous creature of a nightmare to his bewildered childish senses — was Sally Hope. Sally, who in the passing weeks had grown up as a sort of an ideal within him, an object to share his love with Montana. And now she was there beside Tremaine, who was shouting, running the others away. But —

Suddenly the girl had whirled. He caught sight of her face. It was pale as death. Her eyes were blazing. Then she had deliberately slapped Smokey Tremaine across the mouth. He was backing away —

"Get back! Get back!" Another voice suddenly came above the bedlam. "Damn you, I'll —"

A mighty cheer drowned out the threat. But Little Montana had heard enough of that cool and careless voice to know that it could belong to no one but his idol — Montana.

He stood on tiptoe again to see. Tremaine had backed off, stamping away toward the chutes. Sally no longer was with him. The outlaw, Foghorn, was lurching up, Montana still in the saddle. Almost before the brute was on its feet, it resumed its merciless, bone-crushing assault. Lost in admiration for the cowboy, conscious of a wave of hot hatred against Tremaine, Little Montana scarcely heard or saw the finish.

As quickly as it had started the battle was over. The pick-up gun! Big Montana was lifted from the outlaw by a hazer. Wild with joy, unable to restrain himself, Little Montana jerked away from Cousins and started across the field toward the chutes. The announcer was bawling something, but he paid no heed. Over there was Big Montana, grown even more of a hero now in his childish eyes. He caught the name of Smokey Tremaine — and Tiger Rose. Hatred surged up anew within him; childish hatred for Smokey Tremaine.

A new roar of shouting assailed his ears. In it was a note of warning. He stopped. His startled gaze flew about. People seemed to be running in all directions. He sighted Cousins trying to reach him. And Sally. He thought he caught her screaming his name. He tried to go to her. A mob cut in between them. Everyone was crowding back like frightened sheep. And it seemed everyone was suddenly crying out to him. Yet what all the commotion was about he had not the slightest idea.

Then he was certain the shouts were directed at him. But why? The fleeing mob was trying to warn him of impending danger. He turned. His eyes grew wide with terror. Thundering down upon him was a big gray outlaw — Tiger Rose — its hoofs cleaving the ground, slicing the air viciously, its body a bundle of straining iron muscles. So close was the brute that Little Montana could see the savage glint in the eyes of its rider — Smokey Tremaine!

The youngster's terrified gaze swept the crowd for Cousins — or Sally. Somewhere they had been caught in the mad scramble and hustled along. Alone he stood in the path of the frenzied, bawling, blinded horse.

Instinct warned him to throw himself out of the way. But his knees suddenly had turned to tallow. His senses were reeling. He was in the grip of a numbing impotence that left him dizzy and nauseated. He flung his arm across his eyes. His lips trembled.

He risked another glance. The bawling brute was almost upon him. He attempted to cry out — for Big Montana. No sound issued from between his locked lips. Stark terror rooted him in his tracks. His frantic gaze met that of Tremaine, astride the outlaw. A deadly gleam now filled the cowboy's eyes.

Then the outlaw was directly above him. The inherent sense of self-preservation finally drove his

191

paralyzed muscles to obey. The air was filled with flailing hoofs. A terrific blow landed on his head, beat him to the ground.

Then he was conscious that he was in someone's arms. A tumultuous shout drifted from far, far away. He clung desperately to the arms about him. Someone was crying something in his ear. But he could barely hear. His hammering blood had become a sluicing roar, reducing the angry shouts about him to faint whispers. A swaying curtain of darkness before his eyes was shutting out the madly spinning scene.

CHAPTER
TWENTY

A Challenge

Little Montana's first sensation afterward was of the chill of water on his head. He forced his heavy eyelids open to see a flaming sky above him. He was stretched on the ground. Montana was bending over him, bathing his throbbing head. Behind him was a sea of curious faces. Nearest Montana, holding his hand, was Sally. There were tears in her eyes. He tried gamely to smile at her, at Montana.

"I'm all right," he managed to choke out in a tiny voice.

"I'm sure glad, buddy," Big Montana gulped. "We thought you were — a goner. Believe me, I'll settle with that —"

"Tremaine tromped me down," the boy panted. "I couldn't get out of the way. I was too scared. Seemed like my legs wouldn't move —"

"I know he tromped you down." There was a terrible, frozen note in Montana's voice, the crackle of ice. All the pleasantness had left his eyes. They seemed to gleam like the blue barrel of a gun. "On purpose. Damn him, there's something behind all this that you and me aren't wise to. But we will be before we leave Thunder Basin."

Lying now with his throbbing eyes closed against the pain that shot through his head, Little Montana waited for his cowboy buddy to continue. When he did not, he glanced up. Big Montana had disappeared. Cousins was bending over him instead, Cousins and Sally, whose cool white hands seemed to sooth him, whose whispered words of encouragement seemed to give him strength above all else.

"Where's — Big — Montana?" the youngster faltered.

"Lie still, sonny," Cousins urged gently. "You'll feel better in a little while. That outlaw struck you on the head. Don't get excited now." But the cowman's failure to answer his question roused the boy. Jerking away, he lurched to his feet to stand swaying, sweeping the field with eyes that were glazed with pain. The big outlaw, from which the saddle had been stripped, was thundering away across the bowl. The crowd was edging back. Directly before him was Big Montana, coming back from the judges' stand, his forty-five dangling in his hand.

A scream left the lips of the boy and Sally. Facing Big Montana was Tremaine, who also had secured his guns.

"You lousy lobo," Montana was forcing softly through set teeth. "You could have turned that outlaw. You a champion bronc peeler. Why, damn your cowardly heart, I ought to drill you. You've asked for it plenty and you've got it coming."

"Like hell you'll drill him!" It was King Kent coming on a run, roaring like an infuriated bull. "Let the brat stay out of the way if he don't want to —" He planted himself beside the cowboy.

"Brat?" Big Montana smiled — a cold, grim, lifeless smile that was little more than a tightening of his lips across his teeth. "He isn't a brat, and, damn you, it takes more of a man than you'll ever be to call him one. He's my buddy. You get that, you two-bit four-flushing wallopers. My buddy. And no man alive can tromp him down nor abuse him. You keep your bill out of this," he shot out at Kent. "I'm running this show to suit myself for a while and I'll —"

"Like hell you are," Kent bawled. "You can't come down here and start trouble thisaway. It's what you came for. Get the sheriff," he hurled at the crowd, secure in the knowledge that the sheriff could not be reached. "There's a warrant out for this jasper."

"I warned you on the roundup that the minute they try to serve that warrant the jig is up with you," Montana flashed out. "You and Tremaine. Now bust yourself, you white-livered steer."

Kent's rage drove him beyond reason.

"I'll — I'll —" He was shouting at the top of his voice, his face purple with fury. Regardless of Montana's lowered gun he swung a blind and terrific blow at the puncher's head. Montana side-stepped, lifted an uppercut with his left from the ground and plastered it at the base of the bellowing rancher's ear.

That blow stopped Kent in his tracks. He rocked on his heels. The color left his face which grew chalky. His knees sagged, buckled. He crumpled to the ground.

"You don't ever do anything but beller," Montana was panting. "That's all you've done since I first came into Thunder. I've seen your caliber all over cowland — You won't do anything. Any more than this hell-bending Smokey Tremaine. You're two of a kind. Two bob-tailed flushers. You may have the fear of the Lord in the rest of these folks around here but I don't buffalo." He jerked his scathing words from the moaning Kent to Smokey. "Now you, damn you, you tromped my buddy."

But apparently the mighty Tremaine had seen enough of Montana in action, had little stomach left for another encounter.

"I didn't," he cried hoarsely, backing away. "I couldn't hold that Tiger Rose. I tried to holler to the kid. But I couldn't —"

Then Cousins had seized Montana by the arm.

And another voice just at his elbow came low, pleading. It thrilled him with its sweetness, left him embarrassed.

"Cool down," Sally Hope was pleading. "Perhaps he couldn't turn the outlaw. Little Montana isn't hurt badly. More frightened than anything. Don't let us turn this wonderful day into —"

The cowboy dragged a hand across his eyes. Before Little Montana knew what he was about he, too, was running forward, had clutched the arm of his friend.

"Don't, pard!" he begged. "Mebbeso he couldn't help it. Don't have any more trouble over me. Please. Come along."

He was tugging frantically at Montana's arm. And the girl had laid a hand on him, was also attempting to move him along. Cousins, too, was pulling him.

Big Montana shook them all off roughly, stood for a moment eyeing the white-faced Tremaine.

"You snake," he spat. "I won't clean up on you now. But your time's coming when I get ready. You've hated this kid and me ever since you laid eyes on us. You've mistaken us for somebody. And you're gunning for us. Well, you'll have just plenty of chance. I'm giving you fair warning, in front of everybody — here and now — don't ever try to start anything else."

With a contemptuous shrug, he rammed his forty-five into its holster and deliberately turned his back on Tremaine. For a moment it seemed that the Diamond A foreman was going for his guns. But apparently he thought better of it for he spun about on his heel and stamped away toward the chutes, his pock-marked face dark and ugly with anger.

The tragedy averted, again the dizziness assailed Little Montana. Too late he realized that only the excitement of the moment had brought him to his feet. He took a step, stumbled, went down to his knees, fighting gamely against the returning mantle of darkness. But to no avail. He could feel himself going down, was only vaguely aware of being snatched up

197

and lifted in strong arms. Once to him came the voice of the girl, the gruff almost surly answer of Montana. Then his bewildered senses left him.

CHAPTER
TWENTY-ONE

Tempting an Enemy?

Little Montana groped back to consciousness. His eyelids fluttered open. He was on a bed beside an open window. When his aching eyes became accustomed to the light he stared outside. For miles a veritable wilderness of grass and trees met his gaze. He was conscious of a riot of color, yet as he studied them he found but few patches of even buff or white. All the rest was green; more varieties and tones of green than he knew existed, the dark green of bushes ran to the lighter green of cottonwood; here and there was a cluster of aspens, their slender, graceful trunks a chalky white against a background of green leaves. And on beyond, the Big Horns rose from the valley floor, their sides carpeted with the green of pine so dark as to be almost black.

Weary of staring at the mountains, he turned over to look from the open door. It was evening. Outside he could see the buildings of a ranch set in the midst of gigantic cottonwoods. Above was a big house. The Diamond A, he supposed. And below was a great hay barn. Beyond were the stock barns and the corrals of peeled cottonwood.

The air was balmy and sweet with the scent of wild flowers that grew about in profusion; the silence as vast as that found in chambers of the dead — unbroken save for the roar of water. That roar had come to him in his stupor, had been maddening. But now as he listened it soothed him.

He was startled from his meditation by the entrance of Big Montana.

"That's the ticket!" the cowboy exclaimed at sight of his open eyes. "Doc said you would come to pronto if we let you rest. How do you feel now, Button?"

"Shaky," the boy whispered. "Like there wasn't all of me here. Where are we?"

"At the Diamond A. We'll stay here until I talk with Cousins. You can rest up. Then we'll pull out for the Buzzard spread."

"I'm all right," Little Montana said, rising up painfully on the edge of the bed. "Did you have any more trouble with Smokey after I — I passed out?"

"No." Montana sat down beside the boy to stroke his bandaged head tenderly. "Tremaine is sorer than a dog-chewed skunk. He raised such a stink, claiming his horse fell, that they gave him a re-ride, him being champion. But shucks, I bucked into the finals with him dead easy. We ride it off in a month. And, buddy, I'm going to stick around and win those finals. It will give us a crack at the world championship next summer, and we might kind of lope down toward Cheyenne, you and me, and —"

"I sure hope you do skin the life out of him," Little Montana whispered fiercely. "His horse didn't fall with him. He threw it off its feet trying to tromp me down."

"I know it, buddy," Montana returned. "And I'm plumb sorry for that reason that I didn't make the four-flusher eat more crow before that crowd. But what do you suppose he did it for?"

"I don't know," Little Montana answered. "I figure that he just thinks we are somebody he knows. Either that or he tromped me, aiming to get even with you."

"Damn him," Montana growled. "He has got us pegged for somebody else sure as shooting. Even Cousins made a mistake thinking me a jasper from the sheriff's office. And Kent, the big —"

"Gosh-all-hemlocks, pard, you sloughed that big-mouthed cuss a dirty one," Little Montana ventured admiringly.

"Yeah," Montana said dryly. "Between him and Smokey Tremaine we aren't going to be crowned Queen of the May around this spread, you can just bet the ace. But Cousins is our friend. My ride won the rodeo for him. He's as tickled as a gaunt hog in green alfalfa. And he sure thinks you're some pumpkins, Button."

"And if it hadn't been for me you could have had Kent and Smokey both for your friends," Little Montana said bitterly. "It is me who has gotten you into all this trouble. If I hadn't ever come to that river crossing, you could —"

"I don't want Kent for my friend," Montana interrupted sourly. "Nor Smokey either. And as far as

201

you being to blame, shucks, pards stick together no matter who is to blame or what kind of merry hell breaks loose. Forget that line of talk. We'll —"

"But Montana," the boy faltered, "I'm scared around here. I guess I haven't got much guts, but it just seems like I can't stay here being scared thisaway."

"What are you scared of?" Montana demanded.

"Of Smokey. And Kent. And I'm scared stiff something will happen to you. I'm just scared of the whole layout but Mister Cousins, I reckon."

"I hate to pull out," Montana said, "because that lousy Tremaine will think I'm quitting the flats because of him. But if you are scared you sure don't have to stay, I can tell you that. I'll see Cousins tonight after dark. I'll give him this letter and find out what it says if I can. If it doesn't tell any more than ours did we'll pull our freight in the morning. We'll go where we belong."

"Where is that?" the boy asked eagerly.

"Our own spread, of course." The cowboy grinned. "Now if you are feeling better we'll eat. The cook allowed the beans were spoiling a long spell back. Then you can get to bed here and have a good snooze while I auger with Cousins."

"There's another thing that is kind of worrying me, Montana," the youngster said shyly, lowering his eyes to trace idle patterns on the bed covers.

"That being?"

"Sally." Clem tried vainly to cover his embarrassment. "She was so good to me in Omaha — and there at the rodeo grounds. And if it hadn't been for her —"

202

"Forget her," Montana cut in sharply. "She was with Smokey Tremaine today."

"She just happened to be talking to him," the boy defended. "And she said she liked you awful well."

"Said she liked me?" Montana stared in utter amazement. "Who'd she say that to?"

"To me, back at the rodeo grounds when I said you was the best pal a little shaver ever had. And she said she wasn't sore about mistaking you for Whitey and kissing you at the depot that —"

"Never mind what she said," Montana growled. "Forget the gals, buddy. You're too young. Besides, pards like us haven't got any business hooking up with fillies. We've got work to do."

"But she busted Smokey when he was hollering for those hazers to let that horse alone when it was on top of you at the rodeo," the boy burst out hotly.

"She — busted — Smokey?" Montana demanded. "Well, that's something in her favor. But right now us Two Montanas had better —"

"I've always wanted a sister or something just like her," the lad said wistfully. "Seems like she's the prettiest and kindest girl I ever knew. Far as the Two Montanas goes, we could change that to the Three Montanas if Sally would just —"

"Well I'll be doggoned," Montana ejaculated, lifting his hat to brush moist hair back from a brow that was knitted thoughtfully. "I believe you're stuck on Sally Hope. Darn my pictures, Button, you're too young to be getting moon-eyed over a filly. Just forget her now, and let's put on the feed bag."

203

"I'll eat, all right," the boy said wearily, "but I won't forget Sally no matter what happens, 'cause she was the only woman that was ever nice to me. And you just don't know how a little shaver like me misses a sister or a mother or —"

Montana checked him by helping him to his feet and supporting him toward the door. Once outside Little Montana stood gazing about.

"What's that big building down yonder?" he asked, pointing to a hay barn of mammoth proportions.

"That is the Thunder Basin dance hall, I understand," Montana explained. "Folks come from all over the country to dances every week. They are going to have a big shindig down there tonight. Would you like to see it?"

"I sure would," the boy exclaimed.

"Well, if you feel like it, you can come down there and watch them dance until I get through with Cousins. Then we will roll in and pull our freight the first thing in the morning. How does that strike you?"

"Great!" Little Montana beamed. "Do you suppose Sally will be there?"

Montana shot him a quick, quizzical glance.

"I reckon she'll be there with bells on. If that will make your evening any happier."

"It sure would. That is, it would if I wasn't —"

"Wasn't what?" the cowboy demanded.

"Wasn't so danged scared," the boy blurted out. "But I'm even scared of my shadow up here, it seems like. I hope you won't be tied up with Cousins too long."

"I won't," Montana assured him. "And you don't need to be scared, because nothing is going to happen to you. I'm keeping an eye on Smokey Tremaine, and don't you forget it."

CHAPTER
TWENTY-TWO

A Killer Fails

The dancing already had begun when the Two Montanas came from the mess shanty. The wail of the fiddle and the chording of a tin-panny piano set to sparkling the eyes of the boy, who, by now, was feeling much better.

"Go on down and watch them," Big Montana urged. "But be sure and stick close. I don't know just how long I'll be."

"I'll stick around there all right," Little Montana cried, starting toward the dance hall. "I'll find Sally and —"

The rest of his words were lost to Montana. With time weighing on his hands until darkness fell, when he was to meet Cousins, Montana idled about the ranch, which he found to be a miniature village. Its size and well-kept appearance struck him favorably, but thought of what he had been forced to endure at the hands of the Diamond A robbed the place of any attraction it might otherwise have offered.

Through his mind stalked the events of the preceding hours that had crowded down upon him with such amazing rapidity. From these unfortunate incidents his thoughts traveled on to the mystery of Thunder Basin — that the herder had mentioned the day of his arrival and that Cousins had revealed — the phantom rustler gang, and the note of warning that Cousins had received. The more he mulled over the thing the more convinced he became that it was no mystery at all. Rather, he decided, the cow thieves had eluded detection so successfully that the ranchers themselves had made a mystery out of the thing.

The warning, he was satisfied, had been written in a disguised hand. Probably the left, he reasoned. That the rustlers should take such a precaution when, Cousins had told him, no one ever had laid eyes upon them to know them, made the whole affair even more baffling. Presently he dismissed it from his mind. He was no detective. He would tell Cousins so and let him ferret the thing out as best he could. He had plenty of worries of his own without mixing into new ones. Already he had had too much trouble over things that did not concern him. The letters that had brought him into the Basin were his chief concern. They were mystery enough. The hostility of Smokey and Kent; thought of the two set the hot blood of anger to pounding in his veins. He would like to stay, to battle the thing out with them. But somehow, now, his first and only thought was of the lovable youngster, Clem White, who had admitted that he was terrified at the prospect of remaining at the Diamond A.

He broke off his musing, his mind made up. He would deliver the letter from his Uncle Nat to Cousins, find out its contents — if the rancher would reveal them — then he would —

He glanced at the sky. Twilight had lowered in a blanket of purple over the mountains. One by one the stars were popping forth. Out of the far dusk came the boom of Piney river, a tributary of the Tongue he had learned, the plaintive wail of a coyote, and shouts and laughter from the dance pavilion. Above the voice of the caller and the scraping of feet he could catch snatches of the music. Somehow it seemed out of place in the vast creation that lay about him.

Waiting but a few minutes longer, he looked about carefully to make sure he was unobserved, then made his way to the barn.

True to his word, Cousins was waiting, a sinister shadow that detached itself from the barn and moved stealthily toward him.

"Let's get right down to business now," the rancher said in an undertone. "I gave you a general idea of things today at the grounds. There's a gang of rustlers working here in the Basin, stealing the Diamond A ragged. We've had all kinds of detectives in here. Some of them have disappeared completely. Probably warned, and pulled out. Others have not been able to get head or tail to anything. There isn't a soul who has ever laid eyes on a rustler; but critters are disappearing just the same." He paused for breath, staring through the semi-light at Montana's features, which were expressionless.

Kent and Tremaine flashed instantly to Montana's mind at Cousins's revelation. His experience with the two on the roundup had convinced him. But what would they gain by — He would, however, tell Cousins of the affair, if indeed, he did not already know. Then —

"That sure is too bad," Montana remarked without interest. "It seems a danged shame there isn't anything you can do about it. But as far as me getting in and getting my feet wet, I just want to tell you right off the bat that I am not —"

Still the cowman gave him no chance to finish; no chance to state his position and correct the false impression he had thus far been unable to explain.

"You are my last bet," Cousins said in a whisper. "I haven't even taken King nor Smokey into my confidence this time. I'm playing a lone hand. The only thing that stumps me — It's odd that I didn't any more than write to Sheriff Crowe asking for another detective when I got that last warning from the gang. What do you make of it?"

Genuinely sorry for the old fellow, whose sincerity he could not question, and who, like a child, seemed to be laying his whole problem before him innocently, more to humor him, draw him out, than for any other reason, Montana asked, "How did you get the warning?" The instant he asked the question he regretted it. It was none of his affair. He had decided not to mix into it. Yet, somehow, he had taken a great liking to this cowman who plainly needed help so badly.

"In the mail."

"Do you recognize the handwriting?"

"I never saw it before."

"Have you any suspicion as to who wrote that note?"

"Yes." The word came almost breathlessly. "After all these years of being robbed I have a damned good idea who is doing it."

"So have I," Montana said definitely. "But who do you —"

Cousins sidled closer. But what he was about to say was never uttered. A jet of flame stabbed the darkness behind him. The report of a revolver, crashed down upon them. Cousins took a faltering step, pitched head-long into Montana's arms!

Stunned for an instant by the suddenness of the attack, half blinded by the pencil of light that had come streaking out of the gloom, Montana stood motionless supporting the form of the rancher. Then he laid him down, whipped his forty-five from its holster and flattened himself against the side of the barn. He peered into the darkness, eyes straining, ears alert to every sound, ready on the instant for a movement by the mysterious gunman.

Seconds dragged by. Seconds without breath or motion. But no alien sound broke the vast stillness. Only the roar and boom of the river, the distant hubbub from the dance pavilion. Even above those sounds Montana caught the thin small whisper of a cricket, the croak of a bullfrog. But no sound of moving feet. Apparently Cousins's assailant had been gone with the shot, his footsteps drowned by the laughter and music from the dance hall that now seemed to rise in a crescendo tumult in his straining ears.

210

Realizing that the sound of the shot also had been lost in the din, Montana lifted Cousins in his arms and made his way awkwardly to the ranch house. There he quickly summoned the cook and set to work on the unconscious cowman.

A hasty examination showed that the bullet had but creased Cousins's scalp. While the wound was bleeding profusely, it had done little damage. Even before Montana had cleansed and bandaged it with hot water and rags, supplied by the frightened cook, the rancher opened his eyes.

"Get Kent," he gasped out. "And Smokey. Then scout around. Don't tell anybody I've been shot. Nor disturb the dance. I'll be all right as soon as I get my wind."

Satisfied that the cowman had suffered more from shock and pain than from the wound itself, Montana left him. Making his way outside, he strode down across the yard to the dance hall. A grim and determined Montana who looked neither to the right or left, but whose fingers rested lightly on the butt of his forty-five. At the door of the dance hall he crowded into the jam of perspiring swains and stopped to look around.

"Hammer on a fence post, roll your dough —"

His face aflame with the heat, which even darkness had failed to dissipate, a gaudy kerchief tucked in his wilted collar, one booted foot tapping time to the music, the square-dance caller sent his hoarse voice rasping away into the night.

Everyone was gay. The orchestra was playing with an abandon never found beyond the confines of rangeland. Town girls laughed and danced with town men dressed in an extravagant attempt at cowland fashion, or flirted outrageously with the real punchers. The hall was a blaze of color. Suspended coal-oil lamps gleamed on silk gowns that seemed sadly out of place among the bright calicos and ginghams. Slim-waisted, demure little maids balanced shyly on the corners with boisterous punchers, who had sacrificed only their guns for the occasion and who dragged their spinning spurs across the floor with each movement, or who yipped and howled with every change of chord.

At the far end of the hall Montana's roving gaze came to rest on Sally, almost surrounded by cowboys. In spite of himself, his eagerness to locate Kent and bring him to Cousins's side, he stared. She was dressed in a simple frock of white that accentuated her willowy slenderness. There was no denying that she was pretty, as Little Montana had said; and, the boy also had said, she liked him, but Montana tore his gaze from her with something of anger. He had no time to frivol away. No doubt with her pretty face — which he could not help but note was even prettier in the shadows cast by the flickering lights — pleasant, compelling with its rapidly changing color — she could attract men. There was something about her. Another time perhaps — Still she was pretty — the prettiest woman he ever had seen. And she had kissed him — unintentionally it was true, but — The memory of that kiss had haunted him. He

212

wished for a moment that he was one of those nearest her, clamoring for a dance.

Off to one side of the girl he sighted Kent. Elbowing his way through the crowd he reached the cowman's side. After a time he was able to whisper into his ear Cousins's instruction. Kent whirled on him, anger in his eyes. Then, with a sullen grunt, he moved away toward the entrance.

Montana looked about for Little Montana. But the milling throng was so dense he could not locate him. Satisfied that the youngster was somewhere in the house, he set about in search of Smokey, deciding that when he had located Smokey and told him that Cousins wanted him, he would find the boy and turn in.

But a thorough search of the hall revealed no trace of either Smokey or the youngster. Suddenly prey to a growing apprehension that, for some unknown reason, tightened his nerves, he started about asking if anyone had seen them.

Breaking through the cordon about Sally he approached her with embarrassment.

"Pardon me, Miss Sally," he essayed. "I was just wondering —"

She turned quickly at sound of his voice. A strange light flared into her eyes. Brown eyes, he now noticed abstractedly. Great brown eyes that somehow — And she was smiling at him. A friendly sort of smile that upset him greatly. Far different from when she had left him at the station.

His own eyes swept over her. Without comparison she was the belle of the ball. The color came and went in her face like the changing colors on the mountain peaks.

"Montana!" she exclaimed, happily, he could have sworn. "Are you dancing?"

The question nonplused him, for the moment left him speechless. There was an invitation in that voice — an invitation that for a moment sent the suitors edging back.

"No ma'am," he said, almost ruefully. "I'm looking for my buddy. He came down here to watch the crowd —"

She glanced around quickly, startled.

"He was here only a moment ago. He has been with me. Why, I'll help you look for him."

"Thank you, just the same," Montana said hastily. "He can't be very far away. I'll locate him pronto." Before she could answer he elbowed away through the crowd which quickly wedged in about her.

But a thorough search of the dance hall revealed no trace of either Smokey or the boy. Prey by now to a rapidly increasing apprehension, Montana went about asking if anyone had seen them. But no one he approached had seen them, or, if they had, they had failed to notice them in the crowded pavilion.

Convinced presently that neither of the two was in the house, Montana went outside to stand peering into the darkness.

It was a night of charm, a night typical of the mountains. A cooling breeze, which after the long drought at last gave promise of rain, had sprung up to come whining down from the canyons. A new moon was sinking in the west — a thin, golden crescent that yet shed enough light to touch the trees with a soft pale glow, bringing out the shrubbery in gigantic spectral shapes and moving the mountains deceptively near.

Thoroughly alarmed by now, Montana set out in search of the grounds. He had gone but a short distance when the glow of a cigaret caught his eye. He moved nearer, stopped to listen. His nerves jerked tight. Little Montana was speaking.

"That's my name, I tell you," the boy was saying in a voice high-pitched with fear. "And that is all I know."

"You're lying, you brat," came the snarl of Smokey Tremaine. "And I'm going —"

Montana did not wait for him to finish. He lunged forward, seized hold of the startled Smokey, spun him around and sent his fist crashing to the puncher's jaw. Tremaine went sprawling to the ground.

"You let this kid alone," Montana whipped out. "You tried to tromp him down once today. Seems like just warning you don't do any good. I don't want to kill you if I can keep from it, but now, damn you, I'm telling you, and backing it up with gunplay. You understand, Tremaine?"

Seconds passed; tense, deadly seconds that struck terror to the heart of the frightened boy who cowered in the shadows, panting. In the wan light he caught sight of Montana, his features set, drawn. On the ground crouched Tremaine, his own face twisted hatefully.

"Don't be scared, Button," Montana was reassuring the youngster. "I'm watching this lobo. You travel," he threw at Smokey. "And another break toward this kid and I'm shooting to kill."

The Diamond A foreman got to his feet, face livid, gloved fingers dangerously near the butts of his. forty-fives, which even at the dance, like the others, he had failed to discard. The boy's terrified gaze flew back to Montana. He was standing with legs spraddled wide, the same steely glint in his eyes that he had seen at the rodeo grounds.

"I wasn't hurting the brat," Tremaine found his voice to snarl. He suddenly withdrew his hands from his cartridge belt to slap the dust from his clothes.

"Mebbe not," Montana warned, "but get this straight. You ever make another break as long as we're around this spread and I'm shooting to kill. Cousins wants to see you. Quick. You hit the grit."

"I'll get even with you for this," Tremaine growled between clenched teeth. "And I'll get even with this brat, too." Muttering curses he spun about and strode away into the darkness.

Montana stood stock still watching him until he was swallowed up in the gloom. Then he faced the boy.

"What is the idea, Button?" he demanded. "I thought I told you to stay in the dance hall."

"I did," the boy faltered through chattering teeth. "I sat there and waited for a long spell. Then I saw Sally. She talked with me for a time. Smokey came along and started talking with me. He was nice and I figured we might have made a mistake this afternoon; that he didn't really try to tromp me down. He got to telling me about all his horses. Asked me if I didn't want to see them. I didn't see any harm in that, and besides I'd gotten over being scared of him, so I started to the barn with him. He stopped out here and wanted to know my name. I told him it was Little Montana and he just seemed to get sore all of a sudden. He was getting pretty tough when you came up. Gosh, I'm glad you came, Montana."

"The thing has got me plumb stumped," Montana said blankly, lifting his hat to run his fingers through his hair thoughtfully. "I just can't get head or tail of it. But let's walk around a spell, buddy. I want to look this place over." Taking hold of the frightened boy's arm, he started away along a trail that ran into the gloom beyond the dimly lighted entrance to the dance pavilion. "What else did Tremaine have to say to you?"

"Nothing," timidly, "only just asked who I really was. I told him, Little Montana. And he called me a liar."

In silence Montana walked on through the shadows that lay thick and ominous about them.

"What the devil is eating on that jasper?" he mused aloud after a time. "Hell — this whole spread is crazy as a herd of locoed steers — crazy as we ever were to come down here in the first place."

"I think so, too," Little Montana agreed, hugging close to his side. "Let's go away from here. I'm scared worse than ever now."

"We'll go," Montana said grimly. "Tomorrow. I tried my damnedest to shut Cousins up long enough to give him this letter tonight. But just seems the old fellow is

217

like you, scared plumb to death about things — so scared a jasper can't even talk sense to him. And — something happened."

"What?" the boy asked fearfully.

"Cousins got shot."

"Shot? Who did it?"

"Your guess is just as good as mine." Montana paused to glance about cautiously. "I just wish I knew, or even had a hunch."

By now the lights of the ranch had vanished in the gloom behind them. They were enveloped in darkness unpierced save for the feeble rays of the setting moon, which caused the vegetation to rise up in eerie, unreal shapes about them.

CHAPTER
TWENTY-THREE

Wrong Trail

"I reckon we had best be milling back," Montana said presently. "I'll get this letter to Cousins yet tonight if I have to ear him down long enough to listen; then we'll skin out — go back with Whitey and —" He broke off shortly to seize the boy's arm and hurl him to the ground. "Lay still," he warned in an undertone.

Frightened half out of his senses, Little Montana sprawled breathless. The crack of a six-shooter out of the night set his nerves to singing. He cringed in terror. Came a crackling of underbrush from behind. Silence.

The boy leaped up. Montana took an uncertain step forward, threw out his arms and pitched to the ground.

"Shot in the left arm," he gasped. "We were sky-lined right in here. I ought to have known. But you. Get away from here quick. Go back to the ranch. Find Sally. Stay in the dance hall with her. Don't leave her for anything, even if you have to go to town with her. Tell her I'll make it right when I come."

"But you're shot," the boy protested, forgetful of his own fright at thought of Montana's predicament.

"Never mind me," Montana panted. "Take care of yourself."

219

"That would be a fine way for a pard to act," Little Montana flung back. "I can help you." He dropped to his knees. "Who do you suppose did it?"

"I don't know," Montana gasped. "But I'm not hurt very bad. The shock knocked me off my pins, I reckon. But — light out, Button. And keep your mouth shut."

"I want to help you," the boy said through chattering teeth. "But if you want me to go —"

"I do," Montana whispered. "I'll get back all right. As soon as I catch my wind. Take care of yourself until I'm able."

Little Montana waited to hear no more. Leaping up, he sped away, determined, no matter what Montana said, to bring help.

Until the breath was tearing at his lungs he ran, his only thought of Montana. For all his exertion now he was cold, shivering in the chill night air, now hot, burning with resentment against the coward who had shot down his friend. Not once in his childish mind could he picture anyone but Tremaine as that assailant. The affair between Montana and Smokey at the rodeo grounds, the set-to outside the pavilion, Smokey had slung away threatening. Even now the swarthy-faced foreman of the Diamond A might be lurking in the brush to waylay him.

The notion lent speed to his feet. On and on he ran until he was reeling with fatigue. Then he stopped to look around, striving to pierce the ominous darkness until his eyes ached with the strain. The moon had set behind the mountains. The heavens were starless and black with clouds. Trees loomed like hulking ghosts about him. Out of the far dark came the boom of the river. Yet the lights of the Diamond A had vanished; the music and laughter were drowned in the noises of the night. He turned slowly in all directions. But for the life of him he could not tell where he was. He walked on, then paused to listen. No sound reached him save the crash of the river and the moaning of the wind through the pines.

The stark reality of the thing began to dawn upon him. He was lost! The shadowed mountains suddenly had become hideous prisons that held him in a grip as firm and horrible as anything he could conjure up in his childish mind. Panic descended upon him, terror of the darkness, of Tremaine, that the wounded Montana would die before he could return with aid.

He plunged on again only to pitch headlong into a thicket. Not until his clothes were almost torn from his body was he able to extricate himself. He was aware that he was crying, crying loudly for help. Yet no answer reached his straining ears.

When he was able he arose. He found that by standing still he could see a short distance ahead. The thread of silver at his feet, he reasoned, must be the trail he had followed with Big Montana. Yet he wondered at the distance they had come.

Cautiously he started along it, filled with hope that now he could find Sally and get help for his wounded comrade. His terror increased, urging him on until he was running swiftly. Again the swarthy face of Tremaine leered at him from every thicket of brush. And

Montana — He stopped to cry Sally's name at the top of his voice. Still no answer came out of the blackness.

He stumbled on. Again and again he plunged headlong into the brush which tore his face and filled his arms and hands with thorns. Vaguely now he realized that he was going away from the ranch. Time and again he imagined he had changed his course. But he was not certain. His sense of direction had deserted him. The darkness overwhelmed him. His voice was husky from his constant calls for help. To add to the horror of the moment thunder began growling in the ebon void above the towering mountains. His strength was ebbing swiftly. Manfully he forced his logy muscles to respond. He must get aid for Montana!

Then he became aware of the chill of water on his feet. His boots were soaked. The cold reached above his ankles. No longer could he see the trail. He seemed to be crossing a stream, picking his way along slippery cobblestones, managing miraculously to maintain his balance. Above and below was a mighty roar.

Then the chill on his feet ceased. And the going required greater effort. He must be climbing. It sapped his little remaining strength and breath. Still he struggled on, now possessed of a grim stubbornness that took no notice of time or distance.

Came a blinding flash of lightning to dazzle him with its brilliance and leave its glare for several seconds before his eyes. A deafening crash of thunder sent him cringing to the ground. For an infinity of time he lay in a daze. When he had collected his wits he was conscious of a vast and foreboding silence about him.

222

Below he could hear the river, its roar lessened with distance. The air, which had been cool, suddenly seemed inert, suffocating.

Came another streamer of lightning followed by a clap of thunder that seemed to rock the mountains. A deluge descended from the inky heavens. Too weak to rise, he began crawling along in the rain that drenched him to the skin, made his teeth chatter with its biting cold. But now he seemed to have lost all sense of the things about him. His terror had become so deep-rooted that he was merely an automaton, the victim of some hideous nightmare.

After an endless period of desperate struggling he became aware that the rain had ceased. He could still hear it, but strangely it had stopped beating down upon his helpless form. He stared around in the darkness. By a vivid bolt of lightning he found that he had crawled beneath a ledge of rock where he lay spent and fighting for breath.

Once he thought he heard a shout. In vain he tried to hear it repeated above the sluicing roar of the blood in his ears. Convinced finally that his fancy had tricked him, he sank back down, weary to the point of death, beaten, drenched, bruised, stricken with the thought that he had failed Montana who was lying along the trail, his life perhaps depending on his aid.

Through the chimera of his tortured mind he became aware that someone really was shouting. He screamed, then held his rasping breath until he was faint, listening. Nearer and nearer came the cry of a voice. He tried to answer. But after his first outcry he could only reply in almost inaudible gurgles. Then the one who had shouted stood directly above him. A bolt of lightning revealed him clearly. The blood in Little Montana's veins seemed to turn to ice. He cowered back beneath the ledge. It was Smokey Tremaine!

CHAPTER
TWENTY-FOUR

Lost in the Storm

The chill of water on his face and a numbing pain in his left arm were the first sensations of Big Montana. He forced his weighted eyelids open only to close them quickly against the rain beating down upon him. He was lying in the trail, half drowned, shivering violently. Yet he was thankful for the downpour that had revived him. With difficulty he raised himself to a sitting posture, felt gingerly of the hole in the flesh of his forearm that seemed on fire.

Despite the shock to his wits, Montana knew that he had not been wounded seriously; that the bullet pinging out of the dark behind luckily had missed the bone of his arm. Slipping off his neckerchief, with awkward fingers he bound the bleeding wound and knotted the bandage with his teeth.

He labored with feverish haste, praying the while that no accident had befallen the boy along the trail and that he had reached the ranch ahead of the storm. Once he was on the point of shouting. But caution warned him to silence. His unknown assailant might still be lying in wait for him.

To his mind flew the note Cousins had received. One sentence of the scrawl beat on his brain. *If another pussyfoot comes in here we'll get you and him, too!*

That the rustlers had mistaken him for a detective, as Cousins had done, and made good their threat, was possible. This also would explain the shot that had creased Cousins. Yet, somehow he could not shake off a suspicion that Smokey had fired at him out of revenge. But if this were the case, who had shot Cousins? Certainly not Smokey, whom he had found with the boy outside the dance hall a short time afterward. And who was it that Cousins was about to name when the mysterious bullet sent him down?

Determined to find out, he climbed to his feet. His good hand fell to his holster. It was empty. He felt around on the ground for his forty-five, which he recalled having drawn just before he dropped. But he could not locate it in the darkness. He abandoned the search presently. Getting the wound attended to and satisfying himself that Little Montana was safe were far more important at the moment than recovering his Colt.

He started along the trail toward the Diamond A, pausing now and then to get his bearings by the flashes of lightning, and listen for the sound of any footsteps behind.

After an infinity of time the lights of the dance hall burst into view. Careful to avoid a chance meeting with anyone until he could reach the ranch house and have Cousins or the cook care for his wound, he kept well in the shadows and made a detour of the entrance. He had gone but a short distance when a shout halted him.

"Montana!" It was Cousins calling.

Surprised to see the cowman about so quickly, Montana waited.

Cousins ducked out from the pavilion and hobbled toward him through the rain.

"What did you find out?" he demanded, stopping beside Montana to huddle in his great yellow slicker, his back to the downpour.

Montana thrust his wounded arm behind him.

"Where is Little Montana?" he asked anxiously.

"Nobody seems to have seen him," Cousins answered. "I got worried about the little shaver in this storm and I've been trying to locate him. He isn't at your bunkhouse nor in the dance hall. Some of the folks thought they heard a shot just before the storm. Did you hear it?"

"Little Montana isn't here?" Montana cried blankly, ignoring the question. "Where is Sal — Miss Hope?"

"She left for town before the storm, along with a lot of the Elbar people," was Cousins's disturbing reply.

"And Smokey Tremaine?" Montana blurted out, prey to a dread fear that grew mightily upon him.

"Smokey hasn't been seen since before the storm either," Cousins answered.

Montana's heart sank within him. The girl gone to town. Smokey missing. Little Montana missing. The discovery set his nerves to strumming, brought a steely light into his eyes.

"You're the jasper we want!" Kent shouted, sighting them and coming on a run. "The fellows say they heard a shot just before the storm. Smokey is missing. Where is he?"

"To hell with Smokey!" Montana snapped. "I don't know where he is."

"You'd better be telling," Kent cried threateningly. "You've had it in for Smokey ever since you hit the Basin. You aimed to kill him and I'll bet —"

"Go to hell!" Montana struggled with his mounting anger. He jerked as a blinding flash of lightning rent the sky to be followed by a clap of thunder that seemed to rock the earth. His wounded arm came from behind him. He flinched with the pain of the movement, swayed on his feet. Cousins seized hold of him to keep him from falling.

"You're hurt, Montana!" the rancher exclaimed. "What is it?"

"Just a scratch," the cowboy answered weakly.

"It's a bullet wound!" Cousins cried. "Did they get —"

"A bullet wound?" Kent snarled. "Then that accounts for things. I warned you against this damned trail-drifter, Al. He's killed —"

"I haven't killed anybody," Montana cut in to retort, gritting his teeth on the pain that was streaking like livid flame through his arm.

"Then who shot you?" Kent demanded.

"I don't know," Montana flung back. "But I'm going to find out!"

"Like hell you are!" Kent roared. "You arrest this fellow, Al, or I'll kill him."

Cousins whirled on him.

"What for?" he snapped.

"Smokey is missing," Kent shouted furiously. "We've searched high and low for him. Now this drifter sneaks in here wounded. The dancers heard a shot. He's drilled Smokey!"

"You're crazy!" Cousins snorted. "Wait —"

"And let him get away?" Kent blazed. "Not on your life. You'll arrest him or —"

"You'll play hell arresting me, jasper!" Montana flared before Cousins could stop him. "I knocked down your cob pile once and saw you didn't have any guts under it and I'll do it again if you get funny."

"Don't threaten me!" Kent thundered. "Cousins, I'm holding you responsible."

Cousins ignored him.

"Hold on, Montana!" he cried. "Where you going?"

"To find Little Montana," Montana flashed, striding away.

"Arrest him!" Kent bawled. "I tell you he's killed Smokey."

"Don't be a damned fool all your life," Cousins growled. "He isn't to be monkeyed with. Especially not now while that boy's missing. He's shot, man. And knows something. We'll never find out the way you're going at it. To hell with that talk of him killing Smokey."

He stood glaring at Kent through the dripping rain. Presently the sloshing of a horse's hoofs in the mud broke in upon them. Montana jerked his mount to its haunches in the slippery earth.

"Halt!" Kent cried, flying into a new fit of rage. "You're under arrest."

"Arrest, hell!" Montana snorted. "There aren't enough men in Thunder Basin to arrest me till I find that kid!"

"What's happened, Montana?" Cousins put in.

"I don't know," the cowboy answered. "But I'm going to locate Little Montana and Tremaine. And if anything has happened to that boy I'll go through this dump like a white-faced bull through a herd of billy goats."

"See, I told you!" Kent roared. "There he goes threatening again. I tell you —"

A streak of lightning that shivered across the sky to leave a blinding glare of light behind it silenced him. A mighty clap of thunder crashed down upon them followed by a terrific gust of wind. The lights in the dance pavilion flared up and went out. Pandemonium broke loose. Women were screaming. Men were shouting hoarsely. The crowd broke frantically for the entrance only to become hopelessly jammed and driven back by the lashing storm.

"Montana! Montana!" Cousins shouted to make himself heard above the uproar. "Hold on!" He paused, straining for some sound he had caught through the howling gale. "It's the river!" he cried. "Piney is coming up. For God's sake, Montana, ride the river for that boy!"

"Damn the brat!" bawled Kent. "We've got to find Smokey."

But Montana did not hear him. His horse had snorted under the gouging rowels and lunged away into the night.

"Every hand on the place get going!" Cousins bellowed. "Patrol that river till the flood comes down. Go all directions. For God's sake, hurry. Find that boy before the flood!"

When he had all the employees of the ranch breaking from the mass and running toward the corrals to secure their mounts, and had succeeded in getting the crowd quieted in the pavilion, he came back to Kent, who had not moved.

"You've sure showed your hand tonight," he said scornfully. "If you'd have kept a dally on that tongue of yours we might have gotten somewhere. But you had to blow off and that poor little kid —"

"Damn the brat!" Kent interrupted to snarl. "To hear you talk a fellow would think it was your kid instead of a drifter's brat."

"It doesn't make any difference whose kid he is, he is going to have help!" Cousins flared. "For ten years I've let you run off at the head around here. But I'm still boss of this layout; and from now on you aren't any better than anybody else. Climb onto your hoss and patrol that river or I'll bend a scantling over your mullet head!"

Dumfounded by Cousins's first explosion in years Kent recoiled. "That drifter has poisoned you against me," he cried hoarsely. "Having that brat around —"

"Brat or no brat you're going to hunt for him!" Cousins cut in savagely. "I've held in till I'm busting. Now I've cut loose. This here hurt of mine on the head wasn't from falling down like I told you. I was shot. Shot from behind the same as I'll bet Montana was. And when they come on to my place and go to shooting, damn me, the rag has plumb flew out."

Whirling, he hobbled away toward the corrals, leaving the thunderstruck Kent staring after him.

CHAPTER
TWENTY-FIVE

The Search

Away from the hubbub at the Diamond A, regardless of the pains shooting along his wounded arm, unmindful of the cold, Montana roweled over the ground at a reckless pace, the wild running of his horse seeming to ease his violent emotions.

The storm increased in fury. He humped up in his saddle, head bowed to the sheets of rain that drenched him to the skin and ran in rivulets off the brim of his hat. The wind screamed through the trees and brush about him. But he heeded it not. Blood-red passion consumed him, blinded him to things about him.

Thought of the boy, helpless and alone, lost in the storm-swept wilderness that had claimed the lives of many — even though they were familiar with its dim and lonely trails — haunted him. And somewhere out there, too, was Smokey Tremaine.

He urged his horse to greater speed toward the spot where he had last seen Little Montana. After a time the wind and rain began to cool his boiling blood. The chaotic thoughts in his brain took definite form. He began to reason sanely.

At a dangerous pace he reached the point where the bullet had sent him down and from which Little Montana had started back to the Diamond A. Dismounting, he squatted on his heels to strike a match. The wind killed its tiny gleam even before it had made a flare in the darkness. And the rain had obliterated any footprints.

"There is only one way he could of gone if he didn't go back to the Diamond A," he mused, nursing his throbbing arm. "That is toward the mountains. And if he did go that way he'd have had to cross the river!" Arising, he pulled himself painfully into the saddle and sat peering into the darkness.

"It all depends on how fast he could travel," he reasoned, coolly now. "He'd have gone like the devil to start with because he'd have figured he was on the right track. Then he'd be played out by the time he got to the river. Reckon though, he must have crossed it, for he'd have had time to get to the ranch if he'd turned back. Or mebbeso Smokey —" A grim smile braced his lips across his teeth. He set rowels to his horse and started toward the mountains.

The din and fury of the storm increased. The lightning shivered across the sky to tear and snap savagely about him. Crash after crash of thunder blasted the heavens until his ears pounded with the deafening reports. The ferocious wind bent double the pines and aspens which creaked ominously and threw new deluges over him as he passed beneath.

Then ahead he caught the sound of the river, a roar no louder than that of the storm, yet more sinister and deadly. Its challenge warned him to greater caution. He pulled his horse to a walk and moved forward, alert to the first sign of the flood. As he neared the stream he began calling to Little Montana. But no answering voice came back above the tumult of the storm-lashed mountains.

Presently he reached the bank of the river, leaned over in the saddle to peer down into the water that swirled and hissed beneath him. Dark as it was he could see that it was up and rising rapidly. Time and again his horse shied away violently. It was only with great difficulty that he succeeded in forcing the snorting brute to the water's edge. Finally, after a persistent fight, he roweled the animal ahead. The water was barely to its knees as yet, but the current was terrific.

"It's a cinch he got this far before the storm hit," Montana reasoned aloud, straightening up in his saddle and giving his pony rein. It lurched around and sidled away from the stream, fighting the bit in an attempt to go back down the trail. "And if he was tuckered out and scared, like as not he ran across this ford on the cobblestones without noticing that he was in water till it was too late. Lost folks seldom turn back; once they start they keep going straight or in a circle."

His conclusions were the result of years of experience on the silent trails. The inner sense that all punchers cultivate now told him that Little Montana had crossed the river. With another look into the swirling water, he rode a short distance above to allow for the sweep of the current, and roweled his unwilling horse into the stream.

The next few moments were filled with struggles, terrific, heartbreaking struggles that several times threatened to defeat the valiant efforts of the two. Then they were in midstream. Once it looked as though Montana would have to quit the fighting brute to lighten its load. But the pony had been there before and held its own until it could right itself, put every ounce of its strength into one mighty effort, and strike for the opposite shore. It floundered out onto the bank, shook itself like a dog and started wearily along a slippery trail, which at that point, began winding toward the peaks.

Away from the crash and boom of the river, Montana began shouting again. Still no answer.

For an infinity of time he traveled, now stopping to let his horse blow, now dismounting to lead it around some boulder where the going was too perilous to ride in safety.

Then the storm went whirling away across the heavens to wreak its remaining vengeance on the lowland world. The stars popped forth to touch the trail with a soft, pale light. Save for the roar of the flooded river and distant grumbling of the storm below, a vast and ominous hush lay over the mountains. Again he shouted. This time he thought he heard the faintest kind of an answer far ahead. But when it was not repeated he decided that his fancy had tricked him.

"It's damned odd," he mused. "I'll lay money he never could have come this far unless Tremaine found him. And if Smokey did, he would head up, feeling certain that nobody would attempt a river crossing till daylight, or mebbeso till Piney went down." Gritting his teeth on the pain in his arm which, now that the excitement of fording the stream was past, had started its throbbing anew, he plunged on.

Dog-tired, weak from loss of blood, aching in every joint from the cold, covered from head to foot with mud where he had gone down during the slippery climb, his clothes clinging like a mantle of ice to his shivering form, he finally succeeded in reaching a ledge of rock at the head of the trail. Here he drew rein and dismounted to rest for a moment before attempting to proceed along the trail, which now was but a narrow passageway scratched in the rock overhanging a precipice that dropped some fifty feet to a boulder field below.

When he had succeeded in catching his breath, he went forward cautiously, leading his horse. Rounding the hazardous point without mishap, he could see the outline of a cabin set in a thick grove of spruce some twenty yards beyond. As quickly as he sighted it he shook off his lethargy of weariness and became alert. Tying his horse to a tree, he went forward afoot. His heart gave a mighty leap. There was a light inside the cabin. Making his way as quickly as he could in his water-soaked boots, he crept stealthily to the single window. Then he straightened up and peered within.

With an effort he stifled the curse that sprang to his lips. Before he thought he reached for his forty-five. But his holster was empty. Unmindful of the pain, he sent his fist crashing against the window. The glass shattered with a loud report.

"Tremaine!" he cried in a strained, unnatural voice. "One move and I'll kill you!"

CHAPTER
TWENTY-SIX

Fight on the Ledge

Smokey Tremaine's swarthy face went ashen at the sound of Montana's voice. He stood for an instant framed in the light of a smutty-globed lantern on a table inside the cabin, his jaws sagging, huge body rigid. Then he spun about to face the window. Little Montana, a forlorn figure in his rain-soaked clothes, leaped up from a chair in the corner where he was crouched.

"Montana!" he screamed. "Montana!"

"Throw down your guns, Tremaine!" Montana snapped, ignoring the startled boy's cry and keeping well out of sight in the darkness. "I've got you covered. One break and I'll plug you!"

Smokey bounded away from the light to peer furtively at the shattered window, plainly undecided whether that voice was real or the trick of a guilty conscience. But whatever was rushing through his mind he went for his forty-fives. Once out of their holsters, he hesitated an instant then dropped them to the floor. One fell at his feet. The other caromed away into the darkness.

In Tremaine's movement Montana saw something that set his jaws like clamps. But he had no time to ponder it. Elated that his ruse had worked thus far, he did not wait to map out a course of action. He only knew that inside the cabin were Little Montana and Smokey Tremaine. Further than that he did not think. A wild and reckless impulse was driving him on.

"Now open the door!" he ordered. "And remember, don't bat an eye or I'll riddle you!"

Before the startled Tremaine could collect his wits enough to comply with the command, Little Montana had sprung forward, dropped a heavy bar from across the door and thrown it open.

In a single leap Montana was inside.

"Now, damn you —" he began.

He got no farther. In a glance Tremaine saw that he was unarmed. He stooped to seize the forty-five at his feet. Before he could pick it up, Montana had bundled himself, hurtled through the air and sent him crashing to the floor. Frightened half out of his senses, the boy cowered back against the wall.

As he bore the big puncher down, Montana made a grab for the forty-five. Tremaine clutched his wounded arm. The pain that raced through it for a moment stunned Montana. Before he could recover himself, Smokey had rolled him off and dropped upon him with a force that knocked the breath from his lungs. For several seconds they lay locked in a death grip, their breath rasping croupily in their throats, their muscles bulging, their strength so evenly matched that neither could gain the advantage.

240

Then the strain began to tell on Montana. The throbbing wound in his arm, the struggle in the river, the difficult ascent of the rain-washed trail, had undermined his strength. Still he knew that to relax for a single instant would allow Tremaine to seize the forty-five that lay within reach of both of them.

"Buddy," he gasped to the boy. "Get that gun!"

For all the numbing fear that gripped him Little Montana somehow managed to start forward.

"Stay back," Tremaine snarled. "You touch that gun and I'll kill you, too."

The brutal threat sent the boy cringing back. A blinding fury possessed Montana. With all his remaining strength he threw the big puncher off and lurched to his feet. He had only time to kick the gun from reach when Tremaine came up. Before he could leap away the puncher's great arms encircled him. Again they went crashing to the floor. With the gun out of the way, Montana fought gamely, savagely. But weak as he was he was no match for the giant.

"Button!" he panted again. "Get that gun!"

This time the boy mastered his fear long enough to obey. Before Tremaine could jerk himself away and spring up he had seized it and covered him. With one mighty sweep Smokey knocked it from his hand, spun about. Setting himself, Montana sent a stinging blow to the point of his chin. The big fellow reeled but came on. Again and again Montana struck him. But his blows lacked steam.

Then, for all he could do, Tremaine's arms were about him again: He was borne backward. They rolled

241

against the table. It upset with a crash. The lantern went flying. Luckily the light flickered out before it could ignite the oil that trickled onto the floor. The room was plunged into darkness. Tremaine was on top, squeezing the little remaining breath from Montana's body with a vice-like scissor-grip, his fingers clawing for a throat hold.

Nearer and nearer came those fingers, groping like deadly tentacles in the gloom. Montana tried to bridge. Tremaine's weight was too great. He attempted to squirm from under the huge body. In this, too, he failed.

Sheer desperation in the knowledge that neither he nor the boy could expect any mercy at the hands of the brutal Smokey, lent him the strength to fight on. Yet he was swiftly nearing the point of collapse.

"I've got the gun, Montana!" the boy's shrill voice burst upon them.

"Don't kill him unless you have to," Montana panted. "He —"

Then Tremaine did the unexpected. His fingers stopped their groping. Releasing his hold he sprang up and threw himself toward the boy. Little Montana managed to elude him and run outside into the night. Tremaine started after him.

Montana lurched to his feet. As the big fellow went by, a huge, hulking form in the darkness, he put all his strength behind a blow. Smokey went crashing against the wall. But the pain that raced through his arm was too much for Montana. He could feel the warm blood spurting from the wound, from which the bandage had been torn. His knees suddenly became tallow. He fought desperately against the ebon mantle that agony was throwing down over his eyes. He reeled across the room. The door suddenly had vanished. Things were spinning crazily about him.

A scream from Little Montana brought him back to his senses. Blindly he located the door, staggered into the night. Directly ahead he could make out the figure of Tremaine struggling with the boy. Instinct warned him that once Smokey got hold of the forty-five the battle would be ended in a twinkling.

Montana never knew how he reached the pair. When he was next conscious of the things about him the boy was nowhere to be seen and he was slugging Tremaine in the face with all his might. And his blows were telling. No longer were the great arms trying to encircle him. They were too busy warding off the savage attack. Montana lost all record of time. The passion that had held him in its relentless sway blinded him. Vaguely he realized that the Diamond A foreman was retreating, step by step, under his blows.

They passed his horse, which snorted and reared back on the bridle reins. Then they were at the head of the trail. In the wan light he could see the rim of the rocky ledge. He sensed that Tremaine, too, had recognized the danger of their position, for he was trying frantically to change his course. Almost on the brink of the precipice, he lunged. For all Montana could do the big arms closed about him. In them was the strength of a beast at bay.

243

Montana fought with his last breath to break that bone-crushing grip. To no avail. Slowly the life was being squeezed from his body. He stumbled, went to his knees in the narrow passageway scratched in the ledge. He got one swift look below. The yawning chasm was black and horrible.

He wrapped himself about Tremaine's legs; hung on with bulldog tenacity while the foreman kicked, rained blows down upon his head, strove frenziedly to topple him backward. For seconds that seemed like hours they fought, their muscles strained to the limit, their breath rasping in their throats, their blows landing with deadly accuracy, each knowing that one false move meant a plunge into the Stygian depths below.

"Let go, Tremaine, or I'll shoot!" came Little Montana's voice from directly behind them.

Tremaine's hold relaxed. He spun about, slipped, hovered for an instant on the precipice, then with a hoarse cry went over the brink.

Montana lurched up.

"You came just in the nick of time, Button," he panted when he could catch his breath. "Another minute and I'd have been a goner."

"I — I — couldn't tell who was on top," Little Montana cried. "I — I —" Words failed him. He reeled dizzily.

Leaping to him, Montana dropped an arm about his shoulders.

"Good old Button," he said huskily.

"Where — did — he — go?" the boy faltered.

"Over the ledge, I reckon," Montana replied. "And we can't find him till morning."

"Is — he — dead?"

"I hope not. But it was one or the other of us. I was all in. He'd have killed me in another minute. And you too."

"I didn't mean to — to kill him," Little Montana sobbed. "I only wanted to help you." It was apparent that his emotions were sweeping beyond control. Montana patted his sagging shoulders awkwardly in an attempt to quiet him. Presently he had him soothed, although the dry sobs that racked the youngster filled him with apprehension.

"Where did you come from?" Little Montana gasped. "I thought —"

"We can talk about that in the morning," Montana said. "You're going to rest now. You've had too much excitement already. You —"

He got no farther. With a little cry the boy pitched into his arms. Weak and spent though he was, he took the gun from the limp fingers, lifted him and carried him toward the cabin.

CHAPTER
TWENTY-SEVEN

Temporary Truce

Half dead with fatigue and pain, Montana finally succeeded in reaching the cabin with the boy. Entering, he groped about in the darkness until he located the bed, where he laid him down. Then recovering the lantern — the chimney to which had been broken and from which most of the oil had leaked — he lighted it, righted the table, and set it down.

He turned to surprise the eyes of Little Montana upon him. There was something in the way the boy looked at him that brought him quickly to his side.

"What is it, Button?" he asked anxiously. "Are you hurt or sick or something?"

"I'm scared," the lad faltered through chattering teeth. "Scared clean out of my socks."

"And it isn't any wonder," Montana said sympathetically. "Tremaine didn't hurt you, did he?"

"No. He found me during the storm. He put me on his horse and he walked. Said he was taking me back to the ranch. I didn't know any different till he came to this cabin. We'd just got here when you came."

"What in the hell did that jasper have on his mind?" Montana blurted out blankly. "What did he bring you up here for? What —"

"I don't know," Little Montana put in, "but I do know I'm a hoodoo. You've had trouble ever since you tied up with me. First at Elbar, then at the rodeo. And now this. I'm a fine pard to have, I am."

"Shucks. You aren't in nowise to blame," Montana said sharply. "It's just one of those streaks every jasper bucks up against at some time or another. If I could figure Tremaine out I'd feel a heap better. But we'll auger the thing in the morning. You get quiet now."

"I can't," Little Montana said, arising. "I'm too danged scared. Besides you were shot. Your arm —" He broke off in affright at sight of the blood covering Montana's sleeve. "Is that where —"

"Never mind me," Montana said. "You get quiet or the boss of this here Two Montana gang is going to raise particular hell." He crossed the room to set about kindling a fire with wood from a box near a small camp stove. "As soon as the fire burns up you skin out of those wet duds of yours. Hang them up to dry. Then you can bed down."

"Why can't we go back to the Diamond A?" the boy asked. "I'm able. Please, Montana, let's go back."

"We can't," Montana replied shortly. "The river is up and rising rapid. And —"

"And what?" the boy demanded when he hesitated.

"We'll probably have to do something for Tremaine come daylight."

A wild, hunted look flared into Little Montana's eyes at mention of Smokey, but he recovered himself.

"All right," he said resignedly. "But I'm sorry you ever tied up with me; you wouldn't have had all this trouble."

"And there would only have been one Montana instead of two." Montana grinned. "You aren't to blame, I tell you. I might have run up against Smokey Tremaine if I'd never seen you. And hell would have popped just the same. But I'll figure out that jasper's game somehow, Button. And if I ever get a chance I'll give this danged letter to Cousins and find out what's in it, too."

"I don't care what is in it," the boy blurted out. "All I want to do is get away from this range. Where — where you going, Montana?" as the cowboy moved over toward the door. "Aren't you going to sleep in here with me?"

"I'm going to sit right outside," Montana answered. "Or mebbeso roll up in my saddle blanket and smoke and look down yonder toward the world and the folks who claim to be civilized. Shucks, I'm like a cow, Button. I don't need much sleep. But I figure it would be safer to keep an eye peeled while you get some. If you want me for anything, holler."

"Good night, Montana," the boy whispered.

"Good night, Button. Sleep tight. And don't let me hear any more talk about you being a hoodoo. Pards don't figure that away. Now I'll be right outside. Could spot somebody moving in on us a sight quicker from the dark than we could from inside here. Don't be afraid." With that he was gone into the darkness, leaving the boy alone.

For a long time Little Montana sat staring about the cabin, which apparently was a line camp. Save for the disorder caused by the grim battle between Montana and Smokey, it was neat and clean, although it had the musty smell of unused places. A bedstead with tarp bedroll, the camp stove, a small cupboard, a table and one chair made up the furnishings. At least it was a refuge for the night. Yet, thought of remaining filled him with terror. In the gloomy corners he seemed to see the leering face of Tremaine.

Arising hastily, he walked over to the fire, which now was roaring in the stove, and huddled in a chair. In a short time the heat began to make him drowsy. Getting up again, he fell to pacing around the room, fighting against the sleep that was numbing his senses, fearful to lie down lest some other harrowing incident occur.

Coming to the shattered window, through which the chill night air was whining, he peered out. A short distance away he could see the glowing point of a cigaret and make out the form of Montana. Reassured by his friend's nearness, he undressed, wrung the water from his soaked clothing, hung them up to dry, blew out the light and slipped between the blankets of the bedroll, there to lie, trembling and staring into the blackness. Finally he fell into a fitful, dream-disturbed sleep.

It was broad daylight when Little Montana awoke. He started up, unable, for a moment, to recall where he was. Then he remembered. Springing out of bed, he hastened to the window. A brilliant sun was flooding the mountains. Clouds hung on the peaks above him. Raindrops, like diamonds, sprinkled the needles of the pine. The grass was bowed under its weight of moisture. He took a deep breath. The air was sweet and cool and seemed to sparkle like the water that gurgled in a small stream beside the cabin.

Fagged out in mind and body, but at least feeling more secure in the light of day, he crossed over to the stove. During the night his clothing had dried. He dressed quickly and stepped outside into the sunshine.

Wondering at the whereabouts of Montana, he made his way through the drenched grass to the stream where he washed himself. Then he started walking around. Presently he came to the ledge of rock that dropped away precipitately from the head of the trail.

Below, the vast plains stretched to the verge of sight, a vivid panorama of color, the reds and blues and oranges of clay banks blending in perfect harmony with the buff of flats, grays and browns of cutbanks and stream beds and the greens of foliage. Thrilled in spite of an uneasy fear that haunted him he sat down on the rim of the ledge and fell to staring off across the limitless expanse.

With his eyes he traced the cottonwood-fringed course of the river. Even at that great height he could tell that it was on a rampage. Great pieces of driftwood still were pitching along with the current. Trees and brush were matted with debris. Lowlands were flooded.

Suddenly to the left, nestled in a grove of pine, he caught sight of a cluster of buildings that he took to be

250

the Diamond A, although they were but pygmy structures set in a gleaming fairyland of green and white.

Tiring of this survey presently, he arose to look for Montana. Not until then did he recognize the ledge which he had seen before only in the darkness. He experienced a moment of panic. It was the ledge over which Tremaine had plunged!

The sound of voices put an end to the wild tumult that started in his mind. They seemed to come from directly below. Summoning his courage, he fell to his hands and knees, crawled to the edge of the precipice and peered over. He drew back to lie flat down until his head quit spinning. His glance had revealed a dizzy drop. And at the bottom he had caught a glimpse of two figures. Montana! And — his heart seemed to skip a beat — Smokey Tremaine!

For an infinity of time he lay, too frightened to move. The memory of the fight came rushing back to him with startling vividness. The terror of the day and night before crashed down upon him. His nerves suddenly went to jumping. The blood became a sluicing roar in his ears.

Then the voices of the two were coming nearer — up the trail.

"Shot Cousins?" Smokey snarled. "Hell, I didn't even know Cousins was shot."

"Where did you go after I told you at the dance hall he wanted to see you?" Montana flashed.

"You aren't riding herd on me," Smokey retorted defiantly. "I don't have to account to you for anything.

251

You're locoed. I don't even know what you're talking about."

"You'll find out plenty quick when we get back to the Diamond A," Montana snapped. "And let me tell you something else. The next time you pull anything you want to do a damned sight better shooting than you've done so far, because we won't both have game arms and I'll be loaded for bear. And I'm saying that you are going to spill your guts," he heard Montana's angry growl. "From the start you've had it in for us Two Montanas. I don't know who you figure we are but, damn you, you thought you knew us. You tried to tromp that kid at the rodeo. And now you've brought him clean up here in the mountains, claiming you were taking him back to the Diamond A. Just what is your game?"

"I didn't try to tromp the brat," Smokey snarled. "And I did try to take him back to the Diamond A but got twisted in the storm."

"You're a fine foreman to get twisted this way on your own range," Montana snorted. "There is something behind all this. What the hell did you shoot me for?"

"I didn't shoot you," Tremaine denied sullenly.

From his perch on the rimrock, Little Montana watched the two coming up the steep trail. Tremaine was staggering and covered with blood. His right arm dangled sickeningly at his side. And behind him came Montana, the forty-five he had retrieved during the fight, clutched in his good hand.

252

Breathlessly the boy waited for them to pass. At the creek beside the cabin, Montana halted Tremaine. After he had washed the blood from the fellow's bruised face, he tore his own shirt to ribbons and bandaged Smokey's broken arm.

"Now, damn you," Montana said, "lay there till I rout my buddy out. Then we're going back."

"You can't cross the river," Smokey snarled. "Leastwise I'm not going to try with a busted arm and all stove up."

"I've got a bad arm, too," Montana retorted. "And it isn't your fault it ain't busted. You've got a better chance of crossing safe than I have because I've got to help the boy. Thought from the first you didn't have any guts. Now I know it."

"What's your rush?" Smokey sneered.

"I want to get back and get this arm tended to and healed in time for the rodeo finals," Montana flashed. "I'm going to stick around now just to buck you down — I'll tell you what I'll do," he bargained suddenly. "We'll bury the hatchet until after the finals. If you win, I'll quit the flats. If I win, you travel. But meantime I want you to understand if that boy is harmed or molested there isn't going to be room enough in hell for you and me." Wheeling abruptly he strode to the cabin. "Button!" he shouted. "We're —" Then he noticed the open door. He spun about. "Button!" he yelled at the top of his voice.

Little Montana attempted to answer. But sight of Tremaine's evil face seemed to freeze the blood in his veins. He crowded farther behind his refuge. His foot

253

dislodged a stone that went crashing over the precipice. Montana heard it. He came on the run. The boy strove to rise, only to huddle fearfully on the ledge.

Then once again Montana had lifted him in his arms and was carrying him back toward the cabin. But now he laid him down beside the creek while Tremaine looked on, a sneer twisting his lips.

CHAPTER
TWENTY-EIGHT

Downstream to Death?

Little Montana forced open his heavy eyelids to stare about dully. Above him were trees. He was lying on his back in the grass. When he could gain possession of his faculties, he twisted on his side. A cold rag came away from his throbbing forehead. Montana knelt beside him, bathing his temples. Behind was the swarthy face of Smokey Tremaine.

"Shucks, I'm glad you come to," Montana breathed with relief. "I was scared for a while my little pard wasn't going to." He followed the boy's terrified gaze that was fixed on Tremaine. "He won't bother you any more, buddy," Montana said grimly. "Him and me understand each other now. Lay still till you're able to ride. Then we'll try to cross the river and get back to the Diamond A."

"Much obliged, pard," the boy choked. "I reckon I'm not worth —"

"Shut up!" Montana commanded sharply. He rose quickly and walked over to his horse to tighten the cinch with his good hand until the brute snorted and snapped at him.

When he felt stronger, Little Montana got up and joined him, the while watching Tremaine fearfully. But Smokey ignored him and, despite the pain in his helpless and crudely bandaged arm, swung into his saddle.

Without a word, Montana helped the boy aboard, picked up the bridle reins, jerked his thumb over his shoulder to motion Tremaine ahead and started down the trail, leading the horse.

After an endless period of dangerous slipping and breath-taking jolts they finally reached the foot of the mountains. There they paused only long enough to let the ponies blow and went on to the bank of the flooded river.

"It can be made," Montana observed, after studying the turbulent stream for a few minutes. "But it will take some tall riding."

"Got cold feet, huh?" Smokey sneered, breaking a long silence.

"Shucks, the Two Montanas don't know what cold feet are," Montana snorted. "But I reckon we'll wait a while. She's going down. Another hour we'll make it plumb safe."

"I'm not scared of it now even with a busted arm!" Tremaine taunted.

"You're brave, you are," Montana said bitingly. "But it isn't a question of being scared. It's a question of sense."

"You can stay here till you starve to death if you want to," Smokey jeered. "I'm going across. You yaller —"

He got no farther. In a single bound Montana was beside him. "Open your chops again and I'll beat you to death even if you are crippled!" he warned. "Damn you, I can do it. I wasn't thinking of myself. I was thinking of this kid."

"Don't worry about me," Little Montana put in gamely. "I won't be afraid to tackle it."

Montana's teeth clicked grimly.

"Take the lead," he threw at Tremaine. "Any time you back the Two Montanas down you've got to get up early in the morning, you lobo!"

"How are we going to work it, pard?" the boy asked, eyeing the boiling water timidly.

"Kick off your boots," Montana ordered, as he sat flat down to pull off his own. When the boy had obeyed, Montana undid his cartridge belt, which, with his boots and those of the boy, he tied to the saddle.

"Now take your time and don't lose your head," he directed. "I'll swim alongside of you in case you get in a mix-up out there." He led the snorting, wild-eyed horse to the water's edge and looped the bridle reins over the horn. "See that bunch of brush yonder?" he asked, pointing some two hundred yards below on the opposite bank. "The current will just about carry you that far downstream. Keep your feet out of the stirrups so you won't get too wet nor tangle up if anything happens. Let the horse have its head. Don't try to crowd him nor check him. He will follow Tremaine's horse."

Something in the eyes of Smokey, who had roweled up alongside drew his attention. "Don't you try any

257

funny business," he warned. "Because there's always another meeting!"

Tremaine shrugged, spurred his horse into the churning water and started away.

"Sure you're not scared, buddy?" Montana asked anxiously. "If you are we'd better not try it."

"Scared, hell!" the boy flung back with a brave show of fearlessness. "The Two Montanas aren't scared of anything when they're together!"

Montana made no comment as he struck the horse on the rump and crowded it into the stream.

Once out from the bank the muddy water swirled angrily about them, slapped the cantle of the saddle. The motion of the swimming horse was sickening. But Little Montana fought stubbornly to master the fear that was taking hold upon him.

He glanced ahead. In spite of his crippled arm, Tremaine was proving himself a master in the art of fording rivers. Yet when he turned from time to time, there was a strange, scheming light in his eyes. The boy's gaze sought Montana. Despite his wounded arm, the puncher was swimming strongly beside him, his face set, his muscles beating back the terrific current.

"Keep your head!" Montana cautioned, noting the boy's fright. "We're almost halfway across. Let the bridle reins alone!" as the pony lurched dangerously and Little Montana clutched for them. "Trust to that horse. He'll win."

Then they were in the center of the stream. A gigantic undertow caught them. For several seconds Montana battled for his life. When finally he had pulled himself from the deadly tentacles that were sucking him down, he looked around for the horse. It had drifted with the current and was several feet below. But now its struggles lacked smoothness. It was wallowing hopelessly. The boy was deathly white and clinging for life.

A sudden lurch loosed Little Montana's hold and set him to groping about blindly. His fingers closed over the bridle reins. With all his might he yanked. The fighting animal turned part way over on its side. In three powerful strokes Montana was beside him.

"For God's sake hang on to the horn and let go those bridle reins!" he shouted.

But his warning came too late. Little Montana reeled in the saddle, threw out his arms and pitched over the side of the horse, which once free of his weight, quickly recovered its balance and struck out for the bank.

Montana barely had time to grasp the boy by the ankle as he was caught up by the rushing current and swept downstream. Seconds dragged by with maddening slowness. He fought doggedly to keep his head above water while he worked himself in below Little Montana. Time and again he went under, only to come back up, gasping for breath, spewing the muddy water from his mouth and clinging grimly to the drowning boy.

Then finally he managed to stroke abreast and throw an arm about him. Little Montana clutched hold of him frantically. Fighting now to free himself from the death-like grasp, as well as keep them both above water, his struggles seemed hopeless.

259

Of a sudden Little Montana let go his hold on him, tried to push him away.

"Go ahead, pard!" he gasped. "I can't make it."

"Not by a damned sight I don't quit a pal," Montana choked. "Don't grab me that away. You too can make it."

Choking, panting, fighting stubbornly, he succeeded in dragging the boy from the swift current in the center of the river. Once he felt the sucking tentacles let go he relaxed a little in the battle that was sapping his last ounce of strength. Time and again he was on the point of giving up; the burden too great to bear. Only his fighting heart kept him hanging on; his fighting heart and a determination to save the boy.

Then he thought of Tremaine. His gaze flew to the opposite shore. Smokey had forded the river and was seated on the bank watching their struggles, but making no effort to lend assistance.

"Toss your throw rope!" Montana shouted. "Snub it to your saddlehorn!"

"Go to hell!" Tremaine hurled back. "You got in there now get out!"

A savage curse sprang to Montana's lips. But he had not the breath to voice it. He renewed the struggle with a strength born of fury. With a gigantic effort that tore his muscles, he stroked away. Then he caught sight of a landing-place a short distance beyond. Yet in his spent condition it seemed miles. He hung on tenaciously, putting everything that was in him into the fight. With a mighty spurt he reached the bank, groped blindly for something to cling to. There was nothing. The bank

260

dropped away sheer for about three feet. He looked around wildly. Below, it was even higher. Above — Weak as he was, breasting the current was too great a task.

He got a glimpse of Tremaine leering down at them but still making no move to aid them.

"Tremaine!" he cried. "There'll be a reckoning. And when it comes —" A mouthful of roily water checked the threat.

"You've got to get out first," Smokey taunted. "I'll help drag the creek for your bodies. Let's see who's going to win those rodeo finals now!"

His taunting laugh goaded Montana to desperation. "Buddy," he panted. "You've got to help for all you're worth." He worked himself beneath the boy to raise him up suddenly. "I'll boost you. Get out!"

"But you?" Little Montana gasped.

"Never mind me. Now! Up!"

He put his last ounce of strength into the effort. The boy felt himself being lifted bodily from the water. Then he was even with the bank. He lunged out, clutched a clump of brush. He clung desperately, pulled himself dripping from the river. He saw Tremaine, just above him, give a violent kick. The hand with which Montana was groping for a hold disappeared. The boy turned just in time to see Montana caught up by the swirling water and washed downstream beside a great log that pitched like a cork on the crest of the flood.

A scream escaped him. In horrified fascination he watched Montana making a desperate fight to seize the log. Once it seemed he would win. Then the current swept him from sight around a bend.

"You —" Little Montana cried, wheeling on Tremaine. "You could have saved him."

Smokey only grinned.

"You kicked him!" the boy accused furiously.

Tremaine bounded forward, his face livid with rage.

"Shut up, or I'll throw you in with him!" he snarled.

But Little Montana was not to be silenced.

"Go ahead!" he screamed recklessly. "I'd rather be dead than live without Montana. You drowned him — my pard — Montana — Montana —"

Smokey clapped a hand over his mouth to choke the words in his throat. Wrenching himself loose, the boy turned on him with the fury of a tiger's cub.

For several seconds Smokey fought to subdue the frenzied boy. But with one arm useless and maddening him with pain he was powerless to quiet Little Montana who squirmed away to come back fighting and shrieking at the top of his voice.

In desperation Tremaine kicked him viciously and backed off to glance quickly about. The brutal kick stunned the boy. But only for a moment. Again he pitched into Smokey, fighting, clawing, screaming, his frenzied assault on the puncher's legs threatening to upset him.

A violent oath left Smokey's lips. Raising his good arm he brought his clenched fist crashing down on Little Montana's head. With a piteous cry, the boy crumpled to the ground!

CHAPTER
TWENTY-NINE

Lost Memory

With Little Montana prostrate at his feet, Smokey Tremaine backed away, his breath rasping in his throat. He looked about wildly, listening. Only the crash and boom of the river came to his straining ears.

With the air of a cornered beast he slunk back to the inert figure of the boy. A trace of color in the pallid cheeks showed him that Little Montana still lived. For a time Smokey stood staring down at him. Then a savage gleam shot into his eyes. Stooping quickly he worked his good arm beneath the boy, lifted him onto his hip and lurched drunkenly to the bank of the river.

A shout from behind brought him whirling about. Dropping the boy, Smokey fell to his knees and began working with him frantically just as the Diamond A crew, headed by Al Cousins, a bandage on his hatless head, galloped into the clearing beside the ford. At sight of the pitifully huddled figure, Cousins swung from his horse to drop beside it.

"Is — he — dead?" he choked.

"I don't think so," Smokey muttered. "Seems to have color." To hide the pallor that had blotted the color from his own cheeks, he bent over and laid an ear to the boy's faintly beating heart.

"Is — he — alive?" Cousins asked in a hoarse whisper.

"His heart's beating," Smokey announced, lurching to his feet. "I've done what I could for him. I'm all in." Overwhelmed by a sudden weariness that made his knees like tallow, he staggered to his horse to lean weakly against it.

"Get some water!" Cousins snapped, himself again after the shock of seeing the motionless boy. "What happened?" he demanded of Smokey.

"We tried to ford the river," Tremaine jerked out. "The kid got scared. Pulled us both off my hoss. A log hit him in the head. I grabbed him and made shore."

"Good work!" cried Kent, who until now had sat his horse in sullen silence. "I always claimed you was a real jasper, Smokey. Why, what's the matter?" he blurted out as Tremaine's knees buckled. "Help him, fellows!" He leaped down and ran to Smokey's side.

"My — arm," Tremaine gasped. "It's broken."

"Broken?" Cousins straightened up from bathing the swollen head and face of the boy. "How did that happen?"

"My horse fell with me on some rocks," Smokey mumbled.

Cousins shot him a quick inscrutable glance. There was something in that glance that startled the Diamond A men who were trying awkwardly to help. Some there were among them who knew of Cousins's dislike for Tremaine. But never until the disappearance of Little

Montana and Smokey had they known the depth of that dislike. And now the way Cousins looked at him — mistrust, hatred, suspicion all in a single glance — filled them with apprehension.

"Did your horse fall on the rocks this side of the ford?" Cousins demanded in a hostile tone.

"No, the other side."

"And you forded that river holding this boy in one arm?" incredulously.

"Yes!" With the aid of Kent and the punchers, Smokey stayed on his feet, swaying drunkenly.

"Let up on him," Kent cried. "He's hurt. Instead of a bawling out he deserves a reward for what he's done."

"I'm not so damned sure about that," Cousins shot back. "Who bandaged that arm of yours, Smokey?"

"I did, of course," Smokey answered defiantly. "That is — The kid helped me."

At that moment Little Montana stirred. Instantly Cousins had dropped back beside him, thrown an arm about him.

"Feel better, sonny?" he asked anxiously.

The boy's lips moved but his muttered words were incoherent, almost inaudible.

"God!" Cousins blurted out. "He's — That crack on the head did it. Here, you jaspers. Grab hold of him. Tote him to the ranch. Easy, now. One of you skin out for town. Ride like all hell was after you. Get a doc here as quick as God'll let you. And get that nurse — what's her name — the girl whose ma runs the restaurant — Sally Hope."

As the cowboys leaped to do his bidding he wheeled on Smokey.

"Did you see Montana?" he demanded.

"I saw his horse," Tremaine answered. "Him — He must have gone down in the high water."

"When you come through high water and that jasper goes down somebody is lying, Smokey," Cousins accused hotly.

"What do you mean?" Kent blazed before Tremaine could speak.

"Just what I said," Cousins shot back. "Things are too fishy around here of late to suit me. I never did believe this lying snake and I'm tell you now I don't believe his cock and bull story about fording that river with a busted arm and holding that boy." He went over to plant himself in front of Smokey. "And let me tell you another thing," he snarled, "if it ever comes out that you're to blame for this poor little kid's hurt I'll kill you myself — and save a lot of fellows who'd like to the trouble."

"Hold on there," Kent roared. "That's a nice way to treat Smokey after him saving the brat. That kid's made a fool out of you. You haven't been yourself since he came. You —"

"I have been myself since he came!" Cousins snorted. "That's just what I have been. The little shaver made me my old self again; made me wise to what a bunch of lousy four-flushers have been running my business all these years. But I'm through. Smokey isn't sitting pretty as foreman any more."

"If he goes, I go, too!" Kent flared.

266

"You give me any of your lip and you won't stay even as long as he does," Cousins snapped. Whirling, he strode to his horse, mounted and roweled away after the cowboys who were carrying the boy tenderly toward the ranch.

Days passed; days that plunged the big Diamond A into a melancholy silence. Gone was the laughter and song of the punchers who, whenever they were in the ranch, gathered in knots to talk in lowered voices. Old Al Cousins wandered about aimlessly.

The blinds of one room in the ranch house were drawn. From time to time Sally Hope, white-garbed, passed before the door or paused to look out at the mountains which frowned down, grim and cold.

Behind the house, Cousins, his head sunk on his chest, his hands opening and closing convulsively, paced about, stopping now and then to heave a great sigh, then resuming his never-ending pacing.

Stretched on a bed inside was Little Montana, his face devoid of color. For days he had lain thus without speaking save when he would toss and babble deliriously. Doctors who had come from every direction upon the urgent summons of Cousins, had examined him, consulted among themselves and shaken their heads. Cousins fumed and cursed, pleaded and cajoled, offered anything for aid. But without success.

Came a day when Little Montana groped out of the darkness of his coma. The ever-watchful Cousins was beside him instantly, and the one doctor who had stayed on the case, Sally, and Kent, who happened to be present.

"Where — am — I?" the boy whispered weakly.

"God, I'm glad you come to!" Cousins breathed fervently. "We were scared you weren't going to. You're at the Diamond A, sonny. You —"

"Don't excite him," warned the doctor. "He must be kept absolutely quiet for a time."

"But he's come to!" Cousins cried joyously. "He'll live — get well —"

"Quiet," Sally warned, stroking the lad's arm tenderly.

"Regaining consciousness this way is a big part of the fight won, all right," the doctor admitted. "But he has suffered a concussion of the brain and narrowly escaped a fractured skull. There is always the possibility of —"

"You — mean — he'll — be —" Cousins asked in a hollow tone.

"No, no," the doctor interrupted hastily, anticipating his unvoiced fear. "Probably nothing more than amnesia. Perhaps not even a complete loss of memory; only a slight impairment."

Again Little Montana moved. This time his eyes fluttered open, came to rest on the wrinkled face of Cousins. Then they wandered on to the doctor, to Sally Hope, to Kent. The three watched breathlessly. Cousins could not contain himself.

"You remember me, sonny?" he pleaded. "Al Cousins? And the Diamond A." The boy's eyes came back to him. They were bright and clear but there was no sign of recognition in their depths.

"He don't know me," Cousins groaned. "He's — he's —"

"No, he isn't," the doctor said impatiently. "Those eyes are brighter than I had ever hoped to see them. His failure to recognize you may be only a temporary condition which rest and quiet will overcome."

"Damn that lousy trail-drifter, Montana," Kent put in savagely. "He's the one to blame. If I ever run across him I'll —"

"I'd thank you to leave unless you can be quiet, Mister Kent," Sally said sharply. "I happen to be in charge of this case and I do not propose to have my patient disturbed by your cursing."

Kent gulped, blinked, and backed away from the anger blazing in her eyes. On the point of a discourteous retort, he glanced at Cousins. Here again he found eyes that held no friendship, only suspicion, mistrust.

Day by day the breach between Kent and Cousins had widened. And the loud-mouthed King never let slip an opportunity to slur the missing Montana, whom Cousins, and now Sally, were quick to defend.

"Montana isn't to blame for this," Cousins said hotly. "He's taken care of this kid and loved him. That's more than Smokey did. Let me tell you something, Kent. Smokey never carried this boy across Piney in high water with a busted arm!"

"He did if he said so," Kent flared, yet not before he had cast a glance at Sally and modulated his voice.

269

"He didn't," Cousins disagreed stubbornly. "He admits the boy was all right when he took to the water. Says the youngster got frightened, pulled them both off his horse and hit his head on a log. But don't forget, we found Montana's horse back yonder by the ford that day."

"What does that prove?" Kent growled.

"That horse had been in the water, too. And we found Montana's boots and cartridge belt tied to the saddle string — together with Little Montana's boots. That boy rode Montana's horse across that river!"

"You haven't any way of proving it unless the kid can remember," Kent snarled. "Of course, you'd believe anything if it was against Smokey; just because you hate him you are trying to —"

"You're right; I do hate him!" Cousins interrupted. "But that has nothing to do with it. Whatever happened to this little shaver happened right up there on this side of the ford and had something to do with the other Montana. You're so set on clearing Tremaine, I'll just tell you something else that ought to open your eyes. Smokey said he bandaged his own broken arm. But it was bandaged with strips of Montana's shirt!"

"You nor nobody else can turn me against Smokey," Kent snapped. "He found this kid and risked his life to save him in the flood."

"You two settle that some place else," Sally ordered curtly before the reluctant doctor could voice a protest. "Having quiet in here is the most important thing."

"Yes," the doctor chimed in, "our problem now is getting the boy up and —"

"Are you plumb sure he won't —" Cousins began, his fear for the boy again paramount.

"We are never sure of anything," the doctor told him. "But from the clearness of his eyes and the way he has rallied I believe he will suffer no more than a loss or an impairment of memory which, as I have said, may be only temporary."

"But isn't there something we can do to bring him out of that?" Cousins persisted.

"He has had a terrific shock. There have been cases where another shock has brought about complete recovery. If we could locate Montana, for instance, or even his body."

"I'm leaving no stone unturned until I do," Cousins declared. "I liked that jasper and —" His eyes roved to the boy whose big gray eyes were now regarding them curiously. "I love this little kid. Are you sure there isn't something we can do, Doc? Somewhere I can take him?"

The doctor shook his head.

"Rest, quiet, and the assistance of Miss Sally, who not only has proved herself an exceptional nurse, but who, it is plain to see, loves the youngster as you do yourself, are the only things. With her woman's touch and care she can do more for him now than any of us. Of course, there is always the chance that some other shock will clear up this condition as quickly as it came." Taking the sullen Kent by the arm he pulled him outside, leaving Cousins to resume his endless pacing.

Days passed thus; hot, sultry days of waiting, hoping. August gave way to September. The crispness of fall

271

crept into the air. The haze of purple deepened over the sagebrush flats of Thunder Basin. The seared prairie carpet grew brown and drab and gray. Patches of red and yellow sprinkled the green of aspens and cottonwoods.

Under the skillful and loving care of Sally Hope, who was with him constantly, Little Montana gained strength. In time he was up and about, visibly none the worse for his experience. His physical strength was greater than ever before, his endurance marvelous. His eyes were bright and clear, gave no indication of what he had gone through. Only when Cousins questioned him concerning Montana and what had occurred at the ford, did a puzzled light flare into their depths, a puzzled light that showed plainly Little Montana had no recollection of the harrowing experiences that had resulted in his injury. Cousins strove to help him remember, reconstructed imaginary scenes, pleaded, cast about desperately for something that might provide a shock great enough to restore the boy's impaired faculties. To no avail. The past had been completely erased from Little Montana's mind.

CHAPTER
THIRTY

The Reckoning

Then came the finals in the Diamond A rodeo.

Cousins, who now had no thought for anything except Little Montana, was for calling off the exhibition. But Smokey was loud in his demand that it be held on schedule. And, through the insistence of Kent, he won his point.

The same crowds dotted the hillsides of the natural amphitheater. Smokey, his arm done in splints, even insisted on riding. At first Cousins, to the anger of Kent, had refused to allow him to do so, reluctant, some thought, to let the Diamond A foreman out of his sight for a moment. But finally he had consented. And Smokey rode, hampered by his broken arm and heavy cartridge belt with its two thonged-down forty-fives he always carried now.

The fact that the crippled Tremaine was nervy enough to ride won favor with the crowd. When he came out on Crow Bar, he was given a tremendous roar of applause. And, for an injured man, he made a spectacular ride, raking the pitching brute from shoulder to rump and lacing its sides with his rowels. But before they could pick him up the pain in his arm overcame him. Crow Bar won the battle, then went trotting riderless across the field, empty stirrups flapping, hackamore rope flying.

The doctor urged the worried Cousins to attend the rodeo. At first the old cowman had refused, reluctant to leave Little Montana, to whom, along with Sally, he had become a constant companion.

"Why not take the youngster with you?" the doctor suggested. "The color and excitement, now that he is fit physically, might do him good."

Cousins's seamed and wrinkled face brightened. Ordering the buckboard, he drove Little Montana, together with Sally and the doctor, to the rodeo grounds.

"Chuck Wagner, the second rider in the finals, coming out of Chute Number Four on Dirty Cow!" bellowed the announcer just as the four reached the grounds and went into the judges' stand, where Kent already was seated. Making the boy comfortable in a seat between them, Cousins and Sally watched Wagner come out, while Little Montana gazed off across the field, obviously more struck with the thunderous cheers, the blare of the brass band, and the color than with the pitching contest.

Unlike Tremaine — whom they had carried out of the bowl to revive with water beside the chutes — Wagner, a T6 puncher, loudly praised by Hartzell who swaggered about with a new and surprising air of arrogancy, managed to withstand the sledge-hammer assaults of his wild-eyed bronc. But his poor exhibition of riding stamped him as only a pretender in the championship class. After the pick-up he came limping back, a champion for lack of a better one, but nevertheless a sadly disillusioned bronc twister.

The announcer, directly beside Little Montana, arose.

"That ladies and gents, ends the finals for a whirl at the world championship at Cheyenne next summer," he shouted through a megaphone. "I reckon Chuck Wagner will be the lucky boy. There should have been three riders in the finals. But we all know that Montana won't be —"

Cousins leaped to his feet.

"But folks," he cut in on the announcer, while Kent glared savagely. "Let's give Montana a silent tribute. He made a good ride in this bowl to enter the finals. The least we can do is to give him a — Hats off, folks, for Montana, one of the squarest cowboys who ever bucked a snake-eye down on Tongue river!"

A pulsing hush fell like a stroke on the field. The great crowd came up with bowed heads. As they stood in silence two riders dashed onto the field, their curveting horses bathed in lather. One held his hat aloft. The other —

It was Sally who recognized them, started up, screaming.

"Montana! Whitey!"

The crowd caught the name. A deafening cheer went up. Men yelled themselves hoarse. The group in the judges' stand went wild. All but King Kent who only stared with a sneer on his lips. Men and women alike rushed toward the cowboys only to stop in blank amazement. For the newcomers were alike as two peas.

Then suddenly one roweled his horse in the direction of the chutes, threw himself from the saddle. A man lurched to his feet, whirled to face him. Smokey Tremaine!

Minutes passed — poignant, nerve-racking minutes. The two eyed each other without moving. A lane opened between them. From the corner of his eyes, which burned into Tremaine's, Montana could see the chalk-white faces of the crowd about them. Whitey, his pal, who had roweled forward, now sat his horse directly beside him. And Hartzell was on the fringe of the mob, watching every move with hawkish eyes.

With a savage shake of the head Tremaine threw off the trickles of sweat that suddenly had started coursing across his leathery cheeks. Montana smiled, a cold, lifeless smile, but remained motionless as the stones on the hillsides that glared like upturned mirrors in the sun.

An eddy of dust spiraled across the field. Sheltered for an instant, with his good hand Tremaine whipped a forty-five from its holster, fired.

The smile froze on Montana's whitened lips. He advanced a step, a Colt now dangling in his own hand. On he came, body taut, muscles rigid, bulging — a grim-visaged Montana with hard lines at the corners of his mouth, a deadly shafted light in his eyes once cool blue-gray. Seconds dragged — unbearable seconds filled with dread expectancy. Less steady nerves strummed, wavered under the strain.

Tremaine stood it as long as he could. Then he fired again, wildly, nervously. The bullet droned harmlessly past Montana's ear. On he came, step by step.

Again Tremaine's forty-five belched flame. Montana swayed. Tense watchers waited for him to go down. Sally, her face ashen, stifled a scream, clung frantically to Cousins's shoulder.

"Stop them!" she managed to get out in a tiny voice.

Out from the crowd burst the sheriff, who apparently had just arrived. He sized up the thing with a precision born of other desperate encounters.

"Stop!" he commanded, going for his own gun. "There'll be no killing here!"

"Keep your bill out of this, walloper!" It was Whitey Hope who spoke; spoke in a tone that crackled like ice. "You had your chance to clean up this mess; now the Buzzard is doing it, like I warned you we would." The sheriff blinked, backed off. Whitey sat his horse, forty-five on his hip.

But if Montana even heard he gave no sign. Not so Smokey Tremaine. Obviously relieved by the break in the dead tension, he holstered his gun.

Then Montana was before him. The Diamond A foreman was staring into the barrel of a forty-five. A hoarse cry escaped him. He started backing away.

Cousins, with Sally still clinging to his arm, bolted down from the judges's stand.

"I told you so, Kent," the rancher was bawling. "I knew Smokey was lying; his arm was bandaged with Montana's shirt. You can't fool me. I'd have staked my life on that Montana jasper. Down him, Montana!"

But Montana's gaze was all for the man before him. With a snort of disgust, he lowered his Colt, leaped forward and sent Tremaine reeling backward with a stunning blow to the chin.

"You're not worth killing, you crippled coyote," he said softly. "Hell is too full of your breed now. Take off those gloves!"

The light of a trapped beast flared into Smokey's eyes. Montana's gun jerked up, set him to stripping off the gloves. Montana seized them. Two fingers of the right glove were stuffed! The placard in Mother Hope's Cafe the day of his arrival flashed before Montana's vision. The reward for —

The sheriff, too, saw it. He started forward.

"Stay back!" Whitey's voice broke the gripping stillness. "It's our party, feller."

"The lousy coyote kicked me into Piney to drown," Montana was saying. "Shot me from ambush, kidnaped my buddy. I told you there'd be a reckoning, Tremaine."

Plainly fearful to cross the deadly serious pair, the sheriff halted. With maddening slowness Montana's finger contracted on the tigger. Cousins stopped, rooted in his tracks. Sally screamed, the only sound, save the hoarse rasping of Tremaine's breath, to break the piercing stillness — stillness tangible, that clogged men's throats, made breathing difficult.

"But it's Three-Finger DeHaven!" the sheriff roared as the gloves came away to reveal two fingers missing from Smokey's right hand. "Montana — you've got Three-Finger DeHaven!"

278

Montana withered him with a glance.

"You could've caught him long ago, if you'd had any brains, or wanted to," he jerked out. "Him always wearing gloves — I was suspicious the day I came, saw that reward notice. Then a stunt he pulled in the line camp, when I caught him with my buddy. He packed two guns, but he grabbed for his left first — And that night Masterson was killed. His left gun was smoking. He shot at me just now with his left. Of course, his right arm is crippled. But that right gun is just a bluff. He can't use it. He's a two-gun man who shoots with his left — because his right trigger finger is missing."

"Smokey Tremaine — Three-Finger DeHaven?" Cousins gulped incredulously. "Why DeHaven is the worst rustler — Could he have —"

"Sure, he could." Montana cut him short. "And he did. Smokey wrote you that warning. I thought it was written with the left hand."

"And Smokey is —" Cousins began.

"The rustler who has been stealing you ragged for years. There isn't any gang, only Three-Finger DeHaven and — That's why you never got sight of rustlers. And this sneaking coyote is the jasper who plugged you, tried to down me, figuring I was really a detective."

"Figuring you were really a detective?" Cousins cried. "Aren't you?"

"I tried to tell you the day we met here," Montana grunted. "And again at the barn. You wouldn't give me a chance."

Cousins whirled on the sheriff.

"Isn't he the detective you sent when I wrote that letter?" he demanded.

"What letter?" the sheriff asked blankly.

"Did I pick the wrong jasper?" Cousins gasped. "And he turned out to be the best detective of them all." He wheeled savagely on Tremaine, "So the sheriff never got my letter asking for a detective? You're the jasper I told to mail it. That's how you found out I'd asked for a detective? Why you wrote that warning. Tried to plug me, at the barn that night, like you threatened. I suspected you. I was going to tell Montana I suspected you when you plugged me." He turned back to Montana. "If you aren't a detective, who in the devil are you?"

"The man who killed Masterson!" the sheriff yelled. "I've got a warrant —"

"You've got nothing," Whitey snarled. "But you will have if you open that yawp of yours again."

"I came down here from the Yellowstone to bring you a letter, Cousins," Montana was saying calmly. From his pocket he fished the badly crumpled envelope. "I've been trying to give it to you for a year. Seemed like something always came up. Reckon it's pretty badly water-soaked now. But mebbeso you can read it."

"Who's it from?" Cousins faltered.

"From my uncle, Nat Ellis. Know him?"

"Know him?" Cousins shouted. "I'll say I know him. He used to be my foreman. He disappeared about the time —"With palsied fingers he tore open the envelope. As he read the letter a spreading pallor whitened his cheeks. "God," he breathed hoarsely. "He —"

280

Crumpling the letter in his hands, he whirled. "You lousy —" he hurled at Tremaine. "Nat Ellis has squealed. After all these years. You — Stop!" as Smokey started for his horse. "Stop him, sheriff, or I will!"

"I'll take care of him, Al!" the sheriff shouted. "Stop, Three-Finger DeHaven!"

Smokey lurched about with an oath. He started for his gun. A forty-five cracked. Smokey's knees sagged. He went down in his tracks.

"Stay back! Stay back!" It was Whitey Hope warning the crowd away while he blew the smoke from his hot-barreled forty-five. "He isn't hurt bad. I just winged him. A potshot for luck!"

The sheriff blinked up at the cool puncher.

"Call a wagon," he managed to get out.

The onlookers halted, appalled by the swift-moving tragedy. A buckboard rolled onto the field. Smokey was lifted up, placed inside. The sheriff climbed up beside the driver and the team lunged away toward town.

"We don't know what this is all about, but if Al Cousins says it's all right, you can bet your bottom dollar it is," came the voice of the announcer, who had seized upon the moment of calm to reassure the panicky crowd. "I reckon but for it everybody would be happy. But, ladies and gents, let's forget it and make a great announcement. Montana, coming out of Chute Number One on — We didn't figure on you, cowboy. It will have to be Foghorn again. Will you ride?"

"You tell the world I'll ride," Montana shouted. "Bring on that horse."

"Montana coming out of Chute Number One on Foghorn!" the announcer roared.

At the words, Little Montana, who had remained passively watching the affair from the stands, jerked with muscular violence. A cry escaped his whitened lips. Montana, striding toward the chutes did not hear it. But Sally did — and Cousins. They came back to the stands on the run. The girl seized hold of the boy. The doctor, too, was on his feet.

"Say it again! Say it again!" he was shouting to the astonished announcer. "Loud, man! Bellow it!"

"Montana out of Chute Number One on Foghorn!" the surprised announcer fairly bawled.

Little Montana gasped.

"Montana," he murmured. "He — he — Pard!" He covered his face with his hands, shrank back in terror.

Sally gathered him in her arms.

"There, now," she pleaded. "It's Sally, who loves you — your Sally."

He glanced at her and smiled wanly. Then he buried his face against her breast. "Sally," he choked. "I — remember — now."

"Montana. He's coming out of Chute Number One. On Foghorn!" It was the doctor shouting to the dumfounded crowd, which heard him in amazement. "We don't know where he came from nor how; but your pard, Montana, is back!"

Little Montana pulled away from the girl, clutched at his head. He passed a hand weakly across his eyes.

"Montana," he whispered. "Out of Chute Number One — on Foghorn. Sally — It's my buddy!" He lurched up to reel into the outstretched arms of Cousins who, too, was jibbering crazily.

Then, directly below, the chute gate swung open. A thunderous shout rolled across the bowl. Montana came out on Foghorn to hit the ground with a thud that rocked the stands.

Little Montana jerked himself away from Cousins, stared at the outlaw. A new light blazed in his eyes.

"Montana! Montana!" he shrieked. "Give him hell, pard!"

The cowboy dared a glance above, risked his balance to wave.

"Be back in a minute, Button!" he shouted hoarsely. Then he was gone on top of a madly spinning mass of bawling horseflesh.

CHAPTER
THIRTY-ONE

One Mystery Solved

The ride Montana made that day is history on Tongue river. Foghorn uncorked his mightiest tricks. For all of them the cowboy raked him from shoulder to rump, rode him down to a trembling halt then roweled him back to the judges' stand, acclaimed champion by thunderous shouts. Throwing himself from the saddle, he flew into the stands.

"Montana — Pard —" the boy faltered.

"Button!" The name was a joyful cry on the cowboy's lips. He caught the youngster as he swayed forward. "I was scared to ask —" He choked, swiped savagely at his eyes. "I was scared you were — I'm sure glad we're together again. Just us Two Montanas."

The doctor seized Kent's arm, tried to pull him from the stand.

"Don't butt in," he warned. "That youngster will be all right now. It was just what he needed — another shock."

But Kent shook him off violently, whirled on Montana.

"Where did you come from?" he demanded.

Montana started to turn. Then he was conscious of a movement beneath his arm. In seizing the boy he had thrown his arm around Sally, who was trying gently to free herself. A hot flush swept his face.

"Howdy, Miss Sally," he stammered. "I didn't mean to — I —"

"Don't mind." She smiled, her eyes filling with tears. "We're so happy to think —"

But he had swung on Kent.

"From hell to haunt you," he was lashing out, still clinging to the youngster, "after your pal, Three-Finger DeHaven kicked me into Piney to drown. But I fooled him. And you, too! I managed to grab a drift log — washed ashore a few bends down. Laid there most of the day, all in, with my arm where I'd been shot burning bad. When I was able I lit out — so locoed I hardly knew what direction I was traveling. Made the Dunning place. Whitey Hope, the best pal — Where's Whitey?" he broke off to demand.

"Right here," came back the voice of the cowboy. "Just keeping my gun on Mister Kent in case he decided to get wolfy."

Kent's face blanched. A grim smile moved Montana's lips.

"Always on the job, that's Whitey," Montana said. "A brother to be proud of, Miss Sally. He nursed me through a fever in my arm. Got me on my feet for these finals, staked me to a gun — to use on Tremaine — then saved me the trouble. It was Whitey who figured out about Smokey." He stopped to glare at the white-faced Kent, who for once was speechless.

Little Montana looked up to smile weakly.

"I'm sure glad you came through, pard," he said.

"So am I," the cowboy answered softly. "The Two Montanas are back together again. And now we'll wind up things in this country and drift."

"Not by a danged sight you won't drift," Cousins said. "You're staying right here. Nobody will ever get this boy away from me again."

"Nor from me," Sally put in quickly, flushing.

"Reckon I'll have to take him," Montana told them. "I couldn't get along without him and —"

"And neither can I," Cousins cried. "Didn't you read that letter? Don't you know?"

"I'd plumb forgotten the letter," Montana confessed. "No, I didn't read it."

"Nat Ellis was my foreman, years ago," Cousins explained hastily. "He disappeared; my boy also disappeared. We found his hat in Piney, planted just so I'd think he had drowned. And after all these years you brought me this letter." He pulled Little Montana to him. "And brought me back my boy."

"Your boy?" Montana gasped. "Was that what Uncle Nat —"

"Nat Ellis kidnapped him — Nat Ellis and Smokey Tremaine. Kidnapped him so —" He only gazed after Kent who was slinking away. "— so Kent and Smokey Tremaine could get hold of my ranch. They gave Nat five hundred dollars. He took my boy south, tagged him Clem White, and abandoned him at a ranch way down on Powder river. Then Nat skinned out. Nobody around here has heard from him since. But he kept tabs on the boy somehow; and came clean with everything in this letter."

"So that's how Smokey got his drag with Kent!" Montana blurted out. "And that is what Uncle Nat tried so hard to tell me before he died? Why he had me meet buddy and bring him on here? Keep your eye on Kent, Whitey," he shouted.

"He won't get very far," Cousins said wearily. "I haven't been the sucker I've seemed for years. The Diamond A boys are watching Kent, have been for days. They'll drop him if he —" The crack of a forty-five checked him. They crowded over to see. Again Whitey was calmly blowing the smoke from the hot barrel of his Colt.

"Another casualty," he announced grimly. "Just winged like the other. I didn't want him to get too far. Even crippled ducks get away in the grass once they hit the shore. Another wagon!" he bellowed to the crowd, which still stood about, staring. "Here you, Hartzell," he ordered the T6 owner who was hovering about suspiciously. "Here's a job you'll like. Take this walloper to Elbar. Get him a doctor — if you can't get out of it," he finished dryly.

"Whitey has been itching to stage this roundup." Montana grinned. "He wanted that five-thousand reward for Three-Finger DeHaven. I reckon the kid got it — and Kent, your partner."

"Partner!" Cousins spat. "He just tried to be. Went so far as to tell folks he was. But he isn't; never has been."

"I begin to see things," Montana said, brows knitted pensively. "But there is still a heap of explaining to do. I know now why Smokey and Kent had it in for me from the start — and for buddy. They suspected who we were, even though we didn't know ourselves. They were leary of Button here. I must have reminded them of Uncle Nat — Smokey seemed to recognize me. Then when Whitey and I teamed up — You didn't notice any resemblance, did you?"

"I didn't have a guilty conscience," Cousins reminded.

"But that's why Smokey tried to tromp buddy down and kidnapped him," Montana exclaimed.

"And busted me over the head," Little Montana cried in a voice trembling with excitement. "I remember now. It came to me all of a sudden. After he kicked you into the river I scrapped him. He knocked me out."

"And claimed a drift log hit you," Cousins snarled. "But Montana's horse showed him up. He got what was coming to him, thanks to Montana."

"He hasn't got half of what is coming to him," Montana growled. "Nor Kent, either. But the thanks go to Whitey; and to Uncle Nat, who got us Two Montanas together, headed us down here with that letter for you. And we come danged near backing out, thinking Uncle Nat was locoed, didn't we, Button?"

"We sure did." The boy grinned happily. "That day outside of Elbar."

"But we bulled her through," Montana said. "And I reckon you did find out something that interested you,

288

after all. Found your real pa — and found out you were in line for a big ranch. But there's other things to do and here we stand chewing the rag."

"Other things?" Cousins asked quickly. "Haven't we done enough?"

"There's still a murder," Montana told him. "The lowest murder ever committed in Thunder Basin. I'm going to pin it on the man who did it. We're heading for town, Whitey and I. We've got such a good start now we're going to clean up Elbar."

"Would a little trip to town hurt us, Doc?" Cousins asked, an excited gleam in his eyes.

"It will do you good, Al." The doctor smiled. "And the boy too, now that — Well, I guess I'd better be leaving. I'll see you all in Elbar."

He quit the stand. Sally, who had grown singularly quiet and moody, and the puttering Cousins, prepared the boy for the ride. Montana lifted him into the buckboard, helped the girl up over the wheel, then, with Whitey, who was grinning broadly, waited until Cousins had secured the reins and started. Then Montana and Whitey lifted their horses along the dusty trail that wound up the river toward Elbar.

CHAPTER
THIRTY-TWO

Gunman's Bullets

Once again Elbar was in a tempest of excitement. A soft prairie moon, sliding up in the east, cast a haze of silver over the broken plank walks, routed the creeping shadows about the hulking buildings, made yellow and wan the penciled rays of coal-oil lamps along the street.

Again broad-shouldered, lean-hipped punchers strode that street, spur rowels jangling. Punchers squatted on their haunches or leaned idly against their ponies, which stood three-legged, heads drooping wearily. And again the air was impregnated with a tenseness that threatened momentarily to explode and send the crowd clawing for the guns holstered at every hip.

Montana had come loping into town at twilight, along with Whitey Hope. Their first stop had been at the sheriff's office. Word that the sheriff and the coroner were at the Midway had sent them to the saloon. There they found the two, the sheriff boasting of his capture of Three-Finger DeHaven.

"We're reopening the inquest into the killing of Pop Masterson," Montana cut in coldly to announce. He swept the startled crowd with fearless eyes. "I want

290

every man there who saw the fracas. Figure you've been subpoenaed."

"You can't do that," the coroner sputtered indignantly.

"I am doing it!"

"To make it legal you've got to have subpoenas served," Jerry, the bartender, leaned close to whisper in Montana's ear.

"I'm serving them," Montana snapped. "This is your subpoena." He tapped the butt of his forty-five. "The only kind some of you understand. And it says for every mother's son of you to be at the coroner's office in an hour. You have Tremaine and Kent there," he ordered the sheriff.

"They're wounded," the officer flared hotly. "Besides, you're not giving —"

"They'll be at the inquest if we have to drag them in feet first." The grim-faced Montana planted himself in front of the officer, who backed away. "And you too. Understand? Hartzell," catching a glimpse of the T6 owner edging away through the crowd, "you stick with me. I might need help."

Hartzell stopped short to stare for an instant. Then vanity flamed into his little eyes. He moved over importantly beside Montana.

"Find out if Cousins has gotten in yet," Montana told Whitey. "Take this sheriff and coroner along with you. See that they have Smokey and Kent at the inquest. You wrangle them. I'll wrangle here until you holler." Muttering threats under their breath, the sheriff and the coroner quit the saloon, Whitey at their heels.

"Settle down, jaspers," Montana invited, dropping into a chair. "We'll just auger until things are ready. Meantime, if there is anybody who feels hostile, now's his chance to bark and get it out of his system." But no man spoke.

It was almost an hour later when Whitey returned to find Montana, Jerry, Hartzell, and the punchers laughing hilariously as they swapped yarns of the range. The hostile tension had been broken.

A far different crew, they came trooping into the office of the coroner — a thoroughly cowed crew, yet not unfriendly. The smoking, rough jests, laughter of the other inquest were missing.

Beside the plainly frightened coroner, Montana placed the puzzled Cousins, whose snow-white hair gleamed in the flickering light. Next came the grumbling sheriff, who chewed his lips nervously. Montana, too, took a seat facing the crowd, the boy close at hand. Whitey Hope leaned wearily against the wall, his blue eyes whipping along the line to scan every face.

Montana got to his feet.

"About a year ago," he said slowly, "I ducked out of an inquest in this room, because I knew I was framed. But I told you then that some day I'd call a showdown. I'm calling it, jaspers. And a little different from that other inquest — in case anybody wants to question it — I'm running this show. You all know why we're here. You're not legally subpoenaed, but you'd better be danged eager to get what you know off your chests. Whether he likes it or not, our coroner has reopened the inquest into the death of Pop Masterson. Now I'm asking, who killed him?"

His gaze sought, locked with that of Smokey Tremaine who, despite two splinted and bandaged arms, the sheriff had brought in to seat in the front row facing Montana. But the big puncher never batted an eye. Nor did Kent, who also carried an arm in a sling and who sat beside Smokey, nervously chewing a cigar. There was smug assurance on the peaked face of Hartzell, to whom Montana had given the job of watching the pair, and who made no pretense of concealing his elation at holding the whip hand.

"You've got the guns off Tremaine and Kent, sheriff?" Montana asked. "Break them!"

The sulking sheriff produced the three guns he had taken from the prisoners — two from Tremaine, one from Kent. With fingers that trembled he broke the cylinders. Montana himself dumped the shells from the chambers, examined them closely. He straightened up, a puzzled light in his eyes.

"Smokey!" he shot out. "What did you kill Pop Masterson for?"

"I didn't kill Masterson," Tremaine threw back sullenly.

"There were three shots fired," Montana propounded. "I shot twice. But the second shot was after the killing. You had your two guns out."

"My right gun is a bluff," Smokey admitted hatefully. "I'm a left-handed gunman. Not a cartridge in the chamber of my right gun was fired. I shot once at you and missed. The sheriff can —"

"That's right," the sheriff chimed in. "I examined his gun."

"Your word isn't any better with me now than it was before," Montana silenced him. "You played crooked that night by letting Tremaine and Kent get away. And you'll play crooked again if you get a chance. As for you, Tremaine, you're lying — lying to save your lousy hide, figuring a rustling charge is less than murder."

"You've won, jasper," Smokey cried. "I'm Three-Finger DeHaven. I did the things you claim against the Buzzard. But damn me, I didn't kill Masterson." It was plain that Tremaine's nerve had broken. There was no denying now the sincerity in his words. "I'll take my jolt in the pen. But I didn't kill —" His hoarse voice cracked.

"Just the caliber I figured, Smokey," Montana snorted contemptuously. "A sneaking coyote when you're not filled with the old brave-maker and cornered. You, the jasper who swore to keep the Buzzards out of Thunder Basin! You and Kent —" He stopped abruptly, his roving eyes suddenly centered on Hartzell, who was sucking in every word, an ugly smile of triumph on his thin lips. "Hartzell!" he snapped. "Come up here and break that gun of yours."

The owner of the T6 recoiled.

"Why, I'm your friend, Montana. I offered you friendship that night in the saloon. I'd have quit these wallopers cold. But I figured you were drowned in the river. I didn't have any part in that shooting."

"Get up there and break your gun!" It was Whitey's voice that lashed the color from Hartzell's hawk-like

294

face. "You're the skunk I've picked from the jump. And don't make a crooked move or you're a gone bird."

"You fellows will pay for this high-handed —" the sheriff began furiously.

"Not as dear as you're going to if you bat an eye," Whitey hurled back.

Hartzell cast one terrified look at the cowboy, who though he still leaned carelessly against the wall now had his forty-five in his hand. But the T6 owner made no move to advance.

"I know you offered friendship in the saloon that night," Montana spoke half musingly. "But you offered it too quick, jasper. Whitey has given me a little of your history — about you being the crack shot of the Basin. You didn't offer your friendship, Hartzell, until you figured Smokey was down and I was the best man. Break that gun!"

Hartzell attempted to draw his forty-five. It froze on the rim of his holster. It was Whitey who whipped it out, broke the cylinder and passed the cartridges up to Montana.

"Hartzell!" Montana cried in a strained, unnatural voice. "You're the jasper who fired that third shot. You killed Pop Masterson!"

"I swear I didn't," Hartzell screamed. "I — I — It was Tremaine. He can shoot with both his guns. He —"

Shoving his hand into his pocket, Montana pulled forth a pellet of lead.

"The jasper who shot Pop Masterson was using copper-jacketed forty-fives with niches' in them," he said coldly. "A trick of the old gunmen who shoot to kill. That niche did its work. The bullet didn't glance; it drilled clean through old Pop. I happened to find it under his coat. Here it is, Hartzell!"

Hartzell's peaked face blanched. In Montana's extended hand was a copper-jacketed bullet, the nose of which had been niched. Beside it lay the six copper-jacketed cartridges from the chamber of Hartzell's gun. The noses of all of them were niched!

"That settles that, sheriff," Montana told the officer, who now was staring stupidly. "Hartzell might have gotten away with it if it hadn't been for this niched bullet and the fact that Tremaine carries one gun for a bluff; and for good old Irish Jerry, the bartender at the Midway, who talked me into saving this bullet. We've had Hartzell right under our eyes since we hit Elbar."

"But I looked at Hartzell's gun that night," the coroner ventured with a poor attempt at a sneer. "The chamber was full."

"He had plenty of time to reload before you got that inquest started," Montana replied hotly. "And was smart enough not to reload with niched cartridges. You were so damned set on clearing Tremaine you couldn't bother with facts. I had this bullet that night. But Hartzell tricked me for a while by offering his hand. The jig's up now. He's through."

"I told you Smokey didn't do that killing," Kent found his voice to growl. "And that Buzzard rustling you accused us of, it's a frame-up. Damn you, you'd better —"

"Save your threats," Montana lashed out. "Now that I've found out who killed Pop Masterson I'm ready to start on you. I told you, you were jail bait as quick as I got ready to play my hand. I'm ready now. Your days are numbered on Thunder, Kent."

"I've been here a good many years," sneeringly. "I've seen wild-onion spreads like the Buzzard come and go. You're no different than the rest."

"Only so far as I happen to hold your paper, Kent," Montana retorted coolly.

"His paper?" Cousins put in excitedly. "He hasn't any paper —"

"You'll find out a lot about him before I'm through, Cousins," Montana said. "Because I'm sure you haven't had a part in this thing. Haven't even known what this double-crosser was doing. I hold the paper on the Four Diamond outfit he's slapped mortgages on to keep Smokey Tremaine out of jail. The Four Diamond — the spread King Kent and Smokey Tremaine kept stocked with cattle they stole from your Diamond A!"

The announcement dropped like a bombshell in the packed room. A choking sound left Cousins's lips. But boiling anger held him speechless. Kent slumped down in his chair.

"I could foreclose on that stolen stuff without spilling all this," Montana was saying. "But the Buzzard is on the square, Kent. I'm going to worry you a bit, though, about those critters your phantom rustler gang — that threatened Cousins — stole."

"My stuff is not stolen," Kent shouted. "Not a head. And every bit of my paper is in the hands of the Ranchers' Commission Company of Omaha." He essayed a smile that froze on his chalky face. "I reckon they will have something to say about a wild-onion spread calling that paper."

"They will," decisively. "But it just happened that Pop Masterson was the Ranchers' Commission Company. He was trying to tell you in the saloon that night this skunk" — he indicated the cringing Hartzell — "plugged him. Pop didn't know you'd stolen the stuff to start your spread. Didn't know that you'd robbed your best friend, Al Cousins. Nor he couldn't know that you and Smokey Tremaine rustled those blackballed Buzzards and branded them Four Diamond; and Whitey caught you at it red-handed. I didn't spring that Four Diamond brand in the roundup camp that morning. But you knew that I knew, damn you. But Pop did know you were having trouble paying. You swore you couldn't. Thinking you were a white man, Pop didn't want to drive you to the wall. But he couldn't figure it out when other ranchers were meeting their bills. So he brought these Buzzards in here to feed, to convince himself you were up against the proposition you claimed you were. He aimed to buy your place — that line shack up above Piney you claim, in the mortgage, is the Four Diamond — build up your herd, work with you. Pop's main reason in coming up here was to pull you out of the hole, Kent."

"Damn you, Hartzell!" Kent blurted out savagely. "I asked you fellows there in the Midway that day if you were plumb sure this Buzzard didn't belong to some commission house. You said no, you lying, sneaking —"

"But it was you who talked blackballing," Montana cut in. "You who ran in the Diamond A's, without

Cousins's consent, to stampede us, you who played poker for our stuff, burned our camp, slapped more paper on your stolen stuff to keep Tremaine — who you thought had killed Pop — from being jailed." His soft voice crackled with coldness. "And it was you, Kent, who trumped up that phoney warrant and paid the sheriff to hound me, then lost your nerve and tried to call him off after we nailed you as a rustler.

"Sit down!" he flung at the sheriff, who started up, face purple with rage. "I'll get to you in a minute."

He swung back on Kent.

"You blame Hartzell for telling you Pop didn't have commission-house stuff. Yet if you'd kept Tremaine's mouth shut for a minute when he was deviling the old fellow you'd have found out. Pop was trying to tell you, to explain who he was, what he'd come for. Tremaine was drunk and wouldn't listen. But that's all over now, Kent. There are only two jaspers in the world who can call your crooked paper. And they're doing it now!"

CHAPTER
THIRTY-THREE

Peace in Thunder Basin

The occasional shifting of a nervous boot, a whistling sigh, the sucking breath of Cousins, who was working himself into a fit of rage at revelation of Kent's double-dealing, were the only sounds that broke the frozen stillness in the room. From outside came the nicker of a pony, the hoof beats of the horse of some later arrival.

"The Buzzard spread is calling your crooked paper, Kent!" Montana repeated.

"What's that to you?" Kent sneered. "The Buzzard spread belongs to Masterson's —"

"Masterson's will left everything to the foreman who was with him at the time of his death," Montana checked him. "Sal — Miss Hope went to Omaha, took my little pard — whom you kidnapped once — to keep him out of Tremaine's way. She sent me all the papers, established my claim. I'll admit I walked into a pay streak blind; but it's mine now. And the dying words of Pop Masterson were to clean you out, Kent!"

A slow crimson stain started working itself across the face of Kent. His hands began opening and closing convulsively.

300

"There are only two jaspers in the world who can call the paper on that stolen stuff," Montana was continuing softly; so softly those nearest him strained to hear. "Me, the owner of the Buzzard spread and the Ranchers' Commission Company, and Whitey Hope, the cowboy you tried to run out of business in Elbar. But it won't make any difference to you. You're going over the road, for blotching Buzzard brands after you fell for our two-man roundup gag, for rustling from Al Cousins, for mortgaging stolen property — not to mention kidnapping, Kent. You and Tremaine, the rustler gang of Thunder Basin. And Hartzell, the nervous killer, who, I am convinced, was driven to the killing of Masterson through fear of Tremaine and to prove, some day, his claim to being a man of Smokey's caliber.

"Lock them up, sheriff. I'm filing the charges. And you," as the officer leaped up with alacrity to obey, "Kent has owned you body and soul for years. You've done all his dirty work. But with Kent gone we're giving you one break. You're coming clean from now on!"

The sheriff blinked, gulped, and nodded. The movement, fraught with fear, brought a chuckle from the crowd.

"We've warned you now," Montana said. "Law and order is moving into Elbar. You're going to do your job and do it right or — Whitey is just snorting to be turned loose. As for you," he captured the coroner's shifty gaze, "you tried to frame me at that other

301

inquest. You're on probation too. One break and you'll —"

"It was all a mistake," the coroner got out hoarsely. "Honest, I —"

"Honest is the word," Montana snapped. "From now on you'd better be."

"And now, jaspers, the inquest is over," he announced. "Whitey Hope told some of you there would be jobs at good money for good men this fall. They're ready, waiting for you at the Buzzard. But not for Diamond A men that Al Cousins needs. The rest of you — we'll look you over any time, for we're really stocking Thunder Basin."

He took the boy's arm, assisted Cousins to his feet and started for the door. Outside the three waited for Whitey, who had helped the sheriff herd the cursing Kent, Tremaine, and Hartzell into jail.

"I didn't get half of what you were saying, Montana," Cousins exploded. "About you owning the Buzzard and —"

"I'll tell you all about it. Go into detail later," Montana answered. "But now, everything is all right. I'm tearing up the paper on that stolen stuff, turning back to the Diamond A every head packing Kent's Four Diamond brand except the Buzzards he rustled." He stood gazing down the shadowed, moonlit street, packed with punchers emerging from the inquest. "Button is fixed now; he's going to have a ranch —"

"I don't want any ranch," Little Montana whispered, clinging to his hand. "I only want to stay with you, Montana, be with you wherever you go."

"And you can, too," Cousins cried. "For he's going into partnership with us on the Diamond A — him and Whitey Hope."

"Will you, Montana?" the boy asked hopefully.

"We'll see." Montana's voice was heavy, almost wistful. "I've got to go to Omaha and look over this Commission Company. Then I'm going to take a whirl at the world bronc-busting championship at Cheyenne next summer. After that —"

"Montana!" The boy stood on tiptoe to whisper in his ear. "Haven't you forgotten something?"

"What?" The cowboy smiled down at him.

"Sally. Sally said when we left her at the restaurant that she'd have supper waiting for us."

"That's right," Whitey put in, coming up at the moment. "Let's eat. Ma will be dying to hear all about this ruckus."

They crossed the street and entered the café. There they found a table spread and Sally, fresh and lovely as an orchid in a spotless starched housedress, waiting to serve them.

After a sketchy detail of the inquest to Mother Hope, they seated themselves.

"Eat hearty," Whitey invited, "because it's the last meal Ma serves in the old stand."

"Last meal?" Mother Hope cried. "Why, Whitey what do —"

"Montana has made me a partner in all of Masterson's holdings," Whitey announced proudly. "It's to be the Ellis and Hope Cattle Company. And we'll want you to take charge down to the ranch, Ma, run the kitchen, handle the help."

Mother Hope's eyes sparkled.

"It just seems too good to be true the way things have turned out." She choked back tears of happiness. "But you boys have earned it. You've certainly done things right in Thunder Basin." Wiping her eyes on her apron, she went back to the kitchen.

After she had left, Whitey and Cousins fell into an animated conversation. The boy was too busy watching the smiling Sally to talk, while Montana was singularly quiet, his gaze riveted on his plate.

"Well, how does that partnership in the Diamond A strike you and Whitey?" Cousins asked him presently.

"I've always had the foot-itch," Montana admitted. "I reckon now I've raised all the ruckus I can on Thunder, I'll just turn over the management of the Buzzard to Whitey. I'll file charges against Kent, Tremaine, and Hartzell tomorrow; then I'll just drift till —"

A stifled scream, the clatter of crashing dishes brought them to their feet. Sally had dropped a tray. Montana and Whitey sprang over to help her. But she fled to the kitchen from which Mother Hope emerged to finish serving them.

"What's the matter with Sally?" Whitey demanded.

"She doesn't feel very well," Mother Hope answered.

The boy leaned over close to Montana.

"Why don't you do something about it?" he asked in a quivering voice.

Whitey heard the question, burst into laughter. Montana gazed about uncomfortably.

"That's the idea," Whitey chuckled. "Why don't you do something about it, Montana?"

"Shucks," Montana stammered, catching the eye of Mother Hope, in which there was a strange twinkle. "There isn't anything I can do unless I trot over and get Doc." He got to his feet, reached for his hat only to be hooted down by Whitey. On the verge of flight, he looked around for the boy. But the youngster had slipped to the kitchen in search of Sally.

Despite the lively conversation of Mother Hope, Whitey, and Cousins, Montana finished the meal in silence.

"Well, I reckon I'll drill on down to the ranch tonight," he said. "You and Button staying in, Cousins?"

"Yes. It's my first trip to Elbar in months. And I guess I'm the only one on the range who hasn't known all the devilment Kent was doing. We'll stick around until after you file those charges tomorrow. But I can't stay any longer. With Smokey and Kent gone I'm shorthanded. Looks like we're going to have to throw in together to rustle enough men to handle the two spreads."

"We'll think about it," Montana said. "Let you know later."

The boy had sidled up beside him quietly. Now he pulled the cowboy's head down.

"Sally knew it was you she kissed at the depot that night," Little Montana whispered.

Montana shot a quick, bewildered glance at the others, who, apparently, had not heard — for which he was thankful.

"She's crying because she thinks you're going away," the youngster rushed on. "She's been so good to me. I hate to see her cry. I don't want the Diamond A, Montana. I want to be with you — and Sally. We could be the Three Montanas. I know she'll come in with us if you'd just ask her." Before the dumfounded cowboy realized it, he was being shoved along to the kitchen. There they came upon the girl, crying softly, her head buried in her arms outflung across a table.

"Don't cry, Sally," Little Montana pleaded, tucking his hand into hers. "He isn't going away. He ain't the kind to quit a pal. I just know he won't go."

"But he said he was," she sobbed, without looking up. "I — guess I'm foolish. I've tried so hard not to care. But I just can't help —" She lifted her tear-stained eyes, sprang up startled, face flaming, at sight of Montana.

"I didn't know my going away would make so much difference to — Button," he said huskily. "I'd stay if I really thought — But you never even looked at —"

"Go ahead, tell him to his face you knew it was him you kissed at the depot," Little Montana prompted the blushing girl.

"He's right," she whispered, her gaze falling before the strange and happy light that had crept into the cowboy's eyes. "I did know; and I wasn't angry at the depot, Montana. You've been so good to Whitey. And

306

I've looked at you every chance — But I didn't want you to know that I was so —"

"And you really kissed me — knowing it was me instead of Whitey?"

"Somebody had to break the ice," bravely.

"Go ahead and tell her you liked it," the boy whispered to Montana. "Gosh-all-hemlocks, pard, if you only knew what a swell pal she is! And she's been crying for you. Sally —" as Montana hesitated, "he liked that kiss. And he wants another one. Don't you, Montana? I know Sally does. She told me so."

"Hush," the girl reprimanded sharply.

"Well, I reckon if a lady really wants to be kissed, it ain't much of a gent that won't oblige her," Montana heard himself saying in amazement.

"If you two could only see," the boy begged. "I never had a mother or sister to treat me nice. I never had a man treat me white like you, Montana. Please, pard. And Sally —" He seized their hands, laid that of the girl in Montana's. "I don't want the Diamond A. I want you and Sally. I'll do anything." He stopped, his voice breaking, struggled bravely to keep back the tears. "I'll even promise to brush my teeth for Sally if you'll —" Tears came in a flood. He threw himself into the girl's arms and buried his face against her heaving bosom.

"Well, when it's put up to a fellow just that way," Montana stammered, "I reckon there ain't much left to be said, Miss — Sally!" The name burst in a hoarse whisper from his lips.

"Montana!" She swayed toward him. The awkward arm he dropped about her shoulder tightened. She cuddled against him, sighed contentedly.

"Skin out there a minute and tell Cousins we'll take that partnership in the Diamond A, Button," Montana jerked out. "Tell him —"

The boy rushed into the outer room.

"Montana is going to stay!" he shouted. "And I'm going to have Sally!"

"Is he?" Montana whispered in her ear.

"That's up to you," she breathed. "Bless his heart. I love him. I'd hate to part —"

"It sure takes a brick house to fall on me to make me see some things," Montana said softly, his arms tightening about the girl, who only snuggled closer. "I know Button really did the proposing. But now that he has it all fixed up I wonder — Do you suppose you could spare a little of that love you feel for him for —"

She drew away from him slightly, lifted tear-damp eyes to his.

"I love you, Montana," she said in her low husky voice that he now knew had thrilled him from the first. "I've loved you from the minute you came into the restaurant and ordered 'all the ham and eggs in Elbar for two hungry Montana wolves that hadn't et —'" She laughed gaily. "I knew then, Montana. There now, is that plain enough?" She twined her arms about his neck and again buried her flaming face on his chest.

"I reckon it is," he said in a voice he himself scarcely recognized. "But it don't seem just real. I've been dreaming about you from that day; but you were so pretty, so different. I'm still scared to believe that —"

"You frightened?" she teased. "After the way you've cleaned up the crooks in Elbar?"

"That's different. You can fight your way out with men. But with women. Your feeling for them kind of hits you where you can't get at it. Just a kind of a dull ache I've had for you, Sally." Once started he was rushing along. "And seeing Button love you the way he did — I didn't dare hope. Then that night at the depot — That kiss has burned my lips ever since. But I thought you meant it for Whitey."

"Girls don't kiss their brothers that way. I thought I could make you see then, Montana. Thought my eyes would tell you. I nearly fainted when you rode onto the rodeo grounds. I'd cried so many nights I just couldn't believe — Then, when you accidentally put your arm around me today — Oh, Montana!"

He folded her closer, bent over. His lips found hers.

"It's my turn now, Sally!" They started guiltily, drew apart at Little Montana's yell. The boy slipped into the girl's arms. Montana whirled. Mother Hope, Whitey, Cousins stood in the doorway, their faces wreathed in smiles.

"A fine partner you turned out to be," Whitey growled. "Introduce you to my family and you steal the best sister I've got. Dang you, Montana."

"He had nothing to do with it," Sally defended quickly. "Buddy did it." She smiled up at Montana. "And I'm awful glad."

"So am I." Montana found his voice as Mother Hope came over to pat him on the shoulder and Sally snuggled back into his arms. "And I reckon if it's all right with Sally we'll just make her the third Montana. What do you say?" He lifted her chin in his hand.

"It would break my heart if you didn't," she whispered. "Any girl who will smash a whole tray of dishes just to wake a man up deserves some sort of a break."